Miranda Jarrett

"A swift, rollicking rom...
—Bestselling author M...

"A vibran...
—Bestselling...
The Very...

Lyn Stone

"Stone has an apt hand with dialogue and creates characters
with a refreshing naturalness."
—*Publishers Weekly*

"...laced with lovable characters, witty dialogue,
humor and poignancy, this is a tale to savor."
—*Romantic Times* on *The Highland Wife*

Anne Gracie

"Ms. Gracie has a knack for delving into people's souls and,
at the same time, tickling our funny bone."
—*Rendezvous*

"Welcome Anne Gracie to the ranks
of excellent romance writers...I want more stories
by this extremely talented author."
—*The Romance Reader*

GIFTS OF THE SEASON
Harlequin Historical #631—November 2002

**DON'T MISS THESE OTHER
TITLES AVAILABLE NOW:**

#632 RAFFERTY'S BRIDE
Mary Burton

#633 BECKETT'S BIRTHRIGHT
Bronwyn Williams

#634 THE DUMONT BRIDE
Terri Brisbin

MIRANDA JARRETT

considers herself sublimely fortunate to have a career that combines history and happy endings, even if it's one that's also made her family far too regular patrons of the local pizzeria. Miranda is the author of twenty-seven historical romances, has won numerous awards for her writing and has been a three-time Romance Writers of America RITA® Award finalist for best short historical romance. She loves to hear from readers at P.O. Box 1102, Paoli, PA 19301-1145, or MJarrett21@aol.com. For the latest news, please visit her Web site at www.Mirandajarrett.com.

LYN STONE

A painter of historical events, Lyn finally decided to write about them. An avid reader, she admits, "At thirteen I fell in love with Bronte's Heathcliff and became Catherine. The next year I fell for Rhett and became Scarlett. Then I fell for the hero I'd known most of my life and finally became myself." After living for four years in Europe, Lyn and her husband, Allen, settled into a log house in north Alabama that is crammed to the rafters with antiques, artifacts and the stuff of future tales.

ANNE GRACIE

was born in Australia, but spent her childhood on the move, living in different parts of Australia, Scotland, Malaysia and Greece. Her days, when not in school, were spent outside with animals and her evenings with her nose in a book—they didn't have TV. She writes in a small room lined with books surrounded by teetering piles of paper. Her first book, *Gallant Waif*, was a RITA® Award finalist for best first book. Her second, *Tallie's Knight*, has been short-listed for the Australian Romantic Book of the Year. Anne lives in Melbourne. She has a Web site, www.annegracie.com, and loves to hear from readers.

GIFTS
OF THE
SEASON

MIRANDA JARRETT
LYN STONE
ANNE GRACIE

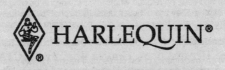

HARLEQUIN®

TORONTO • NEW YORK • LONDON
AMSTERDAM • PARIS • SYDNEY • HAMBURG
STOCKHOLM • ATHENS • TOKYO • MILAN • MADRID
PRAGUE • WARSAW • BUDAPEST • AUCKLAND

ISBN 0-373-29231-7

GIFTS OF THE SEASON

Copyright © 2002 by Harlequin Books S.A.

The publisher acknowledges the copyright holders
of the individual works as follows:

A GIFT MOST RARE
Copyright © 2002 by Miranda Jarrett

CHRISTMAS CHARADE
Copyright © 2002 by Lynda Stone

THE VIRTUOUS WIDOW
First North American Publication 2002
Copyright © 2002 by Anne Gracie

This edition published by arrangement with Harlequin Books S.A.

® and TM are trademarks of the publisher. Trademarks indicated with ® are registered in the United States Patent and Trademark Office, the Canadian Trade Marks Office and in other countries.

Visit us at www.eHarlequin.com

Printed in U.S.A.

CONTENTS

A Gift Most Rare   9
Miranda Jarrett

Christmas Charade   107
Lyn Stone

The Virtuous Widow   199
Anne Gracie

Dear Reader,

Christmas has always been a time of traditions. Whether as old as a medieval carol or as new as Charlie Brown's holiday cartoon, traditions help turn each year into the next memory, to be treasured and recalled long after the decorations are put away. Christmas traditions travel well, too, regardless of how many miles and oceans they must cross. No matter how limited the space for belongings and baggage on a journey might be, there is always room to carry the traditions for this special season: Santa Lucia's candlelit wreath for a daughter from Sweden, a French *grand-mère*'s recipe for *Bûche de Noël*, a Russian uncle's favorite holiday toast, the secret of perfectly folded origami cranes for good luck from a Japanese cousin, or simply Mom's candy-cane Christmas cookies to help a homesick college freshman survive his first final exams.

For Sara and Revell in "A Gift Most Rare," traditions are not only a way of celebrating the holiday, but also their shared past. Like other English expatriates living in India two hundred years ago, they would have been sure to drink Christmas wassail and sing their carols, even though it was beneath the hot Calcutta sun. But new traditions travel back to England with them, and when they decorate for the holiday, there are pasteboard elephants and tigers mixed in with the holly boughs in a joyful union—just like the love that Sara and Revell find together.

A merry holiday to you and your families, and a new year full of love, peace and joy!

Miranda Jarrett

A GIFT MOST RARE
Miranda Jarrett

For Ellen
My bleacher-and-bagel buddy,
who, like every good Hockey Mom, knows that
Christmas (at least the week after) is for Tournaments
Your company & friendship are a treasure
Merry Christmas!

Chapter One

Ladysmith Manor, Sussex
December, 1801

Six years had passed since she'd seen him last, yet with
a lurch to her heart, she realized she'd know him anywhere.

With her hands primly clasped to help mask their trembling, Sara Blake leaned closer to the tall window, her
breath lightly frosting the glass as she gazed down at the
gentleman in black climbing down from his carriage to the
snow-dusted drive. She remembered when he'd not been
so sober and somber, another Christmas when he'd worn
a peacock-blue coat that had made his eyes even brighter
as they'd laughed together, he the handsomest man in the
governor general's ballroom.

Six years. How she'd loved and trusted him then, with
all the fervency that her seventeen-year-old heart could
offer! He wore his dark hair cropped shorter now, another
change to follow the fashion. But as the wind ruffled it
across his brow, she remembered how soft those curls had
been to touch, how she'd relished the silky feel of them
beneath her fingers when he'd bent to kiss her.

"You *do* know who that is, don't you, Miss Blake?" asked Clarissa Fordyce with all the relish of her much-indulged eight-year-old self. "*That's* the gentleman that Mama didn't wish us to invite here for the holiday, until Albert insisted."

"Young gentlemen like your brother often have friends of which their mothers do not quite approve," said Sara, striving to keep her voice properly objective, the way a good governess's should always be, even as the old fears and questions were making her palms damp and her heart race. "Learning to make wise choices in companions is not always an easy skill to acquire."

"*This* one wasn't wise at all," declared Clarissa soundly. With fingers sticky from marzipan, she pressed her plump hands to the glass, eagerly studying the man who was certain to be the most interesting among her mother's guests this week. "Albert says everyone calls him the Sapphire Lord, and that he was the wickedest devil in all of India!"

"Mind your words, Clarissa," chided Sara as her cheeks warmed with a guilty rush of old memories. How could he still affect her like this after so much time apart? "No lady concerns herself with what 'everyone' says. I'm sure the gentleman has another name by which you shall be expected to address him."

"Yes, Miss Blake," answered Clarissa promptly, but without the slightest pretense of contrition or remorse as she pressed closer to the glass. Far below the gentleman was climbing the clean-swept steps, his traveling cloak fluttering back from his broad shoulders as Albert Fordyce hurried forward to greet him. "His true name, Miss Blake, is Lord Revell Claremont, and I shall be perfectly respectful to him on account of him being Mama's guest, and his brother being a duke, and because Albert would thrash me if I didn't. But Lord Revell *does* look like a wicked devil, doesn't he?''

Yet when Sara looked down at Revell Claremont, she saw infinitely more. She saw the man she'd once loved not just with her heart but her soul, as well—but she also saw her own long-gone innocence, and the end of a fairy-tale existence in a faraway land. She saw betrayal and heartbreak and the sudden loss of everything she'd held most dear, and a scandal she'd hoped she'd forever left behind with her old name and life, half a world and two oceans away. She saw her past disclosed and her father's shameful crime curtly revealed, her dismissal from this house swift and inevitable and her future once again made perilously uncertain. Revell Claremont had abandoned her to fate before, when he'd claimed to love her, and she'd absolutely no reason to believe he'd do otherwise now.

Ah, Merry Christmas, indeed.

Revell stood before the fireplace with his legs slightly spread and his hands outstretched toward the flames, pre-tending to concentrate entirely on the fire until he heard the footman's steps leave the room, and the latch to the bedchamber door click gently closed behind him. With a sigh of relief, Revell finally let his shoulders sag, and his sigh trailed off into a groan of exhaustion. He hoped his manservant Yates would return soon with the bath he'd ordered, and a parade of maidservants with steaming pitch-ers of hot water from the kitchen.

Blast, but he was tired, clear through his blood to his bones and his soul. Traveling did that to a man, and Revell hadn't lingered in one place for more than three nights at a time in over a year. Restless as last summer's leaf in the wind: that was how his older brother Brant had described his wandering, and Revell couldn't disagree. He couldn't, not really, not when it was the cold, honest truth.

But then what did Brant know of restlessness, anyway, snug in his grand house in London with his brandy in his hand? Revell had been the one their father had cast the farthest from home, less like a twisting leaf than a worthless penny minted from tin instead of copper. Yet since then Revell had made himself into a wealthy man with the fortune to match his title, a man with power and influence and the awestruck respect of others, exactly the sort of man that, as a boy, he and his two brothers had sworn they would become. Certainly Brant had succeeded, and George, too, and he'd never heard either of them complain of their lot. If restlessness and loneliness were the price to be paid for their success, then so it had been.

Revell shook his head, resisting the lure of the old bitterness, and spread his fingers to take in more of the fire's warmth. He'd been away so long that he'd forgotten how cold Sussex could be in December, or maybe this chill, like the weariness, was only another sign of getting old. He frowned at his reflection in the looking glass over the mantel, half expecting to see his thick black hair streaked with white or his sharp blue eyes turned rheumy with age. He would, after all, be twenty-eight next month, and he shook his head again at how quickly time had slipped by.

From habit he reached into the inside pocket of his waistcoat to find the small curved box, the gold-stamped calfskin worn from touching, and with his thumb he flipped open the lid. At once the cluster of sapphires inside caught the dancing light from the flames, flashing sparks and stars of brilliant blue as he turned the gold ring this way and that. For six years he'd carried this betrothal ring with him, close to his heart, a constant reminder of the one woman he'd thought had been destined to wear it, the only woman he'd ever love, the one who'd spoiled all others for him.

Love. With a muttered oath, he snapped the little box

shut and shoved it back into his pocket, wishing he could thrust aside her memory as easily. God knows she'd been able to forget *him* fast enough, vanishing from Calcutta without explanation or regret or even one last bittersweet word of farewell.

Six years, yet in an instant he could still recall the rippling merriment of her laughter, the way her eyes would grow soft and her cheeks flush when she looked at him, the cherry-sweet taste of her mouth welcoming his.

His dearest, darling Sara....

Six years, hell. He was growing old, and foolishly sentimental, as well, dreading his own company and memories so blasted much that he'd accepted Albert Fordyce's invitation to come here to Ladysmith. They'd been at school together, true, but Revell hadn't seen Albert for years until they'd met by sheerest coincidence last week outside Drury Lane. The promise of a Christmas goose and rum punch and mistletoe in the doorways, a roaring great yule log in the fireplace and a masquerade ball for Twelfth Night: *that* was all it had taken to lure Revell here for a fortnight of weighty cookery, squealing fiddle music, and tedious entertainments with red-faced country squires and their bouncing, plump-cheeked ladies.

And none of it would be enough to make Revell forget Sara, not by half. Nothing ever was.

Merry Christmas, indeed.

For what must have been the thousandth time in this past hour, Sara glanced at the tall case clock that, bedecked with a spray of holly and red ribbon for the season, stood in the corner of the drawing room. Only five minutes remained until seven, when, without fail, Lady Fordyce would marshal her guests for the short procession to the dining room table, and Sara and Clarissa would begin their own little procession upstairs to the nursery for their more humble meal.

Now four minutes were left: could fortune really be smiling upon her like this? Her heart racing, Sara smoothed the small muslin ruffle on the end of her sleeve. If Revell were like the rest of the guests gathered in this room, then he'd be staying at Ladysmith through Twelfth Night. Their paths were bound to cross before then—the manor was simply not so large a house that it could be avoided—but the longer the meeting could be postponed, the better. True, it was unforgivably rude for Revell not to have come here to the drawing room to greet his hostess before dinner on his first night, but for Sara it meant another day and night when her secret was still safe.

Three minutes. There was, of course, also the chance that Revell wouldn't recognize her. Sara knew she was much changed since he'd seen her last. Her sorrows showed on her face, and the plain, serviceable way in which she dressed did little in her favor. Besides, as Clarissa's governess, she was not much different nor more visible than any other family servant. Although she'd been standing here beside the window for the past hour while Clarissa had been petted and indulged by the others, she doubted any of the elegantly gowned ladies or handsome, laughing gentlemen had noticed her at all. She could only pray that Revell would do the same.

"Miss Blake," said Lady Fordyce, sweeping toward Sara. She was a tall, handsome woman, kind and good-natured, who lavished upon her two children with the same fondness and devotion that her husband Sir David doted upon her. "I believe it is time for Clarissa to retire for the evening."

"Yes, my lady," said Sara with an efficient small curtsy to mask her relief. She'd be able to escape with two minutes to spare. "Clarissa has found the holidays most exciting."

"I should blame her brother rather than the holidays," said Lady Fordyce with an exasperated sniff as she watched her children. Held high upon Albert's shoulder, a delighted Clarissa was shrieking Christmas songs as loudly as she could, pumping her arms up and down like a military bandleader and not at all like a young lady.

"Albert," said Lady Fordyce sternly. "*Albert!* Please lower your sister directly so Miss Blake can take her upstairs!"

"Mama, no!" wailed Clarissa as Albert promptly set her down on the carpet with a *shush* of white petticoats. "It's not time, not yet!"

"Alas, Clarissa, it most certainly is," commiserated Sara as she took Clarissa's hand. "Come now, kiss your mama good night."

Clarissa's face crumpled with disappointment as she appealed to the solemn ring of grown-up faces gazing down at her. She was the only child at present in the house, a position that she occupied like a little queen among her courtiers. But even queens could be banished, and Clarissa knew from sorrowful experience she could expect no reprieve from her mother once dinner was being served.

"And a kiss for me, too, Clary," said Albert heartily, the way he did nearly everything. Although still in his twenties, he was already well on his way to being a model bluff English country gentleman, more fond of his dogs and his horses than the leather-bound books in his father's library. "Who's my only sweetheart girl, huh? Who's my best darling sister?"

"That's because I'm your *only* sister, Albert," said Clarissa, but she kissed his ruddy cheek anyway. "As you know perfectly, perfectly well."

"Your sister, Fordyce?" said a deep, low voice that

Sara had thought she'd never hear again. "How could such a charming little sprite have you for a brother?"

Automatically Sara's head turned in response, her heart racing and her feet urging her to flee. Revell was standing so near to her that she could see the tiny half-moon scar, pale against the clean-shaven shadow of his jaw.

Did he see that in his looking glass each morning and remember the night he'd come by it? How he'd cut himself as he'd climbed over the high wall that had surrounded her father's grand white mansion on Chowringhee Road? Did he still recall how often he'd visited her—no, stayed with her, and loved her the glorious night through! Did he touch that scar now and remember her, how he'd slid over the rough stucco and through the thicket of trees and vines to reach the teak bench where she was waiting for him, there in the velvet heat of an Indian midnight?

"Little miss," continued Revell, oblivious to Sara as he bowed to Clarissa. "I am honored."

Fascinated, the girl slipped her hand free of Sara's and stepped forward, spreading her skirts as she dipped co-quettishly before this new admirer. All other conversation stopped while everyone listened and watched, curiosity turning them into eager, avid spectators. Word that the famous—some said infamous—Lord Revell Claremont had joined the party had raced through the house earlier, but this was the first real glimpse of him that most of them had had.

He did not disappoint. Though he smiled warmly enough at Clarissa, his eyes betrayed no emotion, and even standing still he seemed to have the restlessness and grace of a wild tiger, barely contained in impeccable black evening dress and white Holland linen.

Later Sara would overhear the whispers: how the ladies admired the splendid width of his shoulders, the intriguing aura of danger he wore as comfortably as his waistcoat, and the size of the cabochon sapphire—at least as large as a pigeon's egg!—that he wore in a ring on his right hand, while the gentlemen noted the harsh lines fanning from those chilly blue eyes and the ruthless set of his mouth, souvenirs of living too long in a pagan place like India, and to a man they resolved never to cross a coldhearted bastard like Claremont.

But what Sara saw now was how all gentleness had vanished from Revell's face, and how the hardness that had replaced it made her wonder sadly if he ever laughed anymore, or even could.

Lady Fordyce glided forward, resting one hand protectively upon her daughter's shoulder while holding the other outstretched to Revell. The unspoken message in her posture was unmistakable to Sara; Lady Fordyce took her position and her responsibilities as the most prominent hostess in the county very seriously, and Revell had already grievously erred by coming down to the drawing room so late.

"Surely," began Lady Fordyce, "you must be Lord Revell Claremont, yes?"

Revell nodded, lifting her hand to kiss the air over it. "Surely I am, my lady."

"Then just as surely you may now take Lady Lawrence into dinner, my lord," said Lady Fordyce, pointedly withdrawing her hand. "We are most honored by your presence here, my lord, but I do not wish to keep either my guests or my cook waiting."

He bowed again, and turned toward Lady Lawrence, an older widow in lavender silk who was clearly as terrified as she was titillated to have him as her dinner companion. The others fell in by rank with their accustomed partners and followed through the arched door festooned with holly boughs, leaving Sara and Clarissa behind.

"Ooh, Miss Blake, didn't I tell you!" exclaimed Clarissa with relish. ''That Lord Revell *is* a wicked devil, isn't he? He didn't even tell Mama he was sorry, because he *wasn't!*''

''Hush, Clarissa,'' murmured Sara, still gazing toward the now-empty doorway. ''It's not fitting for you to speculate over Lord Revell's character.''

They had stood not four feet apart, and he'd not noticed her. Not a glance, neither a smile nor a frown, no acknowledgment whatsoever that she'd ever meant anything to him that was worth remembering. She hadn't dared hope their first meeting would happen with so little consequence. For now, anyway, she'd escaped.

But how was it possible for a broken heart to break again?

Chapter Two

With his elbows resting on the arms of the chair and fingers pressed together into a little tent over his waistcoat, Revell smiled across the room at Albert Fordyce, striving to project a relaxed *bonhomie* that he assuredly did not feel. They had outlasted all the other male guests tonight and had the room to themselves, though from the unfocused foolishness of Albert's eyes and the nearly empty bottle of brandy beside him, Revell guessed he, too, would soon need help to his bed. If he wanted answers to the questions plaguing him, he'd better ask them now, before Albert was completely beyond coherent reply.

"So tell me of your sister's governess," began Revell, striving to sound idly interested and no more. "What do you know of her?"

"Clary's governess?" Albert frowned, struggling to compose a reasonable answer to what clearly seemed an unimaginable question. "That dry little stick of a female?"

"Yes, your sister's governess." How could Albert speak so slightingly of Sara? And why did it seem to still matter so much that he did? "Though I should hardly call her a 'dry little stick.'"

Albert stared with blank curiosity. "Wouldn't you

now?'' he marveled. ''She's scarcely seemed worth the notice to me.''

''*I* noticed her.'' How could he not, seeing Sara there like a flesh-and-blood ghost come back to haunt him? She was fine-boned and fair-skinned, true—the hot Indian climate often seemed to reduce English women to their very essence—but her delicacy had never seemed a fault to Revell. She'd been light as a fairy in his arms when they'd danced and vibrant with warm-blooded passion when they'd kissed, and lovely enough that every English gentleman in Calcutta had jostled for a favoring smile from her. ''I thought her, ah, rather handsome.''

What kind of blasted understatement was *that?* He certainly wasn't in love with Sara any longer, not the desperate way he'd been six years ago, but ''rather handsome'' didn't begin to explain how he'd felt seeing her again. Where he'd simply grown older, she had somehow grown even more beautiful, her girlish brilliance burnished and refined by experience and time into a softer, more womanly elegance. She'd tried to hide it in those hideous clothes—shrouding herself in grim black and white, her bright curls skinned back beneath a plain cap—but how could she disguise the sunny blue of her eyes or the generous curve of a mouth made for laughing and teasing and lavishing with kisses?

Oh, aye, she was still Sara, still beautiful, still desirable, and still wretchedly, hopelessly unattainable.

''Ah, well, every man must pick his own poison,'' said Albert blithely as he once again reached for the bottle beside his chair. ''And here I thought you were taken with that saucy Talbot girl, the fine plump one making kitten's eyes at you over dinner!''

Revell grimaced. He'd scarcely noticed the young woman sitting at his right until she'd freed her foot from her slipper and brazenly tickled her stockinged toes up and down his calf.

"No, don't scoff," said Albert. "I'd wager you'd find a warm welcome from that one, no mistake. But if Miss Blake's the sort that catches your fancy, Claremont, well, that's a different kettle entirely. I'd no notion that was how you felt."

Thunderstruck, that's how Revell had felt to discover Sara there beside him. Bowled over and blasted and for once so completely unable to trust his own emotions that he'd looked away, down to the little girl holding her hand.

And Sara—hell, Sara had ignored him as if he didn't exist.

"That is her name, then?" In Calcutta she'd been Sara Carstairs. No wonder he'd not been able to find her since. "Miss Blake?"

"So she is called." Albert shrugged carelessly, pouring the brandy in a sloppy arc into his glass. "Missy-Miss Priss Blake."

Revell's fingers tightened on the arm of the chair. When he'd returned to Calcutta from visting the mines in the hills, eager to announce their engagement, he'd been told that Sara hadn't waited for him. The governor's wife, who'd been appointed to tell him, had been as kind as possible, her voice full of pity. Sara's father had died of a sudden apoplexy brought on by the record heat and dust of that last summer, and before the poor gentleman was scarce buried in his grave and his estate settled, Sara had eloped with a cavalry officer and sailed with him back to England.

It had, thought Revell, been the darkest day of his life.

"You are certain she's unwed?" he asked now, praying that Albert was too far in his cups to hear the ancient disappointment in his voice. "There's no, ah, Mr. Blake?"

"Not in this life." Albert grinned, sinking even lower

into his chair. "Mother wouldn't have permitted it, not in a governess for Clary. She's Miss Blake, evermore. Oh, she must have a Christian name somewhere, as well, but I've never heard it."

"Why in blazes not?" asked Revell. He wasn't exactly angry at Albert's attitude, but it did, well, rankle since it was Sara they were discussing. Not that she needed a champion. Whatever she'd done since he'd seen her last, she'd proven herself perfectly capable of looking after herself without him—though, mercifully, without that dashing phantom cavalry officer, too. "The lass lives beneath your own roof, doesn't she?"

"She's a *servant*, Claremont," said Albert firmly. "I don't *have* to know her name. The house servants are my mother's responsibility, not mine. I say, perhaps you've lived too long among the heathens if you've forgotten how things are here at home."

"Perhaps instead I didn't stay away long enough," said Revell testily, rising to his feet. Albert was right. England wasn't India, and the past couldn't be undone and twisted into the present just because he wished it so. "I thank you for the brandy, if not the advice."

But Albert waved away Revell's thanks, frowning a bit as he leaned forward in his chair. "I meant what I said about my mother and the servants, Claremont," he said earnestly. "She won't take it well if you try to tumble Clary's governess. There's no dallying with any of the servants in this house."

Revell smiled wearily, his hand already on the latch of the door. "Ah, but you're forgetting who you're warning, Albert, aren't you? Because I never *dally* at anything."

He left then before he'd say more, or worse, to his well-meaning host. God knows he'd said enough already, and with a muttered oath directed at his own sentimental idiocy, he turned away from the stairs to the bedchambers and instead down the long, darkened gallery. As tired as he was, he knew better than to try to sleep now, and his hollow, echoing footsteps, seemed to mock his loneliness.

Who the devil would have guessed that Sara would be hiding here at Ladysmith of all places, lying in wait to turn him into a babbling, belligerent imbecile? If he'd any wits left he'd make his excuses and leave at daybreak, out of deference to the Fordyces and Sara, too.

Hell, he should leave *now,* and with a disgusted grumble he threw open one of the tall double doors that led to the terrace and the paths to the gardens beyond. In summer this would be a favorite trysting place, with beech trees curving over the terrace, but in late December the branches were shivering bare and unwelcoming, the pale moon stretching their long, skeletal shadows across the snow-covered paths.

Though there was no wind, the air was still icy, sharp enough to make Revell suck in his breath and hunch his shoulders. Yet in a way he welcomed the cold. This, at least, was real, and slowly he walked across the terrace to the stone railing, his shoes crunching lightly on the crusty snow.

Against so much pale snow and moonlight, it was the inky-dark shape that caught his eye, the whipping flicker of a black cloak as the wearer tried to scurry away from him. Even with the hood drawn forward, he knew who it must be, and in three long strides he had cornered her against the terrace's low balustrade. With a little yelp of frustration, she tried to twist past him and the hood slipped back, letting the moonlight fall full upon her startled face.

"Sara," he said, a statement and a question and a greeting and a wish and a prayer combined into the single word that was her name. *"Sara."*

She swallowed, and though she raised her chin with a

brave show of defiance, he saw how she trembled. He understood. He was trembling, too.

"My lord," she said. "Good evening, my lord."

Of course: what the devil had he been thinking, anyway? "Good evening, Miss, ah, Miss Blake."

"Quite." The single word came out in a small cloud, warmed by her breath in the chilly air. No matter how hard she was trying to maintain the same severe governess's face that she'd worn earlier in the drawing room, she was failing: her eyes seemed enormous and liquid as she gazed up at him, the moonlight making spiky shadows of her lashes across her cheeks. "Quite, my lord."

He cleared his throat, then tried to turn the grumbling growl into a cough, painfully conscious of every sound he uttered. What in blazes was he supposed to say next, given so little encouragement? Not that he should need it, of course. The time for careful wooing and well-considered words, or even the most casual flirtation, was long past for them. Now all that was needed was a modicum of genteel chitchat, same as he would venture with any other young lady, or an old one, for that matter.

But then no other lady was standing here before him with her lips parted, the lower one so full as to be nearly a pout, the one above arched like a bow, a mouth that was unforgettably familiar to him, and once had been unforgettably dear, as well?

"It is, ah, a most fine prospect, is it not?" he asked, then nearly cursed himself again for being a half-wit. They were standing on a sheet of crackling frozen snow beneath bleakly leafless branches, in the middle of the night, in the middle of a Sussex winter. Even in the moonlight he could tell that her nose was red with the cold, and that the first trembling he'd thought he'd caused was, on more honest, less flattering consideration, simply shivering. "Allowing for the season, that is."

She nodded as if this made perfect sense. "Exceptionally fine, my lord, for the season."

In silence he thanked her for not pointing him out as the idiot he was. Silence seemed safest.

But then she seemed determined to be safe, as well, lowering her gaze from his face to the buttons on the front of his coat.

"I could not sleep, my lord," she began, her words rushing swift with agitation. "That is why I'm here. Not because I followed you, or…or wished to engage you. I must beg you to understand that what was…was once between us is long done, my lord, nor do I wish it otherwise."

"No," he said, the weight of that denial heavy as lead. "That is, yes, what we shared in Calcutta was long ago."

"Yes, my lord." Another swift, small nod, that was all. "No one here knows of that past, and I would thank you greatly not…not to share it."

Damnation, was she so shamed by having known him?

"I came outside, here, so I would not disturb Miss Fordyce with my restlessness," she continued, her words still tumbling one after the other. "There was not—not any other reason than to calm myself. What other could there have been, my lord?"

"That is why I am here, as well," he said with false heartiness, unwilling to be outdone no matter what it cost him. "A breath of air to clear the head before bed. That is all I sought by coming here, neither more nor less."

She sighed once, and shrugged, little wisps of hair drifting free around her face. The haste and urgency seemed to drain from her, and with it went the reserve that had been her best defense.

"Ah, my lord," she said softly, "then you have found what you wanted, yes?"

"I suppose I have," he said gruffly, longing to brush

those stray strands aside as he tried not to consider any other deeper meanings to this conversation. "Found what I desired, that is."

"I am glad," she said softly, at last returning her gaze to meet his. "You are happy?"

He hesitated, wondering how honest he should be, not only with her, but himself. "Happy enough, I warrant."

"Then I am happy, too," she said, but the bittersweet longing in her eyes didn't agree. "A true Christmas miracle, yes?"

"A miracle?" He swept his arm through the air, desperately trying to clear the unexpected peril from this conversation. "Surely not here in this cold and cheerless place."

She tipped her head to one side, skeptical. "Since when do miracles require sunny days like new seedlings in the spring?"

"They did for us in Calcutta," he said. "Do you remember how even the mornings in the summer would be so infernally hot that we would stay awake all the night, then go riding before dawn, when it was still cool enough for the horses? We found miracles aplenty there in your garden on Chowringhee Road, with the peacocks and the palm trees, gold spangles on your gown and yellow plumes in your hair."

"Chowringhee." The shared memory reminded them both of other intimacies shared, of love and passion in a faraway world ripe with sensual possibilities, and her sudden, wistful smile with the single unbalanced dimple caught him by surprise. "Ah, Rev, you always were a dreamer, and a rover, too. You never could stop searching for whatever magic lay over the next mountain, could you?"

"I never have, Sara." He smiled, too, their years apart slipping away as they used their given names. "Although dreaming and roving are not precisely the most admirable qualities for a man.''

"For you they were," she said promptly. "You never were like the other greedy cadets and Company nabobs in their red coats, Rev. You saw the rare beauty in India, and not just the gold to be stolen away."

"You know too much of me, Sara," he said softly, "and too well at that."

"Too much, too well," she repeated sadly, and as suddenly as her own smile had come, it now vanished. "I know too much of you, and you know too little of me."

"Then tell me, Sara," he urged. "For the sake of what we once shared. Tell me where you have been, how you have come to be here, what makes you happy or content. Tell me whatever you please, and I swear I shall listen. You said yourself there's no better time for miracles than Christmas."

But she shook her head, drawing the hood of her cloak forward over her face and closing him out, as well. "Forgive me, but I must return now to Miss Fordyce. I would not have her wake and find me absent."

"Sara, wait, please."

"Good night, my lord," she said as she turned away. "Good night."

My lord. If she'd struck Revell with her fist, she couldn't have made her feelings more clear, and he drew back as sharply as if she had. He watched her hurry away from him to the door, her black cloak swirling around her white skirts, and he did not follow.

What in blazes had he been thinking, anyway, presuming like that? Did he really believe that a handful of tattered old memories would be enough to overcome the reasons she'd had for leaving him in the first place, or his own doubts about reopening a part of his past that he'd thought permanently—and painfully—left behind? Fate might have brought them back into one another's lives, but not even fate could undo whatever had happened in between.

For that, quite simply, would take another miracle.

Chapter Three

"Miss Blake?" Lady Fordyce paused, the pineapple raised in her hand. "Are you unwell, my dear?"

"No, my lady," said Sara quickly, pulling her thoughts back to the small, sunny room that served Lady Fordyce as her personal headquarters, and where, with Sara's help, she was busily marshaling her troops and resources like any other good general preparing for a major engagement. "The pineapples will be a most handsome addition to the sideboard."

"I was speaking of ribbons, not pineapples," said Lady Fordyce, frowning with concern. "Are you certain you are well? You are most distracted this morning."

Sara flushed, likely the first color to come to her cheeks all day. "Forgive me, my lady," she said hurriedly. "If I am distracted, it is only the usual happy confusion of the season."

Skeptical, Lady Fordyce's frown remained. "More likely it is Clarissa's fault, fussing and worrying at you over what she's to receive for Christmas."

Sara only smiled wanly. If she looked only half as exhausted as she felt, then she was fortunate Lady Fordyce hadn't sent her directly to bed and summoned the surgeon.

But how could Sara look otherwise, considering the miserable, sleepless night she'd spent after leaving Revell on the terrace? She'd truly believed she'd purged him forever from her thoughts and heart, yet the moment he'd smiled at her and begun talking of Calcutta, she'd once again felt that familiar warmth of joy and excitement begin to swirl through her body, the rare happiness that Revell alone had given her, and she'd realized how hopelessly weak—*weak!*—she still was.

In six long years she hadn't learned one blessed thing, not where Revell Claremont was concerned. She might as well be done with it now: throw herself into his arms directly, and beg him to trample on her heart and abandon her again.

"I trust you would confide in me if something were truly wrong, my dear, wouldn't you?" asked Lady Fordyce gently, settling the pineapple back into the basket on her desk so she could rest her hand on Sara's shoulder. "You would tell me if there was a matter I could remedy?"

Oh, yes, thought Sara unhappily, of *course* she'd confide in Lady Fordyce. Governesses for young ladies were supposed to possess unblemished and virginal reputations. She'd never told the Fordyces that she'd spent most of her life in India, or that she'd been forced to leave in a rush of disgrace, let alone spoken of her unfortunate entanglement with Lord Revell Claremont. How could she, when any part of her sorry tale could cost her her place—a place she couldn't afford to lose—even with a kindhearted mistress like Lady Fordyce?

"If there were any ills you could remedy, my lady," she said with careful truth, "then I should always come to you."

Lady Fordyce beamed, and gave Sara's shoulder a fond little pat. "I am delighted to hear it. Ladysmith has always been a happy house, free of secrets and intrigue, and I would like to keep it so. Now, Christmas or not, surely it must be time to begin Clarissa's lessons today?''

With a swift curtsy Sara hurried from the room, down the hall toward the library. She'd already decided that her lesson today would feature Hannibal's ancient journey across the Alps, and she hoped to find a book with illustrations to pique Clarissa's interest enough to make her forget the coming holiday, at least for a moment or two, and make *her* stop daydreaming of Rev Claremont.

With fresh determination she marched into the library. A small fire glowed in the hearth to take the chill from the room for any guests who might venture into it, but Sara was sure she'd have the collection to herself. She certainly wouldn't see Albert Fordyce, or Sir David, either. The current generations of Fordyces were not readers and neither were the majority of their friends and houseguests, and often weeks would pass when no one beyond Sara entered this pleasantly crowded room with the tall bookcases and old-fashioned chairs. Carefully she now pulled a large book of Roman history from the shelf and opened it on the leather-topped table in the center of the room, flipping through the heavy pages filled with text to find the illustrations. At last she came to one she sought, the Carthaginian general Hannibal leading his elephant-borne troops across the Alps, and she leaned closer to study the details of the print.

"Miss Blake," said Revell, his broad shoulders suddenly filling the doorway to the library. He cleared his throat, low, rumbling, and thoroughly self-consciously, as if he needed one more way to announce his arrival. "Good morning, Miss Blake. I did not expect to find you here."

"Nor I you, my lord." Startled though she was, she was resolved to be cool and reserved, a model governess with her hands clasped neatly at her waist. Besides, this time they were in the library, and there wasn't a single moonbeam in sight to addle her wits or to give him unfair advantage.

Not that he needed any. To her dismay he was every bit as handsome here in the bright morning sun as he'd been by the enchanting moon.

"You shouldn't be surprised at all to find me here," he said, leaning one arm against the frame of the door. "Unless you, too, have chosen to believe whatever drivel you hear said, particlarly about me carousing until all hours of the night with most mythical stamina."

"I'm hardly in the position to hear fashionable gossip, my lord," said Sara, striving to sound aloof rather than merely prim. Being a governess and therefore largely invisible, she had, of course, overheard a great deal about the infamous Lord Revell, none of which she wished to repeat to him now. "The only rumors I'm likely to hear in the schoolroom regard new kittens in the stable, or what special pudding is planned for supper."

"It's nothing more than the usual nonsense." He sighed mightily. "Because I lived so long abroad, I am deemed a restless wanderer and no longer quite English. Because I chose to learn the languages of the men with whom I conducted business, I have become somehow wicked and untrustworthy. Because I took care to defend myself against bandits and thugs, I have in turn become as dangerous as they. But then you know how suspicious Englishmen can be of anything that they do not immediately understand, don't you?"

Tugging on the cuffs of his shirt, he smiled so wryly it was almost a wince, and to her amazement she realized that this lengthy explanation was really a sign that he was as nervous as she. He must be sure he was rambling, babbling on like this, and cursing himself in silent misery, but she found it...*endearing.*

"People will always see what they wish in others," she

said softly, knowing that sad truth from her own experience. "Especially if what they imagine is more exciting than the truth."

"Exactly," declared Revell. "Which is why Albert Fordyce fully expects me to go racing about the countryside on one of his skittish overbred nags, laying a breakneck siege to every squire's equally skittish, red-faced daughter in the county simply for the sport of it."

"You wouldn't?" she asked, unable to keep from teasing him in the face of such indignation. "You disappoint me, my lord."

"Well, yes, I disappoint everyone, don't I?" he said as he finally came to stand beside her at the table. "Don't you remember how it was your father's library that drew me to your house in the first place?"

She did. Her father's library had been her favorite place in their house and she had spent endless hours curled in a tall-backed wicker chair near the window to catch any breeze while she read and dreamed of the impossibly distant fairy-tale lands of France and England.

She'd been sitting in that same chair when she'd first seen Revell coming through the doorway with her father. She had not wanted to be interrupted, and had tried to hide, pressing herself more tightly into the chair's curving back and holding her breath to sit perfectly still.

But Revell had spotted her anyway and sought her out, and as soon as he smiled, she'd forgotten instantly about hiding. She'd never seen a more handsome British gentleman in Calcutta, and she'd been as dazzled as every other female in Calcutta by that smile. But it wasn't until later that afternoon, after they'd quarreled—so violently that her father had scolded her for being inhospitable—over the symbolism in Voltaire's *Candide,* that she'd realized that she would love Revell Claremont, too. He had been as fascinated by her bookish wit as by her newly blossoming body, while she had found the handsome gentleman who was equally accomplished at kissing and listening irresistible.

But while the library might bring back bittersweet memories, hearing Revell mention her father only robbed Sara of her composure, forcing her once again to consider Hannibal to hide her confusion and uneasiness. Her poor father's death had changed everything. If only the circumstances around it had been less clouded, then she wouldn't have had to leave Calcutta so hastily, or change her name, or become a governess to keep herself from starving. But how much of this sad truth did Revell know, and how much would he forgive?

"Did you know I bought your father's copy of *Candide* at the auction of his things?" Revell continued, running his fingers along the leather binding of the open book on the table before them. "The one you'd left in the garden, where the dew had dappled the cover? By the time of the auction, you were already gone, of course, but still I wanted something to remind me of the days we'd shared."

"You came back to Calcutta in time for the sale?" she asked, stunned. "But you couldn't have, not when they told me that you—"

"Here you are, Miss Blake!" exclaimed Clarissa, the holiday-red ribbons in her hair bobbing as she skipped into the library. "Mama said I should find you here, and I— oh, Lord Revell, why are *you* here, too?"

"And a fine good day to you, too, Miss Clarissa," said Revell, deftly covering Sara's confusion. "As you can see, I am helping Miss Blake prepare your lessons for today."

Clarissa's cheerfulness vanished, and she heaved a dutiful sigh that must have begun at the tips of her slippers; clearly she'd been hoping for an explanation with more interesting possibilities. "What sort of lesson, my lord?"

"We shall be continuing to speak of ancient generals,

Clarissa," said Sara quickly. "I've found a picture here in one of your father's books to show you how Hannibal used elephants to cross the Alps to reach Rome."

"Truly?" asked Clarissa with more interest as she crowded next to Sara to look at the open book. "I do like elephants, with their funny long noses."

"It's a pity the artist hadn't the slightest notion of how an elephant should be ridden, however," said Revell critically, also crowding next to Sara on her other side, and effectively trapping her between the little girl and himself.

Although he continued looking down at the illustration instead of her, he let his hand brush against hers, doing it as if by accident so she couldn't shift away without making a scene. Carefully he pretended to trace the line of the elephant's trunk with one finger, but Sara knew better. Even that slight touch was enough to send a shiver of sensation racing up her arm, a shiver she most decidedly did not wish to feel.

"This poor fellow here might as well be perched at the top of a sliding board, sitting on the elephant's neck like that," he continued, frowning a bit to prove the seriousness of his commentary. "He'd be tossed off, head over heels, and bouncing down the mountainside before he knew it."

"He would?" asked Clarissa, her eyes round with horrified fascination. "All the way down to the bottom?"

"*All* the way," said Revell solemnly. "In less time than it takes to tell. And oh, how that old elephant would laugh!"

"Artists often make such errors, my lord," said Sara hurriedly. Heaven only knew what Revell would say next if she left him unchecked, and *he* wouldn't be the one who'd have to deal with nightmares tonight. "Artists often must instead rely upon the reports of others because they cannot see everything they must portray. They can't really be faulted if the results are sometimes questionable."

"Questionable?" repeated Revell, his brows raised with exaggerated wonder. "I'd say the results were deuced peculiar, and so would you, Miss Blake, if you dared be honest. You know perfectly well what a proper elephant should look like."

"I also know what a proper one smells like," countered Sara warmly, "not that that is particularly relevant to this discussion."

"Why not, Miss Blake?" asked Clarissa, leaning her cheek on her elbow. "If elephants don't smell nice, then why would Hannibal wish to take them all the way to Rome?"

"Because they are very large and strong and have great endurance," said Sara, eager to move on from the question of elephantine aroma. "They would be exceptionally useful to any army."

"Your Miss Blake is quite the expert on elephants," said Revell, beaming dangerously at Sara. "I doubt there's another governess in Sussex—no, all of England!—that has so much experience with the creatures."

"Miss Blake?" asked Clarissa, simultaneously enormously impressed yet uncertain as to whether she should believe Revell or not. "However would she have any experience with elephants?"

"Because I learn through reading," said Sara quickly, before Revell could offer any additional helpful insight. *Blast* him for teasing her this way! Didn't he realize the kind of trouble he was making for her? "One can learn everything about anything through books."

But Clarissa was paying much closer attention to the elephants than to the wisdom to be gained through reading.

"We should put elephants in Mama's greenery," she said, grinning up at Revell. "Miss Blake and I have been charged with making the greenery in the ballroom more festive for Mama. It's our special task. We were going to make camels for the three kings, but now I think they should have elephants instead.''

"Oh, Clarissa, I do not believe that is the wisest idea,'' said Sara doubtfully. Lady Fordyce's tastes were exceptionally traditional, and likely she would not be pleased to find elephants—even elephants cut from white pasteboard and daubed with colored inks—parading over her mantels and sideboards between the silver candlesticks, through boughs of holly and boxwood.

"Why not, Miss Blake?'' asked Revell blithely. "There are plenty of elephants in the Bible, aren't there? Begin with them, then some tigers.''

"Tigers!'' exclaimed Clarissa with a small roar of relish. "Tigers for Christmas!''

Revell nodded, his eyes glinting with wicked mischief that would have shocked Albert and the others. "What better time of the year, eh? And what of a mongoose or two? Miss Blake knows of them, too, you know.''

"You must come help us, Lord Revell,'' ordered Clarissa. "This afternoon, in the schoolroom. You can help Miss Blake and me cut out the animals and paint them, and then tomorrow we can arrange them in the ballroom.''

"I'm sure Lord Revell has other plans, Clarissa,'' said Sara, silently praying that he did. "Doubtless he'd rather spend his afternoon in the company of the other gentlemen like your brother, not in the schoolroom with us.''

"Not at all,'' said Revell, holding his hand over his heart so gallantly that Clarissa giggled. "I cannot think of a greater pleasure than spending the afternoon in the company of two such delightful ladies.''

"Please, my lord,'' said Sara, almost pleading. "It is not necessary.''

"And I say it is my decision if I choose to splatter

myself with glue and paint for the sake of the elephants and tigers and mongooses, too.'' His grin softened as their gazes met over Clarissa's head. ''Besides, isn't Christmas the time for miracles and magic of every sort?''

Chapter Four

Revell stood before his bedchamber window, watching the two figures make their way in a zigzagging path across the snowy field toward the house. Against the stark black and white of the wintry landscape, the pair stood out in sharp contrast: the little girl in her bright red cardinal and blue mittens, the woman in a cloak of darkest green. But then, for Revell, the two would be the first he'd spot even in the most crowded street in London.

"That be Miss Fordyce and her governess, my lord," said the maidservant, following his gaze as she set the tray on the table beside him. The woman was past middle age, a servant who'd likely been with the Fordyces for so long that she felt entitled to certain conversational freedoms like this. "No matter what the weather, them two always go walking at this time of the day, regular as clockwork after first lessons."

Revell, of course, had discovered this for himself, having already visited the schoolroom as promised to help with the tigers and elephants. The schoolroom had been empty except for a mystified parlor maid who'd informed him of Miss Clarissa's customary walk. He'd have to control his impatience for another half hour or so until they returned, and without much interest he glanced at the plates of sliced cold meat, breads, and cheese on the tray that the cook had sent up to him out of a certain pity.

He knew he was already being regarded as something of an oddity. The other houseguests had scattered for the day, the gentlemen out riding and visiting the local tavern with Albert and Sir David as their leaders, and the ladies, under Lady Fordyce's guidance, putting the final touches on their masquerade costumes at the local milliners and mantua-makers. His polite refusal to join either party had raised eyebrows, and he could only imagine what manner of wicked pastimes the others had imagined for him instead. How wonderfully shocked they'd be when they, inevitably, learned the truth!

"Aye, my lord, that Miss Blake has worked magic with the little miss," continued the maidservant with approval, taking Revell's silence as encouragement. "Like a little wild creature, she was, before Miss Blake came. 'Course 'tis to be expected, being so petted and all, but Miss Blake was the only one to give her manners to match her breeding."

"How long has Miss Blake been with the family?" asked Revell, striving to sound only idly interested. He knew it wasn't wise to encourage such confidential discussions with servants, but he'd learned next to nothing from Albert, and God help him, he'd so blasted much at stake.

"Five years this spring, my lord," answered the maidservant promptly, her hands folded over the front of her apron. "Before that she was with Lady Gordon, whose husband made such a fortune in India. A regular nabob, he was. Oh, begging your pardon, my lord, meaning no disrespect to yourself."

"None taken," said Revell, his thoughts racing. He remembered Lady Gordon—Lady Gorgon, they'd called her, on account of her imperious manner—from Calcutta's small English social world before her husband had retired from the Company and returned home. But how would Sara have become a servant in Lady Gordon's household, and why in blazes would she have left India—and him— so suddenly to do so? "Though I suppose they must have become acquainted in India together."

"Miss Blake in India, my lord?" asked the servant, scandalized. "She's a proper English lass, is our Miss Blake, not one of those wild, brown-skinned hussies from the colonies! Begging pardon again, my lord, but 'tis different for gentlemen. You know how it be, my lord. Lady Fordyce would never have taken Miss Blake if she'd lived wild among the pagan savages like that."

"I understand," said Revell, and he did, far more than the servant could realize. He'd forgotten the prejudice against women who'd gone out to India, let alone the ones like Sara who'd been born there. She hadn't even had the advantage of being sent home to England for education as a girl, the way most British children were, simply because her widowed father hadn't been able to bear parting with her. When he'd teased Sara about tigers and elephants before Clarissa, he'd only meant to remind her of the past they'd shared. Instead, great bumbling ass that he was, he'd put her entire livelihood and reputation at risk.

"If that will be all, my lord," the maidservant was saying as she dropped a quick curtsy, the edges of her apron clutched in her hands.

"Yes, yes, and thank you," said Revell, then shook his head as he thought of the final question. "About Miss Blake. She's never been wed, has she?"

The servant grinned widely. "Nay, my lord, nor could she have taken a husband and still be Miss Blake, could she? Neither husband, nor followers, not since she's been with the Fordyces. I tell you, my lord, she's a good, quiet lass, and a credit to this house.''

"That is all, then," he said softly, and turned back to the window. Sara and Clarissa must be inside now, for the haphazard trail of their footprints through the snow led to the kitchen door in the yard below. Soon he could venture back to the schoolroom, and be sure to find them there.

And then what? He'd learned more of Sara's past from the maidservant, true, but he'd also realized he didn't want to ask any more such questions. It had been one thing to make inquiries when he'd no notion of where she was, but quite another when fate had so conveniently placed her once again beneath the same roof. Now he should be asking her himself, directly and without guile; anything else seemed distastefully like spying, and Sara—Sara deserved better than that from him, no matter what happened next.

Still gazing out at the flurried footprints in the snow, he lightly touched the waistcoat pocket that held the sapphire ring. She could talk all she wished about Christmas miracles, but surely finding her again like this, across six years and three continents, was as truly miraculous as anything he could ever have dreamed.

Perhaps this is why he'd been drawn so inexplicably to Ladysmith. Perhaps some subtle tug of fate had made him trade London and a liquor-sodden bachelor Christmas with Brant for another chance with Sara. Living in India had loosened his distinctly English faith in a world based on logic and reason, and made him trust more to the mysteries of fate.

But not even that could explain why Sara had abandoned him the first time, or why he seemed so damned eager to let her do it again. He thought he'd sensed the old magic between them again, but for her part, she hadn't exactly been overjoyed to see him. Pleased, yes, but not overjoyed, and not at all eager to trade her life as a governess for one with him—a sobering, if not downright depressing, thought. Yet he couldn't deny that when he was with her, he felt happier, younger, more content and yet more excited, too, more at peace with himself and the world.

He might even still feel in love.

He gave the box with the ring one last rueful pat. All he could do was ask Sara for the truth, and let the rest fall where it would.

And believe with all his heart in miracles.

Never had Sara doubted that Revell Claremont was an extraordinarily accomplished gentleman. He rode well— both horses and elephants—shot well, and was as skilled with the short, curved blade of a Gurkha's *kookree* as he was with an English cutlass. Unlike most sons of dukes, he had survived on his own since he was fourteen, and made his first fortune before he'd turned twenty-one. He was as well read as any university man, spoke five languages with ease and grace and swore in several more, and while he could demonstrate all the *politesse* of a career diplomat, he could also be a ruthless negotiator and trader, as able to conduct business in a rough tent with Bengali brigands as he was with the equally cut-throat factors of the East India Company.

But as Sara soon saw, he was hopeless—absolutely, abjectly hopeless—with a pair of scissors, a pot of paste, and a pile of colored paper squares.

"*Not* like that, my lord," said Clarissa, scowling down at the tiger's head, newly attached at a peculiar angle to his body and oozing a fatal blob of paste from his throat, or what should have been his throat if his head had been placed more accurately. "You've put it on all wrong."

"I have?" Revell stared balefully at the tiger, heedless of another paste blob smeared across the sleeve of his superfine coat. He had insisted on sitting beside Clarissa at the child's table, his oversize frame hunched forward and his legs bent awkwardly to fit the short chair. "I thought he had rather a rakish air about him."

"No, he doesn't," said Clarissa crossly. "It's just *wrong.*"

Considering the discussion complete, she reached across Revell and pushed the offending head into a more anatomically pleasing position, using her small thumb to wipe away the extra paste.

"There," she said, propping the tiger to stand upright. "*Now* he'll do. Mama is most particular, my lord. She doesn't want her ballroom cluttered up with any old rubbish, and she'll tell you so, too."

"I doubt she would tell Lord Revell quite as rudely as you have, Clarissa," said Sara. She didn't dare look at Revell, sitting there with his knees beneath his chin and the most wounded look imaginable on his face, or risk giggling out loud. "He has been most kind to offer his help, you know."

"Well, he hasn't helped at all," declared Clarissa, hands on her hips and without a morsel of gratitude. "First he cut the ear off that lovely elephant you'd drawn, then he didn't wash the red paint from the brush before he put it into the blue and made it all nasty and purple, and *then* he tried to ruin this tiger, too, by putting the head on so crooked."

"Clarissa," warned Sara. "I believe Lord Revell deserves an apology from you for that."

Revell sighed. "No, I don't," he said humbly. "I did muddy the paints, exactly as Clarissa said."

"That's not the point, my lord." As sternly as she could, Sara frowned at Clarissa. "Clarissa, an apology."

"Very well." Now Clarissa was the one to sigh, flopping her hands at her sides to duck the slightest possible curtsy. "Forgive me for speaking so rudely to you, my lord. You didn't mean to be clumsy and bumbling. You just were."

"I know," admitted Revell as he tried to scrape the paste from his sleeve. "It's quite a problem with me, isn't it? But perhaps Miss Blake can help me. Surely there must be some task you'll trust me with, Miss Blake? Something that not even I could ruin?"

Though Revell's expression remained serious and properly penitent for Clarissa's sake, his eyes sparkled with such amusement that Sara realized he, too, was dangerously close to laughing. The blobs of paste and ruined paint were like another secret they shared, another connection—albeit an untidy one—and she felt such a warmth of fresh affection swirling between them that she couldn't keep from smiling.

If they had wed as they'd planned, they could be husband and wife in a house of their own, instead of guest and governess in this one. They could be laughing with *their* children, making plans for *their* Christmas together, sharing the paint and paste and mangled elephants, trust and love and happiness.

Oh, Sara, Sara, take care! A smile is not a promise for the future, nor an explanation for the past, and not once since he found you has he mentioned love....

"He could make the paper chains to hang over the looking glasses, Miss Blake, couldn't he?" suggested Clarissa. "Even babies can make those. Here, my lord, it's quite simple. You cut the strips of paper and loop them together like this."

She demonstrated importantly, showing Revell exactly how to make the chain's paper links tie into one another, as if she were a conjurer revealing a complex trick. "You do have to use the paste again, my lord, but it goes inside, where no one will see if you use too much."

"As you wish, *memsahib*," said Revell, dutifully bending over the strips of colored paper with more success than he'd shown with the animals; as Clarissa had noted, even a baby could make paper chains.

But Clarissa's attention had already bounded forward. "What did you call me?" she asked. "Mem what?"

"*Memsahib,*" he said, concentrating on making the paste stick. "That's what fine ladies are called in India, as a form of respect. Your mother would be *memsahib,* while your father would simply be *sahib.*"

"*Memsahib,*" repeated Clarissa, relishing the sound and feel of the foreign word. "Do you know other Indian words?"

"Oh, an entire wagon full," said Revell expansively. "Instead of a gown, you would wear a *sari.* Your mother's grand ball would be called a *burra khana,* and Miss Blake here would be your *ayah.*"

Sara laughed, wrinkling her nose. "I do not know if I wish to be anyone's *ayah.* All the *ayahs* I ever had were cross-tempered old women who'd pinch my arm to make me obey."

"Did you truly know *ayahs,* Miss Blake?" asked Clarissa curiously. "Or is it like the elephants, and you only mean from books?"

"From books, I am sure," said Revell quickly, rescuing Sara from her misstep. "I'm the one who's more at home in Calcutta than London."

"Which is how you've come to know so many peculiar foreign words, I expect," said Clarissa, leaning closer to admire his handiwork. "Why, my lord, that is almost a proper chain after all. Here, let me put it with the others."

Gingerly she gathered up Revell's chain and carried it across the room to add it to the other decorations they'd made, pausing to admire the animals once again.

"We need to talk, Sara," said Revell, his voice low and

urgent as he touched her arm. "When can we meet alone?"

Startled, she blushed, and pulled her arm away. "We shouldn't, Revell," she whispered. "That night on the terrace—wasn't that enough?"

"Not by half, it wasn't," he said. "Tonight, after Clarissa is in bed. Ten o'clock, say, by the same door to the terrace."

"Please, Rev, I do not—"

"I'll not take no, Sara," he said firmly. "Tonight, on the same terrace. Don't fail me, lass."

But before she could answer the door to the schoolroom opened and in swept Lady Fordyce.

"Look, Clary, look what I've brought you from town!" she called gaily, holding up an elaborate mask decorated with gold beads and red plumes. "It shall be the perfect accompaniment to your costume for—oh, my, Lord Revell! You surprise me, my lord!"

She might have been surprised, but Sara was beyond that, to out-and-out speechless horror. To have Lady Fordyce discover her like this, in Clarissa's schoolroom, with Revell standing so guiltily close to her that there could be no respectable explanation possible.

Not that Revell wouldn't venture one. "I didn't intend to surprise you, Lady Fordyce," he said, remaining beside Sara as if there were nothing at all remarkable about such proximity. "I was simply helping your daughter with the elephants."

Lady Fordyce's face went cautiously blank. "Elephants?"

"Yes, Mama, look!" Gleefully Clarissa held a paper elephant in one hand and a tiger in the other. "For the ballroom! Miss Blake and I made the animals, while Lord Revell made chains!"

"Even babies can make chains," explained Revell modestly, stepping to the table to drape one of his chains from one hand across to the other. "And so, therefore, can I."

"But elephants and tigers, Miss Blake?" asked Lady Fordyce, disapproval frosting her voice. "For my masquerade ball?"

Sara nodded, resolutely determined to put the best face on what now seemed a disastrous decision. "Yes, my lady. The elephants were inspired by our lessons on ancient Rome."

"But your lessons are one thing," said Lady Fordyce, her expression growing darker still, "and my Christmas masquerade is quite, quite another."

"Ah, but there will be no more appropriate creatures imaginable," assured Revell as he idly swung the chain back and forth. "You've only to see how the Prince of Wales himself is covering his walls with peacocks and tigers everywhere, and my own brother is having the dining room of Claremont House painted all over with frolicking monkeys."

"Your brother the duke?" asked Lady Fordyce, reconsidering the elephant in her daughter's hand. "His Grace would approve? And the Prince, too?"

"I should not be surprised if you set a new fashion, and all on account of your daughter's lessons," said Revell, his smile shifting toward Sara, as if to thank Clarissa's governess for such a splendid notion.

But at the same time his gaze seemed to warm as he found Sara's, giving his words another meaning that only she would understand, and that would remind her once again of the meeting he sought with her later.

"You know, Lady Fordyce," he continued, determinedly not looking away and not letting Sara do so, either, "that in England today there is nothing more choice, more desired, than that which comes from India, and never more so than this Christmas."

Chapter Five

By the single candlestick in her chamber upstairs from the nursery, Sara took one final look at her reflection in the small looking glass over the washstand. Did her eyes truly seem brighter, happier, her mouth more ready to curve into a smile? Or was it no more than the most wishful hopes and the wavering candlelight that had made the difference, and not Revell?

Lightly she touched the crooked head of the paper tiger that she'd hidden in her pocket, now tucked into the frame of her looking glass, and as she ran her finger along the hardened paste on the tiger's neck, she smiled, thinking of how gamely Revell had struggled at the low schoolroom table. Tomorrow, when they began decorating the ballroom in earnest, she'd sworn to herself that she'd return the tiger to the other ornaments. Deciding what to do next about Revell wouldn't be nearly as easy.

From the hall below she heard the ten echoes of the case clock chiming the hour, and swiftly patted her hair one last time. She'd dallied long enough; now that she'd made up her mind to meet Revell—though only for the briefest few minutes imaginable!—she didn't want to keep him waiting.

She hurried down the back stairs, keeping her footsteps as soft as possible so that no one else would know she wasn't asleep. Not that anyone was likely to notice. With the house so full of guests, most servants were still busy helping in the kitchen or with serving, and from the voices and merry laughter in the drawing room, the Fordyces and their friends weren't likely to retire to their bedchambers until midnight at the earliest. She paused to press herself against the wall to allow two footmen to bustle past with covered trays.

Around this corner, she thought as she fastened the front of her cloak, then down the last hall to the terrace doors, and to Revell. As hard as it would be, she meant to tell him the truth, as quickly and with as few words as possible, and then she would—

"Miss Blake!" called Lady Fordyce breathlessly behind her. "Oh, Miss Blake! How vastly fortuitous that you are still awake!"

Reluctantly, Sara stopped, her anticipation crumbling. As much as she wished to run ahead, to pretend she hadn't heard her mistress, her conscience wouldn't let her.

"I couldn't sleep, my lady," she said, her explanation mechanical with disappointment as Lady Fordyce joined her. "I was only going outside for a brief walk."

"Then how glad I am to have found you first," declared the older woman, her round face flushed and glistening with a hostess's duress as well as the wine from dinner. She took Sara firmly by the arm to steer her back toward the drawing room, clearly unwilling to let Sara even consider escape.

"Miss Talbot wishes to sing," she continued, "and none of the other ladies seem to be able to cope with the stiffness of our sorry old pianoforte's keys. But now we have *you*, Miss Blake, a born accompanist if ever there was one! You *must* play for Miss Talbot. Come, come,

come, you cannot wish to keep such a splendid company waiting a moment longer!''

Miserably Sara thought of Revell, of keeping him waiting far more than a moment, of dreams of her own that had waited for six years and more. But that was nothing tangible, nothing definite, and nothing that could be explained to Lady Fordyce without risking her position and her livelihood. And so, with her head bent in dutiful unhappiness, Sara went to her fate, and the pianoforte.

She hadn't come.

For over an hour Revell had waited for her on the terrace, letting the cold wind flail away at his body through his coat as well as the hopes he'd held somewhere near his heart. He'd come early, not wanting to miss her, and he'd stayed late, in the ever-dwindling possibility she'd been delayed. He'd stayed until he'd lost the feeling in his hands from the cold and his face had settled in an icy grimace, and he'd given up only when he could invent no more excuses on her absent behalf.

She hadn't come because, quite simply, she hadn't cared.

Now he sat at the breakfast table, listlessly prodding at his toasted rolls and shirred eggs while the purposelessly cheerful conversation rolled around him. He wondered what he'd do to pass this day, and all the ones that would follow. He reminded himself that Sara hadn't promised to meet him, or anything else, for that matter. He tried to compose a suitable greeting for her when they met again, one that somehow wouldn't put his disappointment and bitterness on public display. He considered inventing some sort of family emergency and leaving this afternoon, and never looking back. He endeavored not to imagine how his older brother would jeer and call him the greatest, most sentimental fool in Christendom, and how, this time, Brant would be right.

"Like the rarest, sweetest nightingale!" the man next to him was gushing. "Ah, Miss Talbot, how we were blessed to have such a songbird in our midst last night!"

Miss Talbot, the plump and amorous blonde who, to Revell's dismay, persisted in trying to catch his attention, now giggled, balancing a teaspoon delicately between her fingers.

"You are too, too kind, Mr. Andrews," she simpered. "I do my best, I do, even when you gentlemen do make me go on and *on!*"

"'On and on,' my word," said Mr. Andrews, chuckling as if this were the greatest witticism in the world. "I could have listened to your sweet voice all the night long!"

He leaned into Revell, suddenly confidential. "Such a gem of a voice you missed last night, Lord Revell, oh, what you missed!"

"Indeed," said Revell, as dry and discouraging as he could be, but the other man plowed onward undaunted.

"Indeed, yes, my lord," he maintained, slyly winking at Miss Talbot and her décolletage. "Why, I hate to consider the pleasure we would have missed if Lady Fordyce hadn't drummed her daughter's governess into playing the pianoforte so Miss Talbot could have her music—"

"She made her governess play for Miss Talbot?" asked Revell, incredulous. "Last night, in the drawing room?"

"Oh, my, yes, my lord," answered Miss Talbot, practically purring to have finally gained Lord Revell's attention. "I must have sung for simply *hours*. The kind gentlemen wouldn't let me stop, my lord."

"And Miss Blake—the governess—played for you the entire time?"

"Yes, my lord." Miss Talbot smiled winningly. "It was Lady Fordyce's wish and order that she accommodate me.

And though I am more accustomed to the touch of a true
lady's hand upon the keys, for one evening that sour little
wren's skills were adequate enough for—''

"Forgive me, Miss Talbot, but I must, ah, leave, leave
directly." Revell rose so fast he nearly toppled his chair
backward, and as he bolted from the room to amazed gasps
and outraged murmurs, he didn't bother to look back, leaving Andrews to console the indignantly abandoned Miss
Talbot.

At this hour of the morning Sara and Clarissa must be
on their morning walk—"regular as clockwork," the maid
had said—and if he hurried, he might meet them before
they returned home. Having Clarissa there wouldn't let
him speak as freely as he would have done last night, but
it would still be far better than if he had to seek her out
inside the crowded house. He raced to his room for his
coat and gloves, past more startled servants and guests
with his coattails flying about behind him, before he
reached the back door and opened it himself, not waiting
for the footman who belatedly hurried to do it for him.

A light dusting of new snow had fallen in the night,
softening and smoothing the outlines of the landscape, but
also making any new footprints sharp and clean by contrast. Revell crossed the yard near the stables, heading in
the direction where he'd seen Sara and Clarissa yesterday.
A wide trampled path of muddied snow showed where
Albert had ridden out with his friends earlier, but there,
off to one side, Revell found what he'd sought: two sets
of prints walking closely together, one small, one smaller,
and both framed by the sweeping trail of long petticoats.

He found them in a small copse of ancient holly, the
leaves glossy and dark green against the snow, the berries
crimson. In the snow sat a large willow basket that Sara
and Clarissa were filling with branches Sara was cutting
from the holly to take back to the ballroom. The little girl

laughed with excitement, clapping her red-mittened hands
as she kicked her feet in an impromptu dance in the snow.

Yet as pretty a scene as this was, Revell still hesitated
to interrupt. While Sara's role as an impromptu accompanist was certainly a plausible explanation for why she
hadn't joined him, she could just as easily have chosen to
play over meeting him. Nothing was certain, but then nothing concerning Sara was.

Except, of course, that he wished it to be.

Sara turned, tossing another branch into the basket, and
now that Revell could hear the song she was humming,
without thinking he began singing along with her, the
words coming back to him from at least a lifetime away.

"'Green grow'th the holly,
So doth the ivy,
Though winter blast's blow ne'er so high
Blow ever so icy,
Green grow'th the holly.'"

She looked up swiftly, found him on the edge of the
copse, and her face lit with the most radiant smile imaginable, free of any shadow of uncertainty or second
thoughts.

"Lord Revell!" cried Clarissa gleefully, loping through
the snow toward him. "You *did* come! Miss Blake said
you wouldn't bother with us, not anymore, but you *did!*"

"Miss Blake is a wise woman, Clarissa," said Revell
with mock severity, his gaze never leaving Sara's face.
Strange how he was still speaking to the child—even making perfect sense, too—while so much else unsaid was
vibrating between him and Sara. "But not even your Miss
Blake knows everything, especially not about me."

*But if she'd only give him half a chance, a quarter of a
chance, he'd offer her every last morsel of fact that there*

was to learn, plus his heart and his soul and the world in the bargain.

"Sing your song again, my lord," begged Clarissa, hopping up and down with anticipation. "It's exactly right for picking holly."

"It's not *his* song at all, Clarissa," said Sara, rubbing her gloved hands together to warm them. Her cheeks were very pink, her eyes very bright, and the exertion of the bough-cutting along with her hood had tousled her hair into wispy tendrils around her face, most disordered for a governess and, decided Revell, altogether charming. "It's a very famous song written long ago by King Henry the Eighth."

"Then he must be a relative of yours, my lord," said Clarissa sagely. "Miss Blake says dukes are next to princes and kings, which makes you almost family with King Henry himself."

Revell laughed, both at the ridiculousness of the connection and because, in his present giddy—*giddy?*—state, he couldn't help it.

"Not precisely, no," he said. "My family's muddled enough without claiming old King Hal and all his mischief into the tawdry mix. There's only myself and two brothers left among us Claremonts, and I can assure you that that is plenty."

"Then you are an orphan, too, just like Miss Blake," said Clarissa with appropriate solemnity. "*We* are her family now, you know, especially at Christmas. Mama says she has nowhere else to go."

"Oh, my, Clarissa," said Sara, her smile perhaps more poignant than she intended, her unabashed joy clearly faltering. "You would have me be a stray dog that no one wishes to claim!"

"*I* did not say you were a stray dog, Miss Blake," said Clarissa indignantly, "only that you had nowhere else to go, and you don't, and neither does Lord Revell. I suppose we can look after him, too, same as we do you. Mama always says kindness must begin at home. Here now, my lord, bend down.''

Mystified but obedient, Revell bowed his tall shoulders to Clarissa's level. He didn't really consider himself an orphan, not at his age and with his less than warm memories of his long-dead parents, and he hardly felt in need of befriending because of their absence. But then hadn't he accepted Albert Fordyce's invitation for exactly that reason—to experience the kind of loud, cheerful, traditional family Christmas that he and his brothers had never really had for themselves? Wasn't he every bit the foot-loose mongrel dog that Sara had just described, always roaming, without a home to call his own?

"There, my lord," said Clarissa, scowling with concentration as she stuck a small sprig of holly into the top buttonhole of his coat. "Now you truly belong with us all at Ladysmith, at least until Twelfth Night."

Slowly he straightened, patting the holly sprig as he wondered where his lighthearted smile had gone, and with it Sara's rosy-cheeked exuberance. Now she looked as if a score of private sorrows had pinched and drained the color from her face, memories that he didn't share and perhaps never would.

More unexpected strangeness, this, that the little girl's attempts at aping her mother's grand lady-of-the-manor kindness could touch him—and Sara—so deeply. Perhaps they *were* both the stray dogs no one would claim, and though he tried to laugh again at the sheer lunacy of such a notion, he couldn't. Miracles and elephants, stray dogs and plum pudding and holly for Christmas: who could sort out the significance in so much foolishness?

"Mama says to be truly happy, my lord," continued

Clarissa, "you must have someone to care for, and someone to care for you. Isn't that so, Miss Blake?"

But for once Sara left a question of her student's unanswered. "Clarissa, I believe I must have left my scarf back at the walnut tree. Would you please oblige me by going to fetch it?"

"Yes, Miss Blake," said Clarissa, nodding with gleeful anticipation. She was so seldom permitted to go anywhere unattended, even twenty feet to the walnut tree, that she was off before Sara could change her mind, crashing through the brush and snow.

But Sara was crashing ahead, too, her words racing in a breathless rush, knowing she wouldn't have long to explain. "About last night, Rev, about—"

"I don't care," he said, coming to stand close before her, gently pushing back her hood.

She was trembling with anticipation. "But, Rev, I want you to know that—"

"That's enough," he said softly, and then he was kissing her, his lips warm on hers in the chilly air, his fingers tangling in her hair as he cradled her head. She should have pulled away, she should have protested, but instead she closed her eyes and surrendered with only a faint, fluttering sigh that was lost between them.

She tipped her head and hungrily parted her lips, welcoming him deeper as the rush of well-remembered pleasure and intimacy slipped through her body. Her head and her reason might have tried to forget him, but the rest of her had clung to his memory with fervent loyalty, making the years they'd been apart slip away as nothing. One kiss, and she realized how much a part of her Revell still was, and always would be.

"Ah, Sara," he murmured, his voice rough with desire as at last he broke the kiss, keeping her face close to his.

"How can you know how much I have missed kissing you?"

She smiled through a blur of tears, her emotions almost too strong for lowly words. She felt shaken and uncertain, as if she'd been turned inside out and back again, without any notion of what would come next. Yet even so she still heard Clarissa's return behind her, and just in time she pulled away from Revell.

Her cloak blown back from running, the girl rubbed her nose with the thumb of her mitten and gazed up at Sara accusingly. "Your scarf wasn't there, Miss Blake."

"It wasn't?" asked Sara, her heart racing as she self-consciously tried to smooth her hair back into place. Even without turning she could sense Revell beside her, and it took all her willpower not to reach for his hand.

How could one kiss cause so much damage? She'd done well enough for years without Revell at her side. What was it about him that could turn her into such a dreadful, quivering mess, especially when he'd only promised to linger in her life through Twelfth Night? Didn't he realize how disastrous this game could be to her, or did he simply not care? They had to talk: they had to talk *now*, certainly before he tried to kiss her again.

And heaven preserve her if she were still even halfway in love with him....

"It wasn't." Clarissa sighed and pointed dramatically at the basket with the ivy clippings and the missing scarf looped over the handle. "Your scarf wasn't near the walnut tree, Miss Blake, because it was *here* all the while, and if—Miss Blake? Are you ill, Miss Blake?"

"Of course I am well, Clarissa," said Sara quickly, convincing neither the girl nor herself. "Have you ever known me to be ill in all the time I've been with you?"

"You don't look right," said Clarissa warily. "I think we should go home directly."

"Agreed," said Revell, though to Sara his voice didn't sound any more steady than hers. "I told you, Clarissa, that while Miss Blake is vastly clever in most matters, there are times when she is absolutely as mortal as the rest of us. Which is why she needs us to look after her now, exactly as she takes such excellent care of you."

"My mama says so, too." Clarissa nodded, reassured enough to assume, for this once, the role of caretaker, and solicitously took Sara's hand. "Come, Miss Blake. We've been out of doors long enough."

"That is most kind of you, Clarissa, but I'm perfectly well," insisted Sara. "Rev—my lord, please tell her!"

"Not when the lass is correct," said Revell, slinging the basket with the holly over one arm, then offering the other to her. His smile was warm, teasing, yet seductive, too, all attributes she'd no right receiving with a smile from him. "You look peaked, Miss Blake, and we cannot take too much care with you."

Pointedly, Sara ignored his arm. "I am *not* peaked."

"Yes, you are," said Clarissa, turning to Revell with a confidential whisper. "You are most right, my lord, and most kind. It's as Mama says. We cannot take too much care. And I don't care what the others say about you, my lord. You are *not* the wickedest man in India, not when you are being so nice to Miss Blake like this."

He tucked Sara's hand into the crook of his arm, giving it an extra pat, and woefully Sara knew that even if he were not the wickedest man in India, then surely *she* must be the weakest woman in Sussex.

Chapter Six

"So there you are, Miss Blake." The cook looked past her two maids, their hands white with flour from pie-making, as Sara shepherded Clarissa through the kitchen door. "Lady Fordyce's been asking for you all through the house, Miss. Oh, My Lord Revell, forgive me, I didn't see you a-coming there too!"

"He's very hard to overlook, Mrs. Green," said Clarissa, stretching to reach the plate of sliced plum cake destined to accompany some lady guest's tea. "He's even bigger than Albert, you know."

"Your flatter me, Clarissa," said Revell easily, setting the basket of holly on the table as if he were a footman instead of a lord, and making the two young kitchen maids wide-eyed with amazement and admiration, too. "I think so, anyway. Doesn't she, Miss Blake?"

But Sara was already unfastening her cloak, hurrying to make herself presentable for Lady Fordyce. It must be the tigers and elephants being inappropriate for Christmas: she'd already been half expecting to be called to task by her ladyship for that.

"Mrs. Green," she said briskly, stripping off her gloves,

"will you please see that one of your girls takes Clarissa upstairs to the nursery to change her wet things?"

"Lord Revell can take me," suggested Clarissa promptly. "I can show him the way to the—"

"You must not presume on Lord Revell's good nature, Clarissa," said Sara, trying to ignore the waves of curiosity rising from the cook and her maids, and no wonder, either, not with Clarissa treating Revell with all the familiarity of a favorite uncle. "Go along now, upstairs with Bess."

"And what orders for me, Miss Blake?" asked Revell with an easy, fond familiarity that made Sara blush all over again. His smile was warm and winning, his blue eyes so full of affection that she felt it as surely as if he'd kissed her again. Lightly he patted the sprig of holly in his buttonhole, reminding her of far too many things. "Where do you wish me to go?"

If he'd acted like Clarissa's uncle, then Sara didn't want to venture what he must seem to her in the eager eyes of the kitchen staff. No one would believe they'd only just met, and no one—no one—would believe their relationship held all the propriety of the humble governess with a noble-bred guest of the house.

"You shall do whatever you please, my lord," she said, daring him, just remembering to curtsy to him before she left the kitchen. "That is both your prerogative, my lord, and your habit, is it not?"

Oh, that was wrong, wrong, wrong of her to say! If only they'd have ten minutes alone together—ten minutes without kissing—then this would all be sorted out between them! Furious with herself and with him, she bunched her skirts in her fist and marched up the stairs to Lady Fordyce's rooms.

"Ah, Miss Blake, here at last," said Lady Fordyce. She motioned to her lady's maid, waiting with two pairs of slippers in her hands. "The red ones, Hannah, and mind you check that the stitching on the beading is still tight. I shouldn't want them flying off while I danced. Now, Miss Blake, to your affairs.''

Sara squared her shoulders. ''If you mean to speak to me further of the elephants and tigers that Clarissa is making for the ballroom, my lady, then—''

''But I don't.'' Lady Fordyce smiled brightly. ''They are the height of fashion. All the ladies I have asked have said exactly that, and agreed with Lord Revell. You are to be congratulated for your originality and resourcefulness.''

''Thank you, my lady,'' said Sara faintly, wishing she found this more reassuring than she did.

''*Most* original, yes,'' said her ladyship, as pleased with herself as she was with Sara. ''Which is why I have decided that you shall attend the masquerade with Clarissa, in costume like everyone else. As a treat, you see.''

''My lady!'' exclaimed Sara with more dismay than gratitude. Her days for such frivolous entertainments were long past, left behind in Calcutta along with her bright clothes and jewels and plumes in her hair. ''My lady, you are most kind, but—but I have no proper costume of my own, and with the ball being only two days away—''

''Ah, but I have thought of that, too.'' Lady Fordyce clapped her hands together with triumph. ''Off in our lumber room are trunks and trunks of old gowns and petticoats and headdresses and goodness only knows what else. Take Clary with you, and rummage about as you please. I'm sure you'll find exactly what you need to assemble the perfect costume.''

''Thank you, my lady,'' said Sara faintly, taking the plain black mask that her ladyship handed her. ''You are too kind.''

''Not at all, my dear.'' But her ladyship's habitually cheerful demeanor faded, and restlessly she tapped her fingers together. "That, you see, was the more agreeable message for me to deliver. The other is…is more vexing."

She twisted her mouth to one side, searching for the right words in a way that only made Sara more uneasy.

"You know, Miss Blake, that I have always tried to run this household in a fair and agreeable manner, for the good of everyone beneath this roof," she finally began, "and I am perfectly aware that a rogue is a rogue, no matter what his station. But whereas I can dismiss the footman for taking freedoms with the dairymaid, it is an entirely different when a gentleman, a peer, a guest at Ladysmith, is involved."

Sara felt her cheeks growing warm and her palms turn damp as she realized exactly where her ladyship's conversation was heading.

"Oh, my lady, please don't—"

"No, no, this is my responsibility, not yours," said Lady Fordyce firmly. "You should not be put in the position of having to defend yourself against the unwanted attentions of Lord Revell. No, don't deny that it has happened. The entire house whispers of nothing else."

Sara gasped, mortified. Why couldn't this have stayed between her and Revell alone, without involving everyone else at Ladysmith? Why had she once again become the miserable target of talk and gossip? How long before someone learned her real name, and the shameful truth behind her father's death?

And oh, what would Revell say in return?

"You will not—not address Lord Revell about me, will you, Lady Fordyce?" she begged.

"I would never do such a thing, Miss Blake." Her ladyship pressed her lips tightly together. "He is a gentleman. I could hardly scold him, could I? But I believe I have found an, ah, another solution. I cannot explain further, not yet, but I believe you shall find Lord Revell soon ceases his unwelcome attentions.''

But it wasn't as simple as that, not by half, and Sara knew it. For what if she didn't wish Revell to avoid her? What if, in the last two days, his attentions had come to seem not troublesome, but desirable?

Unhappily, Sara stared down at the floor, praying her confusion didn't show on her face for her ladyship to read. She'd told herself that these two weeks until Twelfth Night would be something to endure, and now that same time with him had become something to treasure. That was the truth, if only she'd be honest with herself. She *wanted* to see him, and *wanted* to be with him, however brief that time together would be.

And it would be brief. As giddy as her heart might be, her cold reason hadn't entirely abandoned her. Once Revell learned the truth about why she'd left Calcutta, he'd scorn her, and she in turn had no assurance that in the end he'd treat her with any more loyalty or honor than he had before. Miracles made for pretty talk, but they weren't guarantees of anything.

Yet still Sara felt the pull of the old connection between them, as if they were once again young and blissfully in love, as if nothing in the world were more complicated than that miracle they'd both never forgotten. *That* was what she wanted, to feel like that again, even if it were only for a handful of days. She wanted that, and she wanted it with Revell, and unconsciously she touched her fingers to her lips, remembering his kiss. He had promised to join them in the ballroom, to help arrange the holly and the elephants. Likely he was already waiting for them— for *her*—now.

''I shall expect you and Clarissa downstairs to join me as soon as she can be shifted into dry clothing,'' continued

Lady Fordyce. "I have already called for the sleigh to take us across to Peterborough Hall."

Sara looked up swiftly, jerked back to the present. "Peterborough, your ladyship? Clarissa and I were planning to spend the rest of the day decorating the ballroom."

"Tomorrow will be time enough for that, Miss Blake." Lady Fordyce's smile was serene, satisfied that she'd solved and dispatched yet another thorny problem in her household. "Until the rest of my little plan comes to pass, I intend to remove you as completely as possible from Lord Revell's temptation, even if that means I must take tea with that odious Lucy Peterborough whilst Clary plays with her daughter."

"But Lady Fordyce!" cried Sara with disappointment and dismay. "With all your other guests here, with all you must do for them—this is hardly necessary, not necessary at all!"

"And I say it is." Lady Fordyce took Sara's hand and patted it gently. "You have always been a most virtuous young woman, Miss Blake, and I've no wish to see you changed."

But Sara realized she already had.

"There, Miss Blake," said Clarissa, stepping back to admire their work, her arms crossed over her chest. "I think that looks *most* fine!"

"It certainly does," agreed Sara, gazing around the ballroom. "I cannot wait for your mother to see it."

They had spent the entire morning working to transform the ballroom, relying on three footmen to help put holly boughs along the crowns of the tall pier glasses. More holly and glossy-green clippings from the boxwood had been arranged along the sideboards and draped from the mantelpieces of the four facing fireplaces, while red and white ribbons had been tied in bows from the polished

A Gift Most Rare

brass chandeliers overhead and woven into the rails of the small musician's gallery.

Revell's paper chains were draped across the front of the pianoforte, brought up from the music room in the event any lady wished to play and spell the hired musicians. Tucked into all the greenery were the pasteboard animals that they'd made, a miniature Noah's ark in an English forest, and once the scores of beeswax candles were lit tonight, the effect would be truly magical. She and Clarissa had every right to be proud, and so would Lady Fordyce, for such a spectacle would keep her guests—as well as everyone who hadn't been invited—talking all through the winter.

Once again her glance wandered to the doorway, just as it had done over and over and over again all morning long, and still Revell didn't come. He wouldn't, either; she knew that now, after overhearing one of the footmen telling another that all the gentlemen had gone shooting soon after dawn, even that lord from India.

She sighed, and shook her head ruefully at her own foolish hopes. She missed him. That was the heart of it, wasn't it? She missed him, and these last twenty-four hours seemed to stretch longer than the six years before. Thanks to the visit to Peterborough Hall yesterday, she hadn't seen Revell since they'd cut the ivy together, exactly the way her ladyship intended. Surely she'd served at Ladysmith long enough to know that when Lady Fordyce determined upon an order, there'd be no countering her, and now that she'd deemed it necessary to keep Sara from Revell's path, her ladyship would have boosted him into his saddle this morning with her own white hands.

"Can we go hunt for your costume now, Miss Blake?" asked Clarissa, hopping up and down in anticipation, the only acceptable mood on this, the day before Christmas. "You can't come tonight in your regular old gowns.

You're not allowed to dress plain, Miss Blake, not tonight. No one is. You must look special, like the queen of hearts, or a fairy princess, or—or anyone else grand and rare!''

Sara made an exaggerated frown, wrinkling her nose at her reflection in the tall pier glass before her. ''You'll need far more than antique finery to transform me into a fairy princess, Clarissa.''

''But that is what a masquerade is *for*,'' said Clarissa sternly. She took Sara's hand, tugging her toward the door. ''Come, Miss Blake! The lumber room is the *best* place in the whole house, and I— *Albert, no!*''

With a shriek of anguish, Clarissa raced across the ballroom to where her brother stood in the doorway, a cluster of curious guests peering around him. The men were still dressed for riding in frock coats and light-colored breeches, their boots wet with melting snow and their faces ruddy from the cold.

''No, no, *no*, Albert!'' she wailed, jumping and flailing her arms toward his face. ''You can't come in here, not yet! You *know* no one can see until tonight! It's supposed to be a surprise, Albert, a *surprise!*''

''Just a peek, Clary, eh?'' he said, easily catching her windmilling hands as the others began entering around him. ''I was telling everyone how grand the ballroom looks for Mother's masquerade, and they wanted to see it, that's all.''

''But now you've spoiled the surprise, Albert,'' said Clarissa, her voice quivering with angry tears as she finally pulled free. ''You've spoiled *everything*.''

Sara hurried forward, circling her arms around Clarissa's shaking shoulders. ''It's all right, Clarissa,'' she said softly, wishing she could personally throttle Albert by his thick neck. ''Everything will look much better tonight when it's dark and the candles are lit. You'll see. They'll still be surprised.''

A blond young woman in pink muslin pushed past them and into the center of the ballroom, and as she twirled flirtatiously on her toes Sara realized it was the same lady with the uncertain voice that she'd had to accompany in the music room: Miss Talbot.

"Why, dear Mr. Fordyce," she cooed, making sure her skirts flicked above her ankles, "how charmingly childish this all is! Wouldn't you agree, my lord?"

"I most assuredly would not," said Revell, suddenly there, as well, the sprig of holly once again in his button-hole. "There is nothing whatsoever childish about tigers and elephants, is there, Miss Clarissa?"

"No, my lord." Vindicated, Clarissa sniffed back her tears, and narrowed her eyes at Miss Talbot. "Especially not when they eat you *alive*."

Miss Talbot's smile soured over the arc of her fan. "Goodness, Mr. Fordyce. What an ill-tempered little creature your sister is! If I were your dear mother, I should address the quality of her education directly."

"Rather she should thank Miss Blake," said Revell, "for giving Clarissa the best education imaginable, a model of wisdom and beauty."

"Yes, she has," echoed Clarissa loyally, but there was already question clouding her eyes, a suspicion that things among these grown-ups were not quite all they appeared.

She was right. Revell bowed toward Sara with his hand over his heart and a heavy lock of his hair falling forward across his brow, and making every other person in the ballroom an eager witness to exactly how violently the governess flushed at his lordship's compliment. In return all Sara could do was remember what Lady Fordyce had said, how everyone at Ladysmith was whispering of nothing else than her and Revell, and here, alas, was all the proof anyone needed.

But as delicious as such scandal might be for the other

guests, Sara could also feel a new, uncomfortable tension rippling through the room, marked with nervous coughs and titters. This time, clearly, there was a sense that Lord Revell had at last made his attention too public.

Uneasily, Albert cleared his throat. "I say, Claremont. Mind my little sister, eh?"

Revell's smile didn't change, but the edge in his voice was unmistakable. "What is there to mind, Fordyce? What is it that's not fit for Clarissa to hear? Do you deny that Miss Blake is either wise, or beautiful? Or is it perhaps my own judgment you are doubting?"

"Neither, Claremont, neither at all," blustered Albert miserably, blotting at his face with his handkerchief. "But I only ask that you, ah, that you not be quite so...quite so, ah—"

"Shall I play for us, Mr. Fordyce?" asked Sara quickly, hurrying to the pianoforte in the corner. As bad as it was to be the centerpiece of gossip, this was infinitely worse, having Revell jump to defend her honor like this. "Now that we are all gathered here in a room meant for music, on the very morning of Christmas Eve, wouldn't a dance be a pleasant amusement?"

"A splendid idea, Miss Blake!" cried Albert with all the hearty desperation of a drowning man. He seized Clarissa's hand, practically swinging her into the center of the ballroom. "You won't mind playing for us, will you? Something gay and jolly, fit for the season, eh?"

"As you wish, Mr. Fordyce," murmured Sara as she opened the lid covering the keyboard, trying to sound like the old, usual Sara instead of this new one that interceded so boldly between gentlemen. "It is my pleasure to play, Mr. Fordyce."

"You'll have to grant me more room than this, *memsahib,*" said Revell, suddenly sitting on the bench beside her so closely that his leg pressed against hers. "As Clarissa observed, I am far too large to overlook."

Instantly, Sara scuttled away from him, more to break the contact than to grant him the room he'd asked for.

"Whatever are you doing, Rev?" she whispered urgently. "You can't sit here, and you can't call me *memsahib!* You're supposed to be dancing with the others!"

"And I say I'm supposed to be here," he said easily, sliding along the bench after her. The freshness of the outdoor air still clung to him, sharp and clean and reminding her again of standing among the holly bushes, and of all that holly sprig stood for. "Aren't those my inept paper chains hanging there on the front to mark my place?"

"But, Rev, you can't do this!" she protested in a frantic squeak. "You've already upset Mr. Fordyce and everyone else, and—"

"Did I upset you?" he asked gravely. "That's all I care about."

Oh, heaven help her, she was blushing *again.* "Not the same way, no," she hedged. "But I am not such a public person as you are, and what you did is not—not proper, especially not when it's nearly Christmas like this!"

"And I ask you, whatever happened to Christmas miracles?" Tentatively he curled his fingers over the keys, the sunlight glancing off the sapphire in his ring. "There was a piece for four hands we used to play together, a kind of jig that you'd taught me like a trained dog. I can't promise that I won't make a wretched muddle of it now after so long, but I am willing to try if you will."

His smile was lopsided and surprisingly uncertain, and with a jolt she realized he was asking her for far more than to recall a simple tune. Was she willing to risk that wretched muddle to try to recapture what they'd once done together with such wonderful ease?

"Oh, Rev," she said softly, reminding herself of all that

was still so unsettled and unspoken between them, and how much more likely that muddle would be than anything else. But if he was willing to try, then how could she not? How could she refuse him, or herself, either?

"If you haven't forgotten," she said, choosing her words with the same care as had he, "then I haven't, either, nor do I intend to shame myself and make a muddle."

He grinned, and she plunged into the piece, making him swear as he hurried to catch her. Yet still they played better together than they'd any right to, the awkward notes and missteps forgiven by their enthusiasm. Over and over their arms touched and their fingers bumped into one other's with exactly the intimacy that the long-ago composer had intended, and by the time the fast-paced jig had come to its close both she and Revell were laughing and breathless and completely unaware if anyone had danced to their music or not.

But the sound of one person applauding—only one— broke the spell. Still smiling, Sara turned, then quickly stood, just as Revell also rose to his feet.

The gentleman clapping was newly arrived, his traveling cloak still over his shoulders and his elegant dark clothes creased from his carriage, and from his world-weary, almost arrogant disdain, Sara would have known he was high-born and wealthy even if Lady Fordyce weren't fluttering so anxiously around him, as if he were the greatest prize she'd ever captured.

And in a way he was. Sara had never seen the gentleman before, let alone met him. Yet she recognized him at once: he was older than Revell, an inch or two shorter, and his hair was lighter, but the shape of his face and smile, the ease with which he moved, were so much the same that there could be little doubt.

"Why, Revell, look at you," said Brant, His Grace the Duke of Strachen, his voice deceptively languid as he looked not at his brother, but at Sara. "Such a...a *diversion!* It would seem that I've accepted Lady Fordyce's invitation in the nick of time for a happy Christmas, doesn't it? The very nick, I would venture, for us all."

Chapter Seven

"I am disappointed, Revell," said Brant with a sigh as he dropped into the chair before the new fire in his bed-chamber. "I'd rather expected more from you. Oh, go ahead and sit. It's not as if you're standing in the docket."

"From your manner, why should I feel otherwise?" Revell continued standing where he was behind the other armchair, his hands in fists on the chair's back, which did in fact make him feel as if he were standing in some miserable courtroom, awaiting his sentence. Which, considering his older brother was willing enough to serve as prosecutor, judge, and jury combined, wasn't far from the mark. "Under the circumstances, Brant, I believe I'd rather stand."

Brant sighed, drumming his fingertips lightly on the padded leather arm of his chair. He had changed his traveling clothes for a long silk dressing gown, brilliantly printed with blue and red dragons, that was doubtless in the height of style. Brant was by far the most fashionable of the three brothers, not only in his dress, but in his friends and pastimes, as well, living fast, hard, and expensively. If Brant maintained that Revell was like last summer's leaf, tossed wherever the wind took him, then Revell thought that Brant and his set were more like the sharks that swam in the China Sea, sleekly deadly and ready to tear apart their fellows without a thought.

"Circumstances, circumstances," he now mused. "What precisely *are* the circumstances here, dear brother? You choose to come here in this obscure provincial household instead of spending the holidays with me at Claremont House, after which I receive the most distraught appeal from your hostess, accusing you of being a veritable fox in her henhouse."

"There was no need for Lady Fordyce to have contacted you," said Revell testily. "I am hardly anyone's notion of a fox."

"She didn't contact me," answered Brant, maddeningly mild. "She invited me to join her party. And since you seem to have found the—oh, what shall we say it is? The Christmas plum pudding? Sir Henry's rum punch, famous throughout the county? The salubrious invigoration of the local air?—so thoroughly irresistible, I accepted, and now join you."

"Badger me, you mean." Angrily Revell thumped his fists on the back of the chair. He hated it when his brother lectured him in this bemused paternal fashion, as if there were twenty years between them instead of two. "Damnation, Brant, what kind of idiot do you take me for? I know exactly why you've come, and it's not for some blasted plum pudding!"

Abruptly, Brant's smile vanished. "Then you know what I'm going to say, as well," he said, leaning forward in his chair. "Leave this little chit of a governess alone."

"She is not a chit, Brant," said Revell, his voice clipped with fury. "Her name is Miss Sara Carstairs, and I'll thank you to use it."

"Sara Carstairs?" Brant's eyes glowed with new interest. "The same girl you knew years ago in Calcutta? The one that jilted you at the altar?"

"Miss Carstairs from Calcutta, yes." Inwardly Revell winced, wishing his brother's memory wasn't quite so accurate. "But I did not have the honor of asking for her hand."

"So she is not Miss Blake the governess, but Miss Carstairs the Indian adventuress."

"She is an English lady," insisted Revell. "Her father was a senior officer in the East India Company, much involved in their financial matters."

"She is a woman who left you without a word, now in much-reduced circumstances, while you are still a lord, and, if what our bankers say is true, far, far wealthier than you were when she knew you last." Brant's smile was ruthless. "She must feel as if Heaven itself has dropped you into her lap like a golden plum."

But Revell's tight-lipped smile in return had an edge of its own. He'd already challenged Albert Fordyce earlier in Sara's defense, and he wouldn't hesitate to do the same with his brother.

"Perhaps, Brant," he said, "I'm the one who feels blessed instead."

Brant's expression darkened. "Then why does she need to hide behind another name? Where has she been before she came here? What has she done to keep herself in all that time? No *lady*—especially none who might carry our name—should have so many secrets."

He was, of course, absolutely right, and in theory Revell would agree. But Sara wasn't a theory; she was the one woman in the world that was meant for him. He knew that now, and having so many others disagree only made him more resolute. All he need do was think of how the sorrows and joy to be found in Sara's mobile face so closely mirrored his own, and how, even in these few short days, she had made him feel complete in a way that had been missing in his life for years.

"I do not know where she has been, or what she has done," he said. "Nor do I care. I loved her then, and I love her still, and that is all matters to me."

"Then you are a greater fool than I feared," said Brant sharply. "Remember that you are a Claremont. Remember your place and station in this world. Remember how low our father drove our family, and how you and George and I have worked so hard to restore it to what it should be— what it *must* be."

"But not for me, Brant," said Revell quietly. He'd no business quarreling with his brother. Now that he'd made up his mind, he felt oddly at peace with himself and the rest of the world, and besides, it was Christmas Eve. "I've been away from England too long for that to matter, not for me, or for Sara."

"To hell with such gibberish!" Furiously, Brant shook his head, refusing to accept such a decision. "Listen to me, Revell, and do what is right!"

"I will," said Revell with a slight, final bow of parting, "though I should have done it years ago. I trust you have brought a costume for tonight's masquerade. You will not wish to miss it for the world."

There had been a grand house at Ladysmith Manor for nearly four hundred years, and though the facade of the house in its present form was properly, symmetrically Georgian, hints of its ancient Tudor heritage remained in the twisting dark-paneled hallways of the old wing and the diamond-paned windows of the gatehouse—and, of course, in the leavings of nineteen-odd generations of noble packrats and magpies collected into the sprawling lumber room.

In truth to call it only one "room" was something of a misnomer. Perhaps it had begun as such, but as the servants had been moved out from the uncomfortable quarters directly under the roof to more civilized rooms, the space given over to storage had grown and grown until now nearly the entire attic was given over to musty boxes and barrels and trunks.

"I cannot believe you've not been here before, Miss Blake," said Clarissa as she led the way into the crowded space, holding her lantern high before her. "Whenever my cousins visit in the summer, this is the first place we come if it rains."

"I think I've found you here, yes," said Sara as she raised her own lantern higher, certain that the scurrying they heard was the sound of scores of squirrels and mice running for cover. Though it was still afternoon, the pale winter sunlight made little headway through the dormer windows, and the dusty shadows of so many shrouded, bulky objects seemed murky indeed, and not a little unsettling. "Though I can't say I've ventured very far within."

"One doesn't venture into the lumber room," said Clarissa grandly, her arms outstretched. "One *plunges.*"

Giggling, she darted away, her lantern light bobbing through the shadows as she dared Sara to follow.

"Clarissa," announced Sara, too uneasy for a game of hide-and-seek. "I am not one of your cousins, and I've no intention of chasing you through all this rubbish. If you don't come back directly, I won't find a costume, and I won't be able to attend the ball tonight, and neither shall you."

Instantly, Clarissa reappeared, her contrite face multiplied back and forth in a pair of mottled-looking glasses propped against the walls.

"The clothes are all kept over there, in those trunks," she said, pointing to a row of enormous old traveling trunks, their hair-covered sides nibbled away by mice and their brass studs now sadly tarnished. "At least the best things are. Here, let's open this one first."

Eagerly she unfastened the latches and threw back the curved lid of the first trunk, dust billowing around it. Sara sneezed, reaching for her handkerchief, but Clarissa was already digging inside, pulling out a stiff ivory-colored gown embroidered with faded pink flowers that would have been in fashion at the court of the first King George.

"This would be nice, Miss Blake," she said, pressing it against her waist, where the skirts trailed onto the floor across her feet. "It's only a little spotted, there on the sleeve."

Sara took the gown and held it up to consider. "I should look like the ghost of someone's grandmother," she said, shaking her head. "Especially in such a drab color."

Clarissa frowned, critically studying Sara as if seeing her for the first time, then rummaged once again inside the trunk.

"What of this, Miss Blake?" she said hopefully, producing a dark green silk gown with ruffles like cabbage leaves around the neckline and cuffs, and a waistline cut for a woman double Sara's size. "The color's the same as the holly."

"Oh, Clarissa!" Sara wrinkled her nose, laughing. "I'd be the ghost of someone's *great*-grandmother, and a powerfully stout ghost at that!"

Clarissa sighed mightily and returned to her searching, while Sara opened the next trunk to look on her own. When Lady Fordyce had first suggested she, too, attend the ball in costume with Clarissa, she'd been dismayed by the prospect, considering herself too old, too much a governess, to imagine herself in a gaudy masquerade. But now she felt herself brightened by the magic she'd found with Revell, and knowing he'd be there tonight, too, made her once again long for something rare and special to wear for him, the way she had in Calcutta.

She smiled wistfully, remembering the bright spangled gowns she'd had made from the same silks the Indian ladies used for their saris, silk that was lighter than air and as brilliant as a field of flowers, and nothing like the heavy rustling chintz that the other English ladies had worn. Strange to think how she'd been different from the others then because she'd been so bright, and now how she was set apart because she wore only a governess's proper white and black. But what could she find here now to make herself stand out tonight?

Gingerly she sifted through the layers of old clothing, some of the lace so fragile with age that it disintegrated beneath her fingers. Perhaps she would be doomed to being the dowdy grandmother's ghost after all.

And then she found it, at the very bottom of the chest, wrapped in yellowed linen.

The dark blue velvet gown must have always been intended as a costume, from the style made more than a century ago when King Charles had set the fashion for masques. The bodice was close-fitting and laced up the front with scarlet ribbons, the full, sweeping skirts worked with gold and silver thread and scattered with crystal beads that sparkled like dew drops. The sleeves were as full as summer melons, the velvet slashed to show the red satin beneath and gathered into tight lace-trimmed cuffs, and more lace framed the low, square neckline in an extravagant collar. Sara had never seen anything quite like it, and neither, she was sure, would Revell.

Clarissa gasped with delight. "Oh, Miss Blake! You *will* look like a fairy queen in that!"

Sara grinned, clasping the costume around her to judge its size. There'd only be time for a quick airing to lessen the mustiness, with no alterations, but the length was perfect, and the lacing that crisscrossed in the front would make for a forgiving fit: truly another Christmas miracle, wrapped up in gold ribbon and crystal beads.

Quickly she unfastened her day gown and slipped the heavy velvet costume over her head, drawing in her breath as she tightened the boned bodice around her waist. She'd never worn anything that felt like this, but already she knew it was perfect—*perfect!*—and excitement and anticipation swirled through her as she imagined Revell's reaction.

"Wait, Miss Blake, wait, I know what you need!" Clarissa scurried across the room, returning with a flat square box. Carefully she opened it and lifted out a headpiece with curling plumes and beads that clearly matched the costume. "I didn't know there was a gown to match. We always thought it should belong to a queen, though. And we were right, Miss Blake, weren't we?"

The plumes were a bit bedraggled, and here and there a crystal bead was missing to show that Clarissa and her cousins had in fact worn it, but when Sara settled the headpiece on her hair and turned toward the looking glass, all she saw was the magic: for what other explanation could there be for how completely she'd been transformed?

"No one will know you at all," declared Clarissa, standing behind Sara to see their reflections together. "Every gentleman will wish to dance with you, and that nasty Miss Talbot will be vastly put out."

"Clarissa!" scolded Sara, but without any real sharpness to her voice. "I do not know if the gentlemen will dance with me or not. I'm going to be with you, not them. But if no one recognizes me—why, that is the point of a masquerade, isn't it? To pretend to be someone or something else other that what we are?"

"*No one* shall recognize you," repeated Clarissa emphatically. "Except for Lord Revell. He will know you at once."

"Ahh," said Sara, addressing Clarissa's reflection in the blurry old glass. "And how shall he do that, when none of the other gentlemen can?"

"Because he loves you, Miss Blake," answered the girl solemnly. "I could tell by how he looks at you. It is just like the fairy stories. He was a handsome lord come riding on his steed to rescue you from your lowly life. He loved you from the very minute he laid his gaze upon you. *Exactly* like the fairy stories."

"Life isn't often like fairy stories," said Sara softly, linking her hand with Clarissa's. Once upon a time, in that faraway land of tigers, she'd believed in fairy stories, too. "That's why such tales are so much fun to read. But alas, simply dressing like a fairy queen won't transform me into one for life, nor is Lord Revell about to carry me off to a glittering castle in the clouds. When you wake tomorrow on Christmas morning, I'm still going to be your governess, and nothing more."

"But I want him to carry you away, Miss Blake!" Clarissa's face twisted with urgency. "Next year Mama says I'm to go off to school with the older girls, and you won't be needed here any longer. Who shall look after you then? What will you do when I am gone?"

Sara smiled sadly, lifting off the frivolous headdress. She knew the inevitable last day as Clarissa's governess would come soon enough, the parting already one she dreaded.

"Why, I suppose I shall be most unhappy at first," she said, "and miss you horribly. But then I'll go to another family with another little girl who'll need to learn about elephants and French and the proper song to play after supper, and I'll look after her just as she'll look after me."

"But she won't care for you the way his lordship

would," insisted Clarissa anxiously, her fingers tightening possessively around Sara's. "She *couldn't.*"

She turned and stretched up on her toes to reach Sara's shoulder.

"There, Miss Blake," she said, tapping her fingers. "Right *there.* That's where you need to put the holly tonight so his lordship knows for sure you need him. Didn't you see how he wore it for you?"

"You were the one who put the holly in his buttonhole, Clarissa," said Sara, though of course she remembered it being there, both when they'd been together among the holly bushes and today at the pianoforte. "I didn't."

Impatiently, Clarissa shook her head, unwilling to be diverted. "But it must be the same holly we found outside, Miss Blake, the *exact* same holly from the same bush. I tried to get some for you before, from the ballroom, but after Albert spoiled the surprise this morning, Mama's had the doors locked until tonight."

"And that will be quite soon enough," said Sara, bending to kiss Clarissa on the forehead. The girl's concern touched her, and surprised her, too, coming as it did on Christmas Eve. It wasn't just that Clarissa was striving to emulate her mother; she understood the *magic,* and felt it, too. "Holly leaves stay green the whole winter through, let alone for a single night."

"But you will promise to wear it tonight, Miss Blake?" asked Clarissa, her gaze anxiously searching Sara's face for reassurance. "So that you and Lord Revell will find each other, and not be alone for Christmas?"

"I promise," said Sara softly, wrapping her arms around the girl's shoulders. She could make a promise for tonight, and mean it; it was all that followed that was the mystery. "How could I not, when you've asked me so nicely? Now come, let me change back into my old clothes, and then it's off to bed with you."

"But, Miss Blake, I'm not in the least tired!"

"You will sleep now, or stay in the nursery tonight," said Sara firmly. "Those are your mother's rules, and most excellent ones at that."

With only a bit more grumbling, Sara ushered Clarissa back into the keeping of the nursery maid for her nap, giving her word that she'd return in two hours to dress into their costumes together. Lady Fordyce's rules notwithstanding, Sara didn't really expect the girl to sleep. Who could, when the entire house already seemed to vibrate with excited anticipation?

With the blue velvet costume shrouded in the old linen, Sara hurried downstairs to the laundry room, where a half-dozen harried lady's maids were already toiling to press the last wrinkles from their mistress's costumes, or to stitch an errant pleat or ribbon back into place. Coaxing hundred-year-old creases from velvet was more of a challenge, and Sara steamed and brushed the fabric as best she could, counting on the candlelight in the ballroom to blur and soften the more stubborn spots.

She left the costume hanging on the schoolroom door until it would be time to dress with Clarissa, and, humming to herself, she practically skipped up the back stairs to her room. It had been so long since she'd considered her appearance in anything but the most functional fashion, and she'd forgotten the pleasure to be found in transforming herself for a special occasion—magic of a different sort, she thought wryly, though magic just the same. To match the drama of the costume, she wanted to dress her hair in something more festive than her usual plain knot. Perhaps small braids swept across her head like a wreath, she thought as she unlatched her door, with a few loose curls to—

"Sara, lass, at last, at last," said Revell, coming toward her with his hands outstretched before she'd even entered the room. "I've been waiting here for you forever."

Chapter Eight

He hadn't intended to startle her, yet from the way she gasped, her hand fluttering to her mouth, he realized he'd done exactly that.

"Sara," he said again, more quietly as he reached for her. "Where have you been hiding yourself this afternoon, lass?"

Skittishly she stepped back from his hand, only one step, but still away from him, and glanced nervously through the door to the hall that she'd left half ajar. "I was in the attic with Clarissa, and then in the laundry. Rev, you can't stay here, not in my room like this."

"Whyever not?" he asked, and this time when he reached for her hand, she let him take it. "It's the first time since I've come to this house that I've been able to have you to myself."

Automatically she shifted her glance to her narrow governess's bedstead, then blushed that she'd been so blunt. Not that there was anything provocative about this chaste little room under the eaves. The time he'd sat here waiting for her had been more than enough for him to see by the single candle how pitifully few her personal belongings were, how much reduced her station from when he'd known her in India. It reminded him of the worn, shiny patches that he'd noticed on the fingertips of her gloves, a kind of small, ladylike shabbiness that seemed especially poignant. The change had saddened him, and angered him as well; she was too good, too fine, a woman to live like this.

But there was one detail of her room that had made him smile broadly, there by himself. Tucked into the corner of the little looking glass was the cut-paper tiger that he'd botched so badly, the one that had so offended Clarissa. Clearly, Sara had rescued it, complete with crooked head and hardened blobs of paste, and treasured it now only because he'd made it. He could cover her in sapphires and pearls from the China Sea, yet the one thing she'd taken from him had been his misshapen Christmas tiger.

How could he not love her? How could he not want her with him always?

"It's—it's not right for you to be here, Rev," she said again, though the warm pressure of her fingers around his offered a contrary message. "Not in my room, not like this."

"Because there is a bed only an arm's length away?" he teased. "Or are you remembering other nights with me, Sara? How we'd sit on the hanging teakwood bench in the shadows of the Chowringhee gardens, how we'd talk and laugh all the night long, until the moon set?"

He drew her closer, reeling her in against his body, as he let his voice drop seductively lower. "You remember everything, don't you, here in this cold, snowy place? How the days in Calcutta were so hot that the nights in your garden were our one real favorite haven?"

Gently he pulled her into his arms, his hands crushing the rough wool of her gown as they settled around her waist, another memory that was at once familiar and exciting. With a sigh she swayed into him, coming home, her scent irresistible, her soft, warm body melting against his as if they'd never parted.

"You...you shouldn't be here, Rev," she protested weakly, even as her words were coming in short, husky breaths. "It's not proper, and people will...people will talk."

"People already are," he said, "and what of it? Let them talk, lass, and let us listen. You and I must be the last two in this crowded house who haven't acknowledged what's here between us."

"No," she said softly, touching the sprig of holly in his buttonhole, the same one that Clarissa had given him yesterday. "I suppose that makes us the most dim-witted dullards at Ladysmith."

"Cautious," he said, his fingers spreading lower to caress the soft curves of her hips and bottom and pull her closer against him. "I should rather call us cautious dullards."

She chuckled, deep in her throat where the sound sent a ripple of shivers down his spine, and tipped her chin upward as her eyes looked down, her lashes a shadowy, sooty sweep across her cheeks. She curled her hand around the back of his neck, her fingers making little circles through his hair.

"That hanging bench in the gardens had red cushions," she whispered, as if telling a fresh secret for his ears alone, "and yellow silk tassels that hung down all around, as if it were our secret palanquin to take us wherever we pleased. Do you remember how we'd kick off our slippers and shoes and tuck our legs up when we'd set it to swinging, rocking back and forth to make it fly, as if it were true magic?"

"Like magic," he repeated, kissing the parting of her hair, there at the top. "And I remember, too, *memsahib,* what we did to make it rock like that."

He'd never forget that. They'd been hopelessly young and passionately in love, in a part of the world where even sacred temples were decorated with erotic statuary, and her father had been so trustingly indulgent and distracted as to be out-and-out neglectful.

Some would say that this is what came of ladies reading Voltaire, Fielding, and Rousseau, but Revell knew it was Sara's own dear self and soul. She'd eagerly given her maidenhead to him, and then just as eagerly they'd explored all the ways to give each other pleasure, not only on that swinging bench, but beneath a cloud of white netting in her own bed, as well. She had been charming and inventive and clever, endlessly tender and endearingly thoughtful, and she had spoiled him forever for any other woman.

Now she chuckled again, turning her face so his lips grazed across her forehead, lower, over the neat, feathered arches of her brows.

"Do you remember the little pots of cream custard flavored with rose petals that I'd bring with us?" she asked. "How with a tiny silver spoon, I'd slip the custard into your mouth, and lick the roses from your lips?"

"Like this," he said, his mouth finding hers at last. "Like this."

He had come here to her room with only the most honorable of intentions. He had meant to be respectful, to take only her hand and make the proper, elegant speech that he'd carefully rehearsed and that a lady deserved. Wasn't the well-worn box with the ring still waiting beneath his coat, not far from the sprig of holly? But as soon as he'd seen Sara again, touched her, held her, he'd forgotten everything elegant and proper, and remembered only that she was all and everything he wanted and needed in a woman and from life.

Her lips parted at once for him, welcoming him with an

urgency that matched his own. He kissed her hungrily, starved for what she could give, and he could taste the desire building between them just as he felt the years of separation dissolving around them. His hand slid along the front of her gown to her breast, filling his hand with the soft flesh, and even through the layers of wool and linen he could feel how her nipple hardened at his touch.

With a little moan of frustration, she arched against him, her body taut with the same longing that was racing fire-hot through his blood now. He'd no doubt they could find the same passion on her narrow governess's bed as they had on the hanging teakwood bench, and quickly he slipped his arms beneath the back of her knees to sweep her up into his arms and toward the bed.

"Miss Blake?" The door pushed open with a tentative squeak, spilling more candlelight from the hall into the room. "Miss Blake, are you—*oh!*"

The young maid's eyes were as round as tea dishes, her mouth a perfect shocked *O,* as finally she remembered to drop her curtsy.

"My lord," she said belatedly, her hands twisting with anxiety in her apron as Revell in turn remembered to set Sara back down on the floor. "Forgive me, my lord."

Why the devil hadn't he latched the door? Why hadn't this infernal maid waited another half hour before she'd interrupted them?

"Damnation, girl," he rumbled in frustration. "What in blazes are you—"

"No, Rev, please," said Sara breathlessly as she wriggled free of his arms to stand by herself. Of course she wasn't his yet; she still belonged to the Fordyces, blast them. For them she must strive to sound brisk and efficient, as if her skirts weren't rumpled and her mouth swollen from kissing and her hair coming half unpinned around her face. "What is it, Becky? What has happened?"

"Oh, Miss Blake, it's something terrible bad, and on Christmas Eve, too," said the maid, her voice shaking. "Miss Clarissa's gone missing."

As swiftly as they could, Sara and Revell made their way through the churning crowd gathered on the front steps of the house. Servants, guests, and those arriving early in costume for the party all were jumbled together there, joined in their concern for the missing girl. Everyone seemed to have an idea of where Clarissa had gone, just as everyone had a suggestion for what should be done next to find her. Dogs from Sir David's hunting pack had been brought from the kennels to help, barking with eagerness, and the light from torches and lanterns glinted off the long-barreled muskets of the men gathering for the search. Nor was the weather cooperating: snow was beginning to fall, fat, wet flakes that were perfect for Christmas Eve, but would only hinder the search.

Finally Sara and Revell reached Lady Fordyce, standing on the bottom step with Albert at her side, her face contorted with worry and fear.

"Oh, Miss Blake, here you are at last!" she cried, seizing Sara's hand. "Tell me, tell me, when did you last see my little Clary?"

"We'd gone to the attic, my lady," said Sara quickly, "and then I took her to the nursery to rest, as you wished, with Annie to help her with her clothes."

"Annie." Lady Fordyce's expression darkened as she repeated the nursery maid's name. "Annie did not remain in the nursery, having chosen instead to go meet one of the grooms in the stable."

Sara gasped softly as guilt twisted through her. Staying with Clarissa while she rested had in fact been Annie's responsibility, not Sara's. Yet still she couldn't help thinking of how, knowing Clarissa was unlikely to sleep, she could have remained in the nursery herself, instead of dawdling in her own room with Revell. How could she possibly fault Annie for abandoning Clarissa to meet her lover, when she'd ended up selfishly doing exactly the same?

What if this were some terrible punishment for her dishonesty, for taking pleasure in Revell's caresses and kisses without telling him the truth that he deserved to know?

She felt Revell's fingers around her own, his touch reassuring. "Perhaps Clarissa has gone back to the attic," he suggested. "Children love to hide in such places."

"No, my lord." Lady Fordyce shook her head unhappily. The snowflakes were clustering incongruously in her hair, already dressed in stiff, elaborate curls for the masquerade. "We have searched every corner of the house, and she has not been found. She must have wandered outside, here, to watch the carriages arrive."

"But Clarissa doesn't wander like that," protested Sara, "not without a real reason or purpose."

"Of course she does, Miss Blake," said Albert imperiously. "Clary is the most willful little creature alive."

Sara shook her head, pulling her cloak more tightly against the gusting wind. "I beg your pardon, Mr. Fordyce, but that is what I am saying. Clarissa *is* too willful to have left the house without a reason for doing so."

Albert sniffed dismissively. "Nonsense, Miss Blake," he said. "That is quite obviously what she did, and now I believe she has fallen into the hands of gypsies."

"Gypsies!" Lady Fordyce's voice broke on the single word. "Oh, Albert, no! My poor little baby!"

"Yes, Mother, gypsies," said her son firmly as he took the pistols that a servant had brought him. "I hear there is a pack of the filthy thieves lurking in a field not far from the town. You know how they shall steal any well-bred child they can. Claremont, you'll come with us, won't you? I'd vow you've had experience enough dealing with heathen black devils like this.''

"I'll come if you have more proof than this hearsay," said Revell evenly. "The Romany clans are Christian, you know, and I'll not ruin their Christmas without good reason."

"My sister is missing," said Albert sharply. "That's reason enough for me. But they won't have her long, Mother, I promise you that. Ah, here's Father now with Lord Peterborough and the others."

Purposefully, Albert took his mother's arm and led her to where Sir David, already mounted on horseback, was preparing to lead the neighborhood men in the search for his missing daughter.

"Gypsies," muttered Revell in disgust. "What would they want with Clarissa when they've children of their own? I'd sooner believe she's been borne away by fairies. I'll wager a hundred guineas that she's still somewhere here at Ladysmith."

"I know Clarissa, Rev," insisted Sara urgently, trying to imagine where the girl would go, "and I know she wouldn't have come *wandering* out here, not in the front of the house like this. Oh, Rev, if only I'd—"

"It's not your fault," he said softly, "and I don't want you taking the blame."

But Sara only shook her head. How could she not blame herself? She'd never felt more helpless in her life.

"Clarissa never does anything without a reason, without a—oh, Rev, I know where she's gone!" She clapped her hands, a fierce kind of hope swelling within her. "I know where she *is!*"

"Then show me, Sara," said Rev grimly. "There's not a moment to waste, and the sooner we find her, the better."

Chapter Nine

Revell followed Sara through the garden and across the field, carrying the lantern high to light their way through the dusk and swirling snow. Driven by the wind that tugged at their clothes, the wet, heavy snowflakes stung at Revell's face as they crossed the gardens and fields.

Beside him Sara carried a basket with a blanket, dry socks and mittens. They didn't talk; trudging through the snow was effort enough. Everyone else either remained in the anxious crowd on the front steps of the house, or had ridden off with Albert and Sir David, and the ghostly fields around them seemed by contrast almost unnaturally quiet. No one had offered to come with Revell and Sara, nor had they sought others to help. If Sara's hunch proved right, then they could bring Clarissa home themselves.

Gently, Revell squeezed Sara's fingers through the muffling of their gloves. Though only her eyes were visible between the edge of her hood and the heavy scarf she'd wrapped around her throat and over her mouth, Revell could still feel her determination glowing as brightly as the lantern in his hand. Knowing Clarissa as well as she did—certainly better than her own family, or so it seemed to Revell—her idea of where the girl had gone made perfect sense. All he could do now was follow her, and pray silently that she was right.

Sara loosened her scarf to speak. "We're almost there," she said, pointing to the dark shadow of the familiar copse of holly, "just down that little slope. Clarissa! Cla-*riss*-a!"

Now she was hopping and running down the hill, her heels sliding in the snow. "Clarissa, it's Miss Blake and Lord Claremont! We've come to fetch you home for the masquerade! Oh, please, please, Clarissa, be here!"

She shoved through the dark boughs, scattering clumps of snow, and Revell raised the lantern to light the clearing, shedding its glow over...

Nothing.

"She's—she's not here," whispered Sara, stunned, as she dropped her basket and gazed around the empty clearing. "She's not here, Rev. Oh, I was so *sure* she would be! She insisted I have a holly sprig of my own to wear on my costume tonight to match yours, so you would know that I was...that I—"

She faltered, pressing her hand over her mouth to keep from sobbing aloud.

"Oh, poor lass," he said, setting the lantern in the snow at his feet so he could draw her into his arms. "We'll find her yet. You'll see, Sara. We'll find her, and she'll be fine."

"She could be anywhere." Sara shook her head, no longer bothering to hide her crying as her tears mingled with the melted snowflakes on her cheeks. "But it's my fault that Clarissa's missing at all, Rev! I *knew* how excited she was about Christmas and the masquerade and all, how she wouldn't sleep. I should have stayed with her, I shouldn't have left her for—"

"It's not your fault, Sara," said Revell sharply. "None of this is, and I won't have you—"

"Miss Blake?" The voice from the shadows was faint and quavering. "Miss Blake, is that—that really you?"

"*Clarissa!*" Instantly, Sara turned and ran toward the girl. Clarissa was standing by the edge of the trees, bent from the cold and huddled in her snow-covered red clock, and even from here Rev could see her shivering. "Here you are, my own lost lamb!"

"I—I didn't think it was you, not truly," said Clarissa, her voice breaking with her sobs as she flung her arms around Sara's shoulders. "Oh, Miss Blake, I was so scared!"

"Of course it was me," said Sara softly, her own tears now those of joy and relief as she brushed the snow from Clarissa's cloak and gathered the girl into her arms. "And Lord Revell, too, so you needn't be scared any longer at all. Let me feel your poor little hands—oh, Clarissa, you're an icicle!"

"I—I wanted you to have your holly," said Clarissa, sniffling plaintively as Sara peeled off her wet mittens to replace them with the dry ones they'd brought. "But then the snow started, and it got darker and darker, and then I—I got lost, and—"

"And now you're going home," said Revell, wrapping the blanket around the girl and lifting her up into his arms. He was surprised by how little she weighed, and touched by how readily she curled against him. He wondered if the child realized how close to real danger she'd been: if she'd spent even another hour in this wet cold, then they might all be facing a much more somber Christmas.

Yet he could not be cross with her, the way the other adults in her life were bound to be. He understood wandering better than they ever could, and while his own restlessness might have taken him infinitely farther, he'd also come to realize the satisfaction of finally reaching the end of the quest.

"They'll all be waiting for you at the house," he said, taking care that the blanket was swaddled around Clarissa's legs. "We don't want the elephants and tigers in the ballroom to worry overmuch, do we?"

"But I didn't get the holly for Miss Blake!" she protested weakly. "She *needs* it!"

"What if I give her mine?" asked Revell as Sara gathered up the basket and lantern. "Will that do?"

"Yes, my lord," said Clarissa with a sigh, nestling more closely against his chest. "It will do. Besides, the holly was so you could find her, and you already have, haven't you?"

"Yes, little miss," he said, finding the magic of Sara's smile through the snowflakes. He would ask her tonight to marry him; he'd the best reasons in the world for doing so, and not one that mattered to him against it. "I most definitely have."

They returned to the house through the kitchen, where Clarissa was greeted with cheers and shrieks of rejoicing and amazement. Perfectly content to assume the role of a prodigal little queen, she beamed her red-nosed happiness on a stool before the fire, her arms outstretched as Sara and the disgraced nursery maid Annie pulled off her wet shoes and stockings and clothes and the cook plied her with hot chocolate and milk with biscuits.

But when Lady Fordyce herself rushed through the scullery and into the kitchen, Clarissa forgot all about being a queen among her subjects, and remembered only the warmth of her mother's boundless love, and the contentment to be found in her embrace.

And sadly Sara remembered, too, of how transitory her place was in this little girl's life, and how close she'd come tonight to losing even that. She watched the mother and daughter together, slowly pulling the scarf from around her neck and feeling the icy patches of melted snowflakes as they slid over her throat. It was time, past time, to put her own life into order. She'd lived too long with artifice for protection and fear of disclosure constantly with her. Time to turn toward truth instead, and pray that her own joy might follow—and that Revell would understand, and forgive.

Oh, please, please, if there's one speck of real Christmas magic left in this sorry old world, let it find me tonight!

"So we shall have a grand Christmas masquerade after all," Revell was saying, leaning over so his words were low and confidential, his arm comfortably familiar around her waist, "and only a little delayed. But before you vanish upstairs to dress, Sara, I should like to beg a word alone with you."

She glanced at him nervously, wondering if somehow he'd already guessed the secret she was determined to tell him this night, yet all he did was smile affectionately, and wink in jest, without even a hint of suspicion or judgment.

"This way," she said, taking a candlestick to guide them away from the crowded celebration in the kitchen, back through the low-ceilinged hallway that led to the pantry and cellars. Finally she unlatched the door to the laundry, setting the candle on the edge of the washboard.

"Certainly no one will disturb us here," said Revell heartily, closing the door after them. "Unless it's a tradition of this house to wash the master's shirts on Christmas Eve."

"Oh, Rev," said Sara unhappily, her hands clasped tightly before her. "I've so much to say that I don't know where to begin."

"Then let me start, sweetheart," he said, reaching for her. "I love you, Sara, and I—"

"No!" she cried, shaking her head with anguish to keep

him away. "I've no right to that, not now, not until you first hear what I must say."

"Then at least take this," he said softly, handing her the sprig of holly that had been tucked in his buttonhole, "for courage, and because Clarissa wished it."

She let him place the holly in her fingers, his hand grazing lightly over hers. The shiny, pointed leaves were so very English, and so unlike anything to be found in India: so much a part of the present, and nothing of the past.

In desperation she turned her back to him, the only way she could do this. "Surely, Rev, you must have wondered how I came to be here, in this place so far from Calcutta and with a name not my own."

He didn't answer at first, a pause that tore away at her resolve. "Yes," he said finally. "Yes, I've wondered, but only because I wish to share all things with you."

But not *this,* she thought grimly: what decent man would wish to share such a disgrace? She took a deep breath, almost a gulp, remembering everything with the same horrible clarity as if it had happened six days before instead of six years.

"Soon after you left Calcutta for Madras," she began, the stem of the holly pinched tight in her fingers, "three senior gentleman from the Company came to see Father one night while we were still at table. They sent me away, and then they stayed long past midnight. I knew because I could hear their voices clear in my bedchamber. Not quarreling, exactly, but angry, challenging, with Father's voice the loudest among them, and because of it, I couldn't sleep, and so I heard the gunshot, too."

She felt Revell's hands on her shoulders, yet she was too caught up in the memory to shake him aside.

"The gunshot?" he asked quietly. "Whose gun, love?"

"Father's," she said, her voice quavering. "He—they drove him to kill himself, to put the pistol to his own head.

The servants tried to keep me away, but I pushed through, and I saw him, there on the floor with the pistol still in his hand and all the blood and—and the rest of what was left of him."

"Oh, Sara," murmured Revell. "I never knew."

"No. *No.*" She squeezed her eyes shut and bowed her head, struggling to move beyond that final, hideous memory of her poor father. She had never spoken of that night to anyone, and she'd hadn't dreamed that the pain of her father's suicide would still be unbearably keen. "That was how it was done, Rev, to keep the scandal from the Company—the *Company!*"

She couldn't keep the bitterness from her words. "Those fine gentlemen, the surgeon, even the servants—no one said a word of my poor father's mortal sin, and they let him be buried in the churchyard, as if nothing—nothing were *wrong.*"

She gulped, bracing herself for the last, inevitable part of the tragedy. "But nothing was right, Rev. It wasn't at all. I'd known Father would go with his friends to the taverns in the Lal Bazaar near Tank Square, but I never knew he played—hazard and piquet—at the tables there, or that he lost so much that he'd begun stealing from the Company's accounts to cover what he owed, thousands and thousands of pounds over time. But because when he died, everything we had was sold to make good on what—what he'd taken, no one knew that, either."

"The auction where I bought the copy of *Candide* from your father's library," said Revell slowly. "And all I wanted was something to remember you by."

"I wrote to you, Rev," she said, her voice raw with uncertainty as she turned at last to face him. "When Father died and those fine gentlemen from the Company told me I must take another name and leave Calcutta for London to keep the scandal from ruining me, as well, I wrote to you, my dearest friend. And you did not come, Rev. When I needed you most, you did not come."

"I never had any letters like that from you, Sara," said Revell, his expression black. "Not a single word after your father died."

"But I wrote you letters, dozens and dozens!" she protested anxiously, her heart racing. "They tried to keep the gossip from me, but I heard it anyway, that because I was poor now instead of rich, that you'd never come to me again."

"When I returned to Calcutta, you were already gone," he said, the poignant finality of his words bringing fresh tears to her eyes. "The governor's own lady wife told me you had eloped to England with another man."

The governor's wife had been the one to speak to her, too, soft, silky, soothing words of caution and consolation and comfort. Only now was Sara realizing that they'd been lies, all lies, and one look at the mingled anger and regret on Revell's face told her he was coming to exactly the same appalling conclusion.

"Oh, Rev," she cried softly, "how could I have ever loved anyone but you? All I had with me when I sailed was a single trunk of mourning, and my letters of introduction."

"As hard as I tried, Sara," he said, his voice rough with emotion, "as much as I knew I should, I could never make myself forget you."

She was holding the sprig of holly so tightly that she'd pricked her fingers on the sharp leaves: holly for remembrance, holly that stays evergreen through even the coldest winter.

"You cannot know, Rev," she said, staring down at the shiny green leaves as if seeing them for the first time, "how many times on that long voyage alone I would watch those waves, and be tempted to end my sorrow forever.''

"But you didn't," he said, reaching out to touch the holly in her hand, "so I could find you at last for Christmas."

She curled her fingers around his, looking up at him through the haze of her tears. "They stole six years from us, Rev. Six *years.*"

"But not another day, love," he said, taking the holly from her and tucking it gently into her hair. "Tonight, Sara, I'll find you at the masquerade, just as Clarissa wished. And then I don't intend to ever let you go again."

"Oh, Miss Blake," said Clarissa with a blissful sigh. "How vastly much you *do* look like a fairy queen!"

"Aye, Miss Blake, that you do," said the nursery maid Annie, hovering beside Sara as she stood before the looking glass in Clarissa's room. "There'll be no handsomer lady there tonight, and that's the honest truth."

In wonder Sara stared at her reflection, not quite believing it was her wide-eyed face gazing back. It wasn't only the blue velvet gown covered with winking crystals that revealed curves to her body that no one would have guessed she possessed, or how Lady Fordyce's own maid had dressed her hair in beautifully fashionable curls that seemed to open her face and lengthen her neck for a most elegant effect, complete with the sprig of holly above her ear.

No, the real transformation had come from inside. Years seemed to have slipped from her face along with the harsh lines of propriety that a governess was supposed to show. Her eyes seemed brighter, as full of sparkle as the crystals on her gown, and her cheeks glowed with a happy flush. Her entire body seemed to have lost its habitual prim stiffness, her shoulders now relaxed and her posture as graceful as a willow.

She smiled, and her reflection smiled back: the truth had made this magical change, she thought with amazement, the truth and Revell's love.

"Look, Miss Blake!" exclaimed Clarissa, bounding toward her so that all the ribbons and little bells on her own costume bounced and jostled with her. "A footman just brought these for you! Oh, open it at once, Miss Blake! I want to see what Lord Revell has sent you for Christmas!"

Carefully Sara took the flat, square box, covered in leather, from the girl, and held her breath one delicious moment before she unhooked the latch and opened it with a gasp of stunned awe. Scores of blue sapphires had been matched for a necklace and earrings so perfect and beautiful as to make a queen envious, each flawless stone dancing with blue fire in the candlelight. In the center was a small card with the Claremont arms, and a handful of words from Revell. "Only the beginning, my love."

"So everything they be saying in the kitchen must be true, Miss Blake," said the maid as she helped Sara clasp the necklace. "About you and him, and him being the Sapphire Lord and all."

"Miss Carstairs," said Sara softly, touching the stones ringed around her neck. "My true name is Sara Carstairs."

"You're Miss *Blake*," insisted Clarissa, hopping up and down with impatience. "That's who you've always been, and who'll you'll be unless you marry Lord Revell. Rather, *until* you marry Lord Revell. *Now* can't we go downstairs, please, please, please?"

"Please, please, yes," said Sara, bending to help Clarissa straighten her mask in place before tying the ribbons on her own. A mask was required for entrance to the ball— what else would one wear to a masquerade?—but now Sara was glad of having even that small scrap of black to hide her emotions. There'd be precious little hiding otherwise; if the glittering antique gown didn't draw everyone's attention, then the raja's ransom of sapphires around her neck surely would, and once the whispers began about the jewels being Revell's gift, she would never be a blandly invisible governess again.

Yet though she held her head high as she and Clarissa stood in the doorway to the ballroom, her heart was racing and her mouth so dry she doubted she could speak. Because of Clarissa's adventures, they were so late that the ball was already in full and glorious progress, the music urging the dancers on the crowded floor on at a giddy pace while the other masked guests, all in gaudy, extravagant costumes, watched and gossiped and flirted and drank and laughed from the edges of the room.

And somewhere in this room was Revell....

"Oh, Miss Blake, it's *perfect,* isn't it?" cried Clarissa with delight, lifting her mask to better admire their decorations, the tigers and elephants among the holly made magically alive by the candlelight. "Oh, there's Mama, with the peacock feathers in her hair!"

Before Sara could stop her, the girl was gone, racing off into the sea of guests as the dance ended, with partners bowing and making curtsys and still no sign anywhere of Revell.

"Miss Carstairs, good evening," said the gentleman in red as he claimed her hand without waiting for her to grant her permission—not that His Grace the Duke of Strachen waited for much of anything. "I wish to be the first to commend you on your grand transformation. My brother has always had an eye for the potential beauty in a newly mined gem, and ah, my dear, how you do sparkle once the rough is cut away and the facets polished."

"Forgive me, Your Grace, but you are mistaken," she said, her smile full of happy pride. "Your brother loved me as I was, and as I am, as I do him, and the only 'transformation' you can see has come from the magic of love.''

"Love and magic." Brant smiled indulgently. "Perhaps, Miss Carstairs, you shall do Revell proud after all."

"She shall do our entire family proud, Brant," said Revell, suddenly there. He took her hand, deftly guiding her away from his brother, but instead of taking her to the proper place to begin the next dance, instead he led her to the exact center of the ballroom. Every conversation ended abruptly, just as every head turned expectantly toward them.

Sara laughed nervously. "What are you *doing,* Revell? Everyone's watching."

"So they are," he said easily. "But I found you, didn't I, exactly as Clarissa said I would."

He pulled off his mask and stuffed it into his pocket, then did the same with hers. From the same pocket came a small rounded box covered in worn calfskin, and as he flipped open the lid to take the sapphire ring from its nest of satin, she wondered how this moment seemed to be passing all too quickly, yet at the same time stretching into a blissful eternity she would never forget.

Magic, she thought crazily. *Magic and love and Christmas and a paper tiger with a crooked head, and Revell,* her Revell for always.

With infinite care, he took her hand in his. "Ah, Sara," he said, his eyes bright with the same joy welling up inside her. "I cannot recall a time when I did not love you, nor imagine a time when I won't. Please, please, sweetheart, say you'll marry me, and let me love you forever."

"Yes," she said, not waiting for the ring to throw her arms around him. "Yes, yes, forever and always!"

And a merry, merry Christmas, indeed.

* * * * *

Dear Reader,

Shortly before I wrote "Christmas Charade," I had the opportunity to visit London and stroll through Hyde Park, visit the museums and all the other famous sights about town. Comparing my old nineteenth-century maps of the city with the new ones proved to be an eye-opener. So much has changed, yet so much has stayed the same! I didn't even have to close my eyes to imagine carriages crowding the streets or high-collared dandies tipping their hats to the ladies.

My husband and I had afternoon tea in a small shop in the Cotswolds and there discovered a route to some beautiful villages that were off the tourist-beaten path. This is definitely one of my favorite areas in England, so I have included it in my story.

What a gift it was to be invited to participate in this anthology with two authors whom I admire so much! I adore reading about the Regency era and it has been great fun writing about it. I hope you enjoy "Christmas Charade" and that you will visit a bit farther north with me soon in my upcoming historical, *The Scot*.

With a flutter of my fan and a deep curtsy, I wish you the happiest of holidays!

Lyn Stone

CHRISTMAS CHARADE
Lyn Stone

This story is for my good friends
Charlotte and Robert Ballard, in honor of those fine
Christmases we celebrated together once upon a time.

Chapter One

London, 1815

"So which do you think is the new earl?"

Bethany Goodson disguised her interest by plying her fan and pretending to scan the entire ballroom before glancing idly toward the entrance two gentlemen were making. She returned her gaze to her cousin, Euphemia, who was jittery with excitement. "The one in evening dress, I would think. A fellow so come up in the world would not don regimentals even if he is fresh from the wars."

"Well, both are as handsome as sin on a jam tart!" Phemie declared. "You may have the one in the uniform," she said, giving Beth's shoulder a nudge with her own. "I shall have the other."

"I have no use for either, as you very well know." But the Keiths, even at this distance, certainly were handsome enough to make Beth bemoan her need to remain unattached. She took a sip of her ratafia and set aside her glass. "If you'd known them as lads, you would be thinking twice about it yourself."

"Never say it," Phemie said. "Why is that?"

"Jack and Colin were double trouble. I heard that their poor aunt who reared them took to her bed when they were in shortcoats and never left it until they were safely away at school. I trust it was so. They were hellions when they came home on holiday."

"You knew them before I came to live with you?"

"Yes. Earl Whitworth's estate is near ours. The countess was related to our vicar. There were a number of entertainments we, as children, were allowed to attend. Wakes, picnics and the like."

"Wakes for entertainment? I so love the country life." Phemie laughed merrily, still staring impudently at the two dark-haired brothers. "They bear a remarkable likeness, though I must say the one in regimentals looks a bit older."

Beth frowned as she tried to recall. "No one ever remarked on their ages within my hearing, really, though I believe they are some four or five years older than I. Surely the one in evening clothes is the elder. Why else would he dress the part of an earl and the other remain a mere soldier?"

She turned aside for a moment to speak to someone in passing and felt Phemie's pinch just above her glove. "Ouch! Whatever is wrong with you?"

Phemie was fidgeting, causing her white-gold curls to bounce, not to mention her half-exposed bosom that men found even more fetching. "They are coming this way, Beth!" she whispered. "Do smile, won't you? Perhaps they will beg an introduction!"

"Beg?" she scoffed. "I shouldn't hold my breath if I were you. And do stop behaving like a child eyeing treats!"

Beth turned away again, wishing she could disavow any kinship with Phemie at the moment.

But Phemie's fingers bit into Beth's elbow, yanking her

back around. She looked squarely into a dark blue-coated chest. Her gaze traveled up a double row of gold buttons, past a jet-black neckcloth framed by wide buff lapels and high collar. Impossibly wide shoulders supported gold-fringed epaulettes.

Slowly her gaze crept upward. His strong chin bore the trace of a cleft and his sensuous mouth stretched into a gentle smile. His brown eyes flashed with merriment.

She immediately lowered her eyes. A mistake to be sure. He wore immaculate breeches, fitted to his lower limbs like a layer of whitewash, leaving little to the imagination and much to stir forbidden thoughts.

Beth rapidly jerked her attention up again where it landed on his mouth. Sweet heaven, where shouldn't she look next?

The mouth moved. "Miss Goodson, I would know you anywhere. Please forgive my forwardness, but since we were once well acquainted..."

Beth felt her face heat and knew it to be red as foxfire. "Sir, I believe you have me at a disadvantage."

She did remember which was which, but an introduction would certainly be the proper thing after so many years. She had not seen either of them since she was thirteen, but there was no mistaking they were the Keiths, dark hair, dimples and all.

"Please offer me your hand, sweet friend," he whispered, "else one of these formidable dowager watchdogs will toss me out on my ear. It's Jack. Jack Keith."

She stuck out her hand. He took it and bowed over it, raising it nearly to his lips. So long he held it, Beth had to pull it from his grasp. "Do not presume! Lieutenant, is it?"

"Correct, and no presumption intended, my dear. I do know you well enough to owe you a hair ornament if I'm not mistaken. Some years overdue, I admit, but restitution is certain, never fear.''

He smiled so charmingly, she had to return it. "Welcome home, sir.''

She noticed Phemie was already engaged in spirited conversation with the other Keith, Colin. The earl. Apparently someone had provided her the requisite introduction and given her permission to gush. Or perhaps that brother was simply as audacious as this one.

Beth could hardly blame her cousin for pursuing the man. Phemie hadn't a farthing to her name and lived entirely upon the charity of Beth's father. Since looks were Phemie's only fortune, she obviously meant to spend them well. No one knew better than Beth how her cousin dreaded returning to a life of genteel poverty, which she eventually would do if she did not marry wealth. Phemie had a good and kind heart, even if she did allow desperation to guide the affairs of it.

Jack took Beth's arm and gained his brother's attention. "Look whom I have discovered, Colin! Remember the Jollit's lawn party when we were lads? The jam cakes we appropriated? Here is our lookout.''

"Ah, yes! And you never peached on us, did you?''

Beth curtsied. "It is true I never told, my lord. Mainly because I was enlisted to aid you in the crime and shared the spoils.'' She inclined her head toward Jack, then Phemie. "Lieutenant Lord Keith, I do not believe you have met my cousin, Miss Euphemia Meadows.''

"Miss Meadows.'' Jack reached out, took Phemie's hand and did the pretty.

Beth shot Colin a look of censure. "I see that you have already met her, my lord.''

He smiled without a trace of guilt for the social infraction and turned the subject altogether. "Now, now, a fellow conspirator must dispense with lordings and call me Colin.''

''I must offer you my congratulations, Earl Whitworth. *Colin*,'' she added reluctantly. ''Though I must say I was grieved to hear of your uncle's recent death. Oh, and your cousin passed on recently, as well, did he not? How awful for you both.''

''How kind of you to say so,'' he replied, obviously not terribly grieved himself.

The musicians began to play and distracted him. ''If you would excuse us, I should very much like to dance with Miss Meadows. Later, we must catch up on the happenings Jack and I have missed being away all these years.''

''If you wish it, my lord,'' she said, not feeling the slightest inclination to renew her acquaintance with the new earl, but unwilling to be impolite.

''Would you care to dance?'' Jack asked her.

Not for an instant did she think she could do so without stumbling all over his shiny black shoes. He made her feel shaky, ill-at-ease. ''No, thank you. It's too warm in here for any sort of exercise.''

She popped open her fan and put it in motion without any thought to the blasted language of it. Did that mean *go away* or *come hither?* Uncertain, she held it still again.

''Fresh air is what you need,'' he told her. ''Come to the terrace with me.''

''Unchaperoned?'' she asked, hoping to avoid going without hurting his feelings. She hated feeling so unsettled.

He smiled reassuringly. ''Oh, there are enough people out there we shouldn't cause a stir. It is a beautiful night for November. Quite warm. Colin and I must have brought the weather with us from the Continent.''

Beth relented. ''So you came here directly from the war?''

''Not precisely. Colin and I fought with the Thirteenth

Light Dragoons at Waterloo, but since Napoleon surrendered, we have been billeted near Paris. When finally notified of our cousin's death, we took leave to come home,
of course.''

She strolled out with him, drawing her thin cashmere
shawl over her shoulders, looking up at the stars and asking the occasional question about his service under Wel-
lington. He answered, making light of his adventures there.
Beneath his jollity, however, Beth detected a note of strain
in speaking of his time at war and suspected he had suf-
fered to some extent.

''Obviously, your brother's duties are set in stone, but
will you retain your commission?'' she inquired.

''No, I plan to take up civilian life again now that the
war is at an end. Try my hand at something else.''

''And what will that be?'' she asked conversationally,
well aware that gentlemen adored talking about themselves. Lesson number one in how to get on with the opposite gender.

He surprised her. ''Enough of my dreary existence.
What of you, Beth? I may call you so, mayn't I? We've
known one another for decades, after all.''

''Decades?'' she asked, pretending to be highly put out
with him. ''Sir, I've scarcely lived more than two of them.
And I only met you once or twice in passing.''

''More than twice,'' he argued. ''And last time we
passed, I snagged your pretty satin bow and tied it 'round
the neck of Uncle's favorite hound. That's a solid back-
ground for intimate friendship if you ask me!''

Beth laughed with him. While she did not wish to wed,
she saw no harm in enjoying his company for a short
while. ''Beth, it is, then, Jack. If you promise to replace
my bow.''

''It was blue, as I remember. I should have kept it as a
token.'' His large, white-gloved hand reached up and

brushed one of her black curls off her forehead. He did it so quickly, she hadn't time to recoil from the too familiar gesture. "May I see you again?" he asked. "Perhaps tomorrow?"

Now he *was* presuming, she thought, and decided she must squelch his interest before it took hold. She wasn't deluding herself that his interest grew out of any real attraction. She *did* have a decent dowry that he would be aware of, and he *was* soon to be unemployed. "Lieutenant—"

"Jack," he reminded her.

"Jack. You had best know from the outset that I have no inclination to accept the suit of any gentleman, no matter how dedicated he might prove or how well I know him. I have decided never to marry, you see, and my decision is quite firm."

He shrugged. "I don't recall proposing, but your refusal is duly noted. Few ladies would run grasping at a man of my poor circumstance anyway."

"Wait and see," Beth advised with a wry smile. If Jack Keith believed none of the young women here would throw themselves at his feet now that he was available, then he must never look in his mirror to shave. "However, your circumstance has nothing to do with my decision. Please do not think so."

"Then could we perhaps renew our friendship if I promise not to deluge you with flowers out of season or write odes to your eyebrows? All I'd like is to drive you through the park tomorrow afternoon. Can't you spare me an hour or so?" He winked to encourage her and set her at ease. It did in a way.

"I suppose I might. So long as you realize this is *only* a rekindling of friendship, nothing more." She granted him a smile of thanks for his understanding.

"I'll contain my disappointment." He took her hand in

his and held it. "Now that's settled, tell me why you are so determined to languish on the vine. Some foolish fellow break your heart?"

Relaxed and satisfied she had made her point, Beth answered readily. "I will not marry a titled gentleman and my father would never allow me to wed anyone not so encumbered."

"Encumbered?" he asked with a curious chuckle.

"That is how I view it. Look around you, Jack. Everyone is so caught up in their own importance, they have no thought for others less fortunate. The men strut about in Lords, making policy that benefits only themselves and their kind. Their wives are so committed to attending and providing entertainments, they scarcely have time to serve their primary function as broodmares. That sort of life is not for me."

"You were born to it. How differently would you live?" he asked, seeming keenly interested in her answer.

"I would try to make a difference in the world instead of wasting a fortune on the latest fashions, pouring tea and exclaiming over the latest *on dit.*"

He considered her declaration for a moment, as if he truly cared about it, then asked, "And what does the estimable Baron Goodson think of this ambition of yours? Not much, I'd wager."

Beth sighed. "You would win, too. Father grows more adamant each day that I marry. Small wonder after financing four seasons for me. He always threatens to drag me bodily to London if I won't come willingly, so I do come to keep peace between us. This time, he has even chosen a man for me."

"Oh? Whom did he choose, if I may ask?"

"Arthur Harnell, third baron of that name. Do you know him?"

Jack's brows drew together in a frown. "I do. He attended school with Colin and me. A dreadful bully. You'd do well to stick to your resolve with regard to him, Beth. I doubt he would make a good husband for anyone. Shall I rid you of him?'' Looking half serious, he ran a hand over the pommel of his gleaming dress sword.

She beamed up at him, thoroughly charmed by his concern. Jack would be a great friend. ''Thank you for the offer, but I can dissuade him myself.''

''You'll need funding to assume the life you plan, Beth. A wealthy husband could provide that.''

''But *would* he?'' she asked with a sad smile. ''If I marry, not only will my husband's wealth be his alone, my own money will become his, too. If I remain a spinster, at least I may spend my inheritance from my grandmother as I see fit.''

''You are naive if you believe you can cure the ills of the world, Beth. There will always be the extremely rich and the very poor. That is the way of things.''

''I know that. But suppose everyone who possessed the means willingly took it upon themselves to make a difference in the lives of as many unfortunates as they could comfortably afford. Do you not think everyone's lot would improve?''

''Possibly, but sadly that will never happen.''

''Certainly not if I wed some fine lord who would trap me where I cannot make my own small effort.''

Jack looked thoughtful. ''Do you include Whitworth in your low estimation of these fine lords? If so, I think you unfair.''

''Look at him,'' Beth said, gesturing to the glass doors of the ballroom. ''Already he is reveling in all the attention. Do not think he will escape his role, Jack. You will soon see a change in how he treats you if you have not already done so.''

''I disagree, but I see your mind is made up. So how

many poor souls have you chosen to improve in your fantastical project?''

"Four, I think. Perhaps more, depending upon the amount due me when I receive my inheritance. If,'' she added, ''I can evade Father's plan for me until then.'' She had grown almost desperate to do so.

"Then we must do something to remedy your situation. At least divert your father's intentions.'' He suddenly grinned and exclaimed, ''You could wed me, you know. I would be happy to let you spend your inheritance, and your dowry, as you will.''

She laughed. "I applaud your sense of humor, Jack, and appreciate your attempt to lighten my mood.''

"I am quite serious, Beth. I have money. In fact, I should confess that I—''

Beth interrupted. "Thank you for the gesture, but I shall inherit from my grandmother when I reach twenty-five. That should be enough if I go carefully. I am thoroughly resolved now not to wed, and am well content with my lot as spinster. If only I can put off Father's plans until my birthday.''

"When is that?'' he asked, frowning.

"The fifteenth of January.''

Beth could see by his expression that he truly wished to help and was pondering some way to do it. How troubled he looked.

Suddenly a plan dawned on her that might benefit them both. "Tell me, Jack, are you set on courting anyone in particular over the holidays?''

"I had thought that I would court *you,* but you've quite disabused me of that notion. What do you have in mind?'' he asked.

"Those plays you and Colin used to get up for our entertainment, do you recall them?''

"Of course I do. We took turnabout at villain and hero.

I'm hardly surprised those raucous spectacles stand out in your mind. You took part in one or two yourself, didn't you?'' He shook one finger at her. ''Yes, you played the faerie queen and Tim Bartholomew captured you from beside the wading pool to hold you hostage. You screamed bloody murder and almost got him whipped before we explained the farce. Brilliant bit of acting.''

''Would you like us to arrange another? As in crying off a betrothal?''

''Whose betrothal would that be?'' he asked, with a definite glimmer of interest.

''Ours!'' she declared with a laugh. ''You'll be free of females grasping the coattails of the earl's handsome brother and I shall shed the dreadful Arthur Harnell. At least until Christmas or perhaps the Twelfth Night revel when we shall end it all with high drama for all to hear and see.''

''How scandalous!''

Beth grew even more certain it would serve. ''Surely by that time, Harnell will have turned his interest elsewhere. I shall inherit Grandmama's money a few days later, which will solve my problem, and you will be free to go your merry way!''

Jack worried his chin, his sensuous lips working as Beth watched him play the notion through his mind.

Beth held her breath, afraid he would find some flaw in the plan. ''Well?''

He abruptly dropped to one knee right there on the terrace, grasped her hand and raised his voice. ''My darling Miss Goodson.''

Conversations ceased and eyes turned their way. A few of the couples strolling about quickly drew nearer to see what was happening. Beth placed a palm to her throat and answered, ''Sir?''

''I am agonized with love for you. Take pity!''

"How so?" she asked loudly, quelling her embarrassment, reminding herself that, as the great Shakespeare once said, *the play was the thing*.

"You *must* agree to marry me. Else I shall return to war a broken man, uncaring of a life without you."

"Jack, the war is over," she whispered through unmoving lips.

"Surely the thought counts," he whispered back.

She covered her mouth with her free hand to catch her laughter, knowing that, to others, she appeared to be aghast at the fervor of his avowal.

"Well, answer me!" he rasped under his breath.

Beth sighed theatrically. "Oh, sir, you do me such honor. How on earth could I *ever* refuse?"

He kissed her gloved hand with passion, then rose abruptly to his feet and pressed another kiss upon her brow.

"Lips would be better," she murmured.

"That would thoroughly put you beyond the pale. Now or never, what do you say?"

"Lips," she hissed, "and hurry while we have the audience."

His mouth claimed hers with a zeal that put any thoughts of play-acting right out of her dizzied head.

A scant hour later Jack climbed into the crested carriage behind his brother and collapsed against the soft leather of the button-tufted seats. It was a grand conveyance, he thought, for transporting two scapegraces who probably didn't deserve it. But then, neither had their uncle and cousin, and someone had to ride in the damned thing.

He flicked a finger over the base of the gilded lantern attached to the wall, Beth's opinion of lords and their self-serving ways preying on his mind. "Think we'll get used to all this?"

"Undoubtedly. I'm rather attached already, if you want the truth. You might play hell reclaiming it," Colin informed him, wearing the haughty earl face he had donned for the occasion.

Jack smiled. "I appreciate your coming to my aid this way. You do it so well. Better than I could have done." He immediately fell serious at the thought. "Colin, do you want the title? I'm certain we could devise a way—"

"Good God, no! Tonight was quite enough, thank you very much. I confess I had nightmares our pretense might stretch out for weeks before you found someone suitable to marry." He tugged off his gloves and tossed them aside. "Now you're as good as shackled, I can lay down this cursed role and let you have it."

"Not yet," Jack said. "The betrothal's a ruse." At Colin's look of stunned disbelief, he explained the plan Beth had devised. "She doesn't know it is I who has inherited. She swears she won't take a noble husband. Or any husband at all, for that matter. This may take time, but I can maneuver best if you keep up the charade a while longer."

"The devil you say! You're mad not to tell her the truth. Surely she wouldn't refuse *you?*"

"Actually, I did propose, but she thought it was a jest. Beth only wants a friend at this stage of the game. She made that very clear," Jack said, recalling her words about marriage. "She intends to remain unwed. I intend to change her mind. I need to make her love me."

"Maybe I will accept your offer to make the switch permanent," Colin said with a grimace. "I don't believe you have the wits to hold your hat, much less the damned title."

Jack ignored the censure and slapped Colin on the knee. "I cannot believe my luck. Found her on our first night out."

"Well, don't expect me to keep this going forever. I only promised to free you up until you located exactly the right woman to wed, one not after your wealth and a coronet. You were right to fear interference in a search. Those ambitious mamas were all over me, not to mention that little pudding-pated Euphemia. What unabashed gall, that girl!"

Jack wiggled his brows. "Methinks thou doth protest too much, old son. You showed quite an interest."

Colin shrugged and sighed. "Yes, but she's forward as any lightskirt." The fact seemed to bother him, but he soon brightened. "Could be she's worth a tup or two, now that I think of it. Perhaps I will give her a go."

"As if that thought just occurred. But you can't follow through," Jack warned. "She's to be one of the family if I play my hand correctly."

"And she will promptly deal Bethany out in favor of herself if she gets wind of our trick. I'm sorely tempted to spill the beans just to watch the fun."

Jack sat up straight and frowned at him. "You gave me your word. Just until I'm gazetted as earl. Six weeks, no more. Then the news will out. By that time, matters will be settled for good. Beth will be mine."

Colin rolled his eyes. "All right, all right. But I want the hunting box in Scotland if I go through with this. And," he added perversely, shaking a finger, "that set of pistols Uncle Martin left."

"Done. But not a word of this until I've won her."

"You selected her rather quickly, Jack," Colin said, a note of worry in his voice. "Almost the moment we walked into the place, she caught your eye and you barely spoke to anyone else. It is so unlike you to purchase the first hat you try on."

"Only if it proves to be a perfect fit and is precisely

what I want," Jack argued. "And what is this with you and hats tonight?"

Colin waved that away and continued to bait him. "She's not even the height of fashion, y'know. Blondes such as her cousin are considered the ideal of beauty these days."

"Though I find her lovely, I did not select Bethany for her looks alone. She's strong and strong-minded, that one. Loyal. Trained to perfection, I'll wager. Countess material. A good head on her shoulders."

"Nice shoulders they are, I must admit," Colin commented. "But I still say you might have looked further just to be sure. This is for life, Jack, not a night at the theater."

"She is the one," Jack insisted. Colin would never understand the force that dragged Jack across the ballroom with but one thought in mind. He wasn't certain he understood it himself. But when he had seen Bethany Goodson, he had known immediately she was the right choice. The only choice.

"Well, so long as you don't commence prating on about love," Colin warned. "We both know you better than that."

"So we do, but love can come later. It will, I believe. I like her enormously." More so than he would admit to Colin at the moment. More, even, than he wished to admit to himself. But somehow Jack felt obliged to ease his brother's mind. He was a part of this, after all.

"If I had not been acquainted with Bethany beforehand, I might have taken things more slowly. But I do know her. You know her, too." He hesitated to ask, but knew he must. "Do you have any valid objection to Beth?"

Colin shrugged and grinned. "None comes to mind, except that you won't allow me to tup her cousin."

Jack laughed with him, now eager to expound on his choice. "Beth will help me whip the estate into its former shape. See if she won't. She's passionate about things. Compassionate, too. Though she is a bit idealistic, even that quality speaks well for her. She isn't like many ladies of her class. Beth's very caring.''

Colin hummed, glancing out the window of the carriage, acting bored. ''Caring, and she kisses well. I see.''

Jack ignored the tease and leaned forward to make his point. ''That caring attitude of hers actually settled the decision for me, Colin.''

''And the kiss. Don't forget the kiss,'' Colin said.

''That, too. Don't discount the ability to show affection when it comes to a wife. And think what a mother she'd make!'' Jack discovered he liked thinking about that. He imagined Beth's rounded body, Beth holding a tiny babe, the two of them gamboling on the lawn with a child. ''Yes, I should like my children to have a mother's affection, not just the bare tolerance you and I endured from ours. And from Aunt Florence. Do you ever recall being hugged when you were frightened? Tucked into bed and wished sweet dreams? I *want* that.''

''For your little 'uns or yourself?'' Colin asked, laughing. ''As I recall, we hugged each other when something scared us. As for the tucking in, I much doubt either of us would have stood for it. We always fell asleep where we ran out of mischief and not always in a proper bed. Speaking for myself, I had a boisterous good time growing up, thank you very much. I wouldn't change a moment of it.''

''Knowing how you avoid the sentimental, I'll forgive you the lie,'' Jack said. ''Though I will tell you I doubt you'll find much true affection or sentimentality in *Cousin* Euphemia.''

''Ah, but she does have such beautiful…*qualities*,'' Colin remarked, while his hands made a graphic gesture to describe her bosom. ''And I daresay she's sentimental over some things. Don't imagine that I'm struck to the heart by her, however. She'll abandon me like a boat with a hole in it once I turn from prince to toad, so let's not delay that transformation any longer than necessary, agreed?''

Privately, Jack did begin to worry. For all Colin's savoir faire, he was no more immune to cupid's dart than any other soul. It would be a shame if he came to care for that cousin of Beth's.

Even on very short acquaintance, anyone not totally blinded by Euphemia's appearance could see at a glance there was nothing but avarice in those pretty blue eyes. Her interest in Colin was all too obvious. She had set her cap for the brother she thought was the earl.

''I'm trusting you'll watch out for yourself in this,'' Jack said.

''Don't I always?'' Colin replied.

No, never, Jack thought with a weary exhalation. Even knowing Euphemia's intent and its certain outcome, Colin had not avoided her tonight. Of course, he truly might have something a bit less honorable than marriage in mind. That would never do, given she was Beth's cousin.

It could prove devilishly awkward if Jack's own brother were responsible for deflowering one of the family. But it would almost be worse if Colin were seriously smitten with her, then lost her because he was the younger brother.

''Keep in mind what she's after. She'll learn the truth eventually, and you'll be devastated if you allow yourself to become attached,'' Jack warned. ''She'll be furious with you.''

As if Bethany won't be, too. Jack dismissed the voice of conscience. When all was revealed, Beth would understand. By that time she would love him. He was sure of it.

Almost.

Chapter Two

Jack knew there would be no rumors to leak the identity of the new Earl Whitworth, not for weeks anyway. Eventually the news sheets would get hold of it, but that would take a while. He had yet to be gazetted by his peers. Birth records must be confirmed and those—which were in York—must be searched out and verified.

Though he now wished he had not concocted this harebrained scheme, he was saddled with it. At least until he convinced Beth he was not like the men she had refused thus far.

He and Colin were a scant eleven months apart and no one of their acquaintance here in London knew their exact ages. With little effort at disguise, they looked enough alike to be taken for twins. Strictly for amusement, they had played upon it many times while growing up.

They had gone off to school at the same time, entered the military together and were seldom seen apart from one another. Orphaned at four and five, they had come all the way from York to the Cotswolds to live under their uncle's negligent supervision. Jack doubted his uncle and aunt ever noticed which boy was the elder. Or even cared which. They'd had their heir.

Aunt Florence had died long ago. Cousin Hubert, seven years older than Jack, had been in line to inherit the title. But he had died of apoplexy only a month after Uncle Martin succumbed to brain fever. Hubert's death left Jack the unexpected heir.

Colonel Doherty had arrived at Abreville near Paris to assume command and had informed them of the news. Since the war was over and the duties of occupation boring after all the excitement, he and Colin had been glad to come home.

For months the earldom had stood vacant and waiting. According to the solicitors, the estate, Whitfield in the Cotswolds, was a neglected shambles. Only the London town house, where both Uncle Martin and Hubert had died, remained in anything like livable condition. The fortune was still intact, thank heavens, but obviously no one had made use of the wealth when it came to maintenance.

The Whitworth solicitors were made aware that Jack was the eldest, of course, but he had ordered them to keep the entire business of the succession private. So there was no one to contradict Colin and him if they played at this pretense. And they would do so, he decided, until his betrothal to Bethany became real. Until she grew to love him.

"No one else will do," he muttered, half to himself. "She is the one."

"Peculiar of you to be so adamant about a particular woman, no matter how charming," Colin observed with a superior sniff. "Always before, you stood apart, played the prize and simply waited for women to approach *you.* And you acted as if you never much cared whether they did so or not."

Jack admitted that was true. The tactic had worked most of the time. "There is too much riding on this, Colin. I mean to have her and I dare not leave anything to whim or fancy."

It was also true, he reflected, that Colin had always been the one to pursue a woman, to form the serious attachment, and to require a great deal of brandy and commiseration to get over it when things went awry. Again Jack thought of the entrancing Euphemia and her pert little bosom that had heaved so charmingly under his brother's admiring gaze tonight.

Perhaps a word or two of further warning might be in order. "Look, Colin, don't go making a cake of yourself this time, will you? I won't have the time to console you."

Colin laughed too heartily. "Get stuffed, Jack. The Goodson chit has a fork in you already, so don't be shaking a finger at me and talking of cakes."

Beth had spent two days and nights listening to Phemie extol the virtues of Lord Colin. If her cousin was not besotted, she gave a good impression. However, they both knew better.

"You are making my head ache with all this chatter," Beth mumbled. She sniffed impatiently as she evened the loops of the satin bow just beneath her half-exposed bosom. "I swear, dressed as we are, we shall both come down with colds in the chest."

Euphemia edged Beth from in front of the mirror and promptly tugged her own neckline even lower. "Well, you needn't be so eager to display your wares as I must. *You* have a betrothed now."

Beth glared at her cousin. "I told you, Phemie, it was all for show. I cannot marry Jack. Primary reasons aside, he's no more interested in a wife than I am a husband. We might as well not have bothered with it all. Father's withholding approval. He is ignoring the scene Jack and I constructed on Lord Randolph's terrace. He even refused to admit Jack when he called yesterday."

Beth felt badly about that. Word might be out by tonight

that Baron Goodson thought Jack beneath consideration. No man greeted that sort of slight with equanimity. She only hoped Jack wouldn't cry off their agreement of mutual protection.

"All the same, you've done your part on the parade field, haven't you?" Phemie said. "Whitworth will be inspecting the troops again tonight and I mean to rise to his expectations!" She preened, lifting one arm in parody of a salute while she inhaled to enhance the thrust of her breasts.

She should measure up, Beth thought with a smile. With that gown of ivory shot-silk flowing over her curves and her blond tresses caught up with faux pearls, she might have been the inspiration for a Grecian statue. If Jack's brother didn't fall over his own feet and eventually land on his knees, it wasn't for lack of planning on Phemie's part.

"It wouldn't hurt you to use a bit of padding, you know," Phemie said with a sage appraisal of Beth's comparatively modest endowments.

Then she squinted at Beth's face, a true concession since she swore squinting caused lines about the eyes. Phemie's one flaw was her farsightedness, an affliction of the eyes that apparently did not extend to her thought processes. "Try a touch of rouge, at least," she advised.

"Pale is all the rage," Beth told her, laughing. Modesty aside, Beth knew she looked well enough. She wore soft blue China crepe accented with a darker blue satin ribbon that matched the slender ones wound within her hair. Her filigree necklace and ear bobs with sapphire chips complemented her ensemble nicely, she thought. For all that she was no great beauty like Phemie, Beth did feel rather pretty for a spinster.

She pinched her cheeks and raked her teeth over her lips to redden them. "There. I am ready."

Phemie rolled her subtly kohl-enhanced eyes in resignation and tugged on her gloves as she left the room. "I swear, you will not even *try* to improve yourself."

"And you overly do." Beth scooped up her reticule and followed Phemie down the hall to the wide staircase.

"Lord Harnell is bound to be there tonight. Do you anticipate trouble over the betrothal?" Phemie asked.

"My hope is that he will immediately find another to plague," Beth said. "I am counting on it."

She could not help but remember Jack's reaction when she had told him of her father's choice of suitor for her. She would see him tonight if he attended the Duke of Cranstonbury's affair. Beth hoped he would so that she could apologize for her father.

Also, it would be comforting if she need not come face-to-face with Harnell alone. But what if matters turned ugly despite Jack's presence by her side? Or because of it?

"Phemie, you don't believe Lord Harnell will cause a scene, do you?"

Phemie laughed. "Just see that he doesn't corner you anywhere. He might be handsome, but Harnell *is* a lecher. I've thought more than once I might have to slap his face."

Beth looped her arm through her cousin's as they reached the foyer to wait for her parents. "Has he done something to offend you, cousin?"

"Indeed! He *leers*," Phemie confessed, dragging out the word and leaning close.

"I shouldn't wonder. You usually invite it." She nudged Phemie, cutting off their conversation to welcome her father and mother.

Mother was perfectly beautiful as always, and as inscrutable as she was lovely. She never criticized or admonished Beth. That had been left to the nurses and later governesses. And now to Father, who took the task to heart. Though he was not unkind, he was firm and uncompromising.

Baron Goodson put much store by appearance and was agreeably generous with his praise when the females under his roof lived up to his standards. However, he also liked to believe he made law as to behavior within the family circle. For the most part, he did. The primary exception being Beth's refusal to capitulate on the issue of choosing a husband.

Accordingly he now issued the expected warning. "Bethany, should you make a spectacle of yourself again, you'll not attend another soiree until next summer, do you understand me?"

"Yes, Father," she said. "You will banish me to the country and I shall never have a moment's fun until next season."

Pray, let him do so, she thought, attempting to look dismayed by the prospect. Going home to the country was her dearest wish. She was needed there.

She happened to notice that Phemie was not pretending dismay, but actually hated the thought of leaving London. Beth felt guilty that her cousin's attempt to catch herself an earl might be dashed out of hand before she got it under way.

"Just so!" her father affirmed. "I shall pack you off in an instant!" He concluded his threat with a sharp nod. "Now let us go. I have never held with this *fashionably late* conceit. Promptness is a virtue. Remember that, my girls." He turned and gestured for Stokes to open the door for them.

Beth and Phemie pulled a face at one another while Mother steadfastly ignored the byplay.

Jack had pondered all afternoon on how he could win the favor of Beth's father without revealing the truth about himself. He could hardly court and convince Beth to make their betrothal real if the old man never allowed them together.

"Do you see her?" Colin asked, peering almost desperately over the heads of those already in attendance.

"Eager, are we?" Jack asked as he straightened his cravat and adjusted his left lapel. Tonight was his last time in uniform. He figured this second public appearance would set in everyone's mind which brother had inherited without actually having to lie other than by inference.

Both Colin and he had been careful to introduce themselves using only the family surname of Keith. Neither was yet used to being addressed as *lord,* though it was quite appropriate for both, even given the ruse they played. Colin was heir until Jack fathered a son.

"There!" Colin exclaimed. "I see them. Hurry." Without a pause, he headed directly for the opposite corner of the room. Jack followed, though he would have wished to wait, meander a bit and see how many swains might be buzzing about his quarry. He liked to reconnoiter, size up the opposition, while Colin was prone to charge indiscriminately. Jack couldn't count the times he'd had to drag him back and out of danger. This might very well prove to be one of those times.

"Good evening, Lieutenant," Beth said to him when he approached her. She wore a wary expression. Her mother stood not two yards away, but her back was turned to them. Why did Beth seem so apprehensive?

"Must we begin all over again? I do declare I thought we were past all this formality." He lifted her hand and kissed it soundly through her glove, not bothering to keep the gap betwixt fabric and lips as was proper.

She snatched it out of his grip, looking right and left to see whether they were observed. "Jack, behave!" she said under her breath.

"What's wrong? Our plans haven't changed, have they?"

"No, but Father is unhappy with me," she confessed, wearing a false smile for the benefit of anyone watching. "He threatened to simply send me out of town—which I would prefer, actually—but at the moment I worry he might proceed with Harnell, encourage his suit even more intensely. They're speaking together at this very moment." She cut her gaze in their direction.

Jack smiled, too. "I see now that I must get this fellow out of the picture once and for all. Leave Harnell to me."

"Nothing rash, Jack," she warned, risking censure by placing her hand on his forearm. "Please."

"What, no duel? I promise to dispatch him neatly. Perhaps even allow him to live, though he won't thank me for it when I'm through with him."

"Jack!" she groaned, the smile gone.

"But that's not a chore for tonight, is it? Come, dance with me, dear heart."

"I dislike bringing it to your attention, *dear heart,* but there's not yet any music."

"Then hurry away with me to the gardens. Soothe my savage breast with the sound of your dulcet tones against my ear. Sweet music enough, I do swear, to set me dancing to your tune forever."

"Stand away from me before you get yourself tossed out!" she hissed. "You are impossible!"

"Quite possible, I promise."

"Possible that you shall be tossed!" she returned.

"Absolutely, but not before they feed us. Where lies the food?" He took her hand without awaiting answer and ushered her toward the next room where the buffet should be. On the way, he caught Colin's eye and gestured for him to follow. As he had feared, the eager Euphemia was in tow.

That mattered little in the immediate scheme of things. At the moment Jack only wanted to remove Bethany from the proximity of her parents and ply his suit for a while.

A half hour to an hour of that endeavor, and then he would corner Baron Goodson to see what might be done to establish an accord with the man.

Unless, of course, Beth proved right and he was thrown out on his ear for an infraction of manners before he accomplished his goals. It was proving devilishly hard to keep his hands off of her. She was delightfully saucy, his Beth.

They appropriated one of the white-clothed tables and sat with Euphemia and Colin. Those two immediately retreated into a small world of their own, making sheep's eyes at one another while Jack tried to ease Beth's anxiety. After a second glass of punch and a sampling of the buffet, she had calmed to the point of discussing their betrothal.

"Father certainly will not announce it in writing," she warned, keeping her voice low so that no one around them could hear. "He doesn't even recognize it. How will we go on with this if he gives the betrothal no credence?"

This seemed a perfect opportunity to leave so he could amend the situation. "I shall try to get him alone and speak with him."

Her beautiful mouth rounded as she frowned. "Oh, Jack, I don't know…"

"Keep these two company while I attempt it," he said as he rose. "And save me a dance when the music begins. Three of them. That should send the flags up."

"I daresay," she agreed. "We shouldn't need a public announcement after that."

Jack left her there and made his way back to the ballroom. No sooner had he stepped inside than he felt a strong grip on his arm. He turned to see Harnell scowling at him. "Come outside," the man ordered.

"Unhand me if you want those fingers to remain intact," Jack said pleasantly. At his meaningful look of warning, Harnell let go.

Jack calmly brushed at his sleeve and proceeded toward the doors opening out to the gardens. It was rather chilly out tonight so they were virtually alone. Only two couples strolled the paths some distance away, fully occupied and oblivious of anyone else.

He faced Harnell. "Speak your piece, then I shall speak mine."

"Leave Bethany Goodson alone." Harnell spat the words.

"Warning me off my own fiancée? How positively gauche of you, but then you always were lacking in good sense when it came to—"

Harnell's fist almost reached its mark when Jack caught it, squeezed sharply and felt a bone pop.

He smiled at his opponent's cry of pain and observed him grasping his damaged thumb. "Bit of advice, old man. Keep the thumb on the outside of the fist. It's only out of joint. Next time you could get it broken if you aren't careful."

"I'll kill you, Keith!" Harnell rasped through gritted teeth.

"Not unless your aim improves." Jack dropped the casual tone and got serious. "Abandon your suit of Miss Goodson and this stops here. Do not and you may expect considerably more than a dislocated digit. Now get the hell out of here and do not let me see you again. My patience is gone."

Sweat stood out on Harnell's brow, he was breathing in gasps and his eyes were narrowed to mere slits. Jack gave him credit for prudence when he said nothing more. Yet he didn't leave.

"This conversation is finished, I believe," Jack told him. "You may go now."

He waited until the seething Harnell had rejoined the assembly within, then followed. The man was nowhere to be seen. Prudent, indeed.

Jack searched the ballroom for Baron Goodson, and saw him exiting alone, ostensibly to find a game of cards in the adjoining chamber set up for such.

"My lord, a word with you?" he said as he caught up to him.

"I have nothing to say to you, Keith." The baron continued across the room.

"Whitworth has a definite interest in your daughter," Jack confided. And that did the trick. Baron Goodson stopped in his tracks and gave him full attention.

"The *earl*, you say?" Curiosity animated his features, then suspicion. "But it was *you* who—"

"Could we find someplace private, sir?" Jack asked politely.

Having a baron such as Harnell sue for the precious Bethany's hand was one thing, but catching an earl's regard was quite another. It must be every father's dream, marrying a daughter up in society. How strange to be the *up*, Jack thought.

Personally, he felt it was ridiculous, allowing so much importance in a man's societal rank, but he knew it counted heavily with a man such as Goodson, especially one seeing to his daughter's future.

Jack had known he might have to use the title, though he wasn't quite prepared to reveal that he was the earl. Bethany was not ready for the truth yet. She mistrusted any man with a title and power. The poor little dear seemed convinced that the loftier a man was, the more he would be set against her philanthropic plans. And she could not afford to wed a man without means, such as she believed him to be.

Jack admitted he probably didn't deserve her. But he would have her anyway. With that objective in mind, he followed where Goodson led and they soon entered a small parlor or morning room just off the conservatory.

The baron promptly drew out a cigar and began fiddling with one end of it. Patiently, Jack waited as the baron trimmed, lit and was puffing away on it. Finally the man spoke. "So the earl has an interest, does he?"

"Most assuredly."

His lordship cocked his head to one side and blew out a blue-gray stream of smoke. "Then how is it *you* were the one kissing her and proposing on the terrace at Randolph's place? And don't believe for an instant I haven't noted your brother's salivating over my niece!"

Jack was ready for that. "Well, sir, it is well known about town that your daughter has refused every titled gentleman who has offered for her. How is one to get to know her if she won't let them near? Colin and I figured that if she were attached to me and he pretended a tendre for her cousin, the four of us would naturally go about together and come to know one another quite well."

The baron frowned as he sorted through this. Then he asked, "Are you saying that you are actually keen on Euphemia?"

Jack put on his best imitation of a love-struck expression. "I will say she *is* quite remarkable, sir."

"Humph. Well, I guess she could do worse. Do you have anything to recommend you if Euphemia returns your feelings?"

Zounds, he was getting in deeper by the moment. "This is not a suit for Miss Euphemia's hand, sir. Not yet, and perhaps not at all." Definitely not at all. The thought of it made Jack shudder.

The baron cocked his head, drew on his cigar and nodded. "I understand that, but I won't allow anyone to court my niece if I know he has no prospects at all. There's the off chance something might come of it."

Jack sighed. "I have my back pay, sir, will have the price of my commission shortly, and my brother will share the Whitworth wealth. We plan to manage the estate together, he and I."

"For you are, neither of you, worth much apart, are you? Not trained in managing anything larger than a curricle, I'd wager. Well, I suppose it couldn't hurt to let you squire my girls about for a time. See if you take with 'em." He mused for a few minutes. "Might be a problem. Harnell has pestered me for some time for Bethany's hand. I did vow I'd encourage her to think on it."

"No, sir, you won't want to pursue that. I know the man well and I assure you he would never suit for a daughter of yours. If he presents any protest, I will see to him."

"No, no, let's not be hasty. Suppose Whitworth decides Bethany's not for him? She must have someone to wed who's appropriate, and I swear she's gone through most everyone else who is remotely eligible."

"Suppose I swear to you on my honor that if Miss Bethany can be brought to the altar at all, she will have the title of countess?"

The baron's eyes went wide. "How can you promise such a thing? Whitworth's his own man, surely."

"I speak for him."

"Why does he not speak for himself?"

This was not going quite as smoothly as Jack envisioned. "Well, sir, I am the man of business. I give you my solemn word Whitworth will wed her if she agrees. She is the one for him, but she must be allowed to know him to know this for herself."

The baron waved his cigar around. ''All this talk of *knowing*...I trust you don't mean in the biblical sense.''

''Good God, no! Sir, I regret if you mistook my meaning. I—Whitworth has nothing but the utmost respect for Miss Bethany.''

Goodson grunted in what passed for a laugh. ''Bit of a jest to see what you'd say.'' He shot Jack a crafty look. ''But you be warned, boy. I remember you well from times past when you and that brother of yours made havoc amongst us there in the county. See you don't make a jest of my girls. I am an excellent shot.''

''We shall draw up the contracts if you like. Whitworth's offer only wants the full agreement of the lady in question and it's as good as done.'' Jack stuck out his hand to shake on it.

The baron was slow to respond, but eventually did. ''Very well. I shall see to the papers. Shall we agree on terms?''

''Anything you wish in the way of dowry will suit. Our estate is healthy. Your daughter will never want for anything.''

''Very well. But if I see any indication either you or your brother has betrayed my trust, I shall have your heads on a plate, Keith, regardless of Whitworth's rank.'' He stubbed out his cigar, signaling that the interview was over.

Jack accompanied Goodson back to the gathering in the ballroom, then went his own way to find Bethany.

Now he had arranged a way to court her, but regretted the deception necessary to gain the opportunity. If the baron didn't shoot him, Bethany well might once the truth came out.

Jack counted on the supposition that Goodson would willingly accept *any* earl for a son-in-law and forgive the ruse once explained.

His one hope for Bethany's forgiveness would be to

make her fall madly in love with him before he had to confess. So much in love that she would accept him title and all.

Sadly, to effect that, he must allow his brother's infatuation with the mercenary Euphemia to continue. That particular attachment was bound to end in disaster, but the die was cast and there was little to be done about it now.

He would simply have to stock up on brandy and prepare Colin as best he could.

Chapter Three

They were hardly settled in the barouche and on their way to Hyde Park the next afternoon when the trouble began. Colin took the seat beside Beth while Jack sat with Phemie. It would appear to anyone observing the outing that the brothers had switched the objects of their pursuit. Phemie protested, and Beth was not certain she liked the idea, either. Had they changed their minds?

"I spoke with Baron Goodson last evening," Jack said with a smile. "He is of the opinion the four of us should remain equal friends and not form any particular attachment as yet."

Phemie scoffed and glared at Colin. "Of course, he would suggest that. He wants you for Beth!" Her bottom lip protruded in a pretty pout.

"No, no, I'm sure that is not the case," Colin argued. He looked adoringly at Phemie. "I think, rather, that he would like to place some distance between Jack and Miss Bethany." He turned to smile apologetically at Beth. "Your father can't be all that delighted that you have tossed aside a baron for a soldier, now can he? No doubt he hopes—"

"That she shall have an earl instead! *You!*" Phemie insisted, firmly drawing Colin's attention back to her.

He reached forward, clasped her hand and patted it. "Now, now, take heart. At the first stop, we shall change places, Jack and I. Will that suit you?"

Beth exhaled sharply, impatient with all of them. "I think I shall sit up front with the driver. This deception is altogether too convoluted for my taste."

Jack laughed as if he thought she were joking. "Mine, too, but it was a condition agreed to so that we would be allowed to escort the two of you." He looked quite pointedly at Colin and Phemie, then back at her.

Beth realized that he was doing this as a favor to his brother who was obviously enamored of her cousin. If she refused to play along, Colin would not be able to court Phemie. And worse, Beth admitted to herself, she would appear available again to the likes of Arthur Harnell.

"Uncle doesn't even credit your betrothal to Jack," Phemie declared. "That should tell you something."

"Ah, but the word is out since the evening at Lord Randolph's," Colin assured them. "Even if it is not in print, everyone is talking."

"Then why must we pretend?" Phemie demanded. A perfectly good question, Beth thought. She smiled and cocked her head at Jack, awaiting the answer.

"All we must do is share our dances equally at whatever functions we attend and go about together as a group rather than as two couples. If we do not, Lord Goodson will not allow us to call. Then Bethany most likely will be subjected to more pressure from Harnell and her father."

"And Whitworth will not be allowed to court me, the poor cousin," Phemie surmised.

No one said anything to that. So, in mutual and silent agreement, they proceeded with their ride.

In the fortnight that followed, Beth discovered she rarely

minded the arrangement. Lord Colin, with his ready sense of humor, kept them laughing with his constant gibes at his brother. And Jack, a bit more clever and reserved, proved devilishly quick with ideas for entertainment.

They rode together almost every morning, stoically parading down Rotten Row as if it were summer and they were showing off their latest equine acquisitions. Then they would burst into a gallop, racing across the green and through the trees, reveling in the freedom not possible in warmer weather when there actually were crowds. Even the little season had ended now and attendance in Town had dwindled sharply.

If nothing else, enforced togetherness with Phemie and Lord Colin prevented Beth's attraction to Jack from getting out of hand. Even so, she often caught herself anticipating his slightest touch. The mere brush of his hand against her back or at her waist sent a thrill of warmth throughout her body.

She had taken to wearing a corset, trying to prevent it, but it was of little help. At least, that was the excuse she used to abandon the stiff, whalebone garment. Most slender women had cast them aside as unnecessary with the French empire fashions. Filmy flowing fabrics and raised waistlines only called for a light chemise that was fitted beneath the bosom and lifted one's chest higher by the straps at the shoulders.

Beth shivered, merely recalling how Jack had once trailed an ungloved finger along the low neckline of her newest Worth creation of delicately embroidered gauze. Though she had brushed his hand away and feigned exasperation, she had been none too swift about doing so. His suggestive smile had her in a tizzy the rest of that night. She seemed to grow more shameless by the day.

At present they were alone again in Lady Raythorn's conservatory and Beth feared Jack had something similar

in mind the way those dark eyes of his all but devoured her.

"We should return to the card room," she said, sounding reluctant even to her own ears.

"Not yet," he whispered, his lips very near her ear. "I
went to too much trouble to get you here." His hands
slipped 'round her waist and cradled her against him.

"Jack, behave yourself!" she gasped, closing her eyes,
relishing the feel of his hands on her. "Where are Phemie
and Colin?"

"Heavily into a game of whist, I expect," he said dis-
tractedly as he nuzzled her neck with his chin. "Do you
care?"

Not really. At the moment she seemed not to have a
care in the world save that someone might arrive in this
deserted place full of dead plants and interrupt them. "You
should not..." She breathed the words only out of con-
vention. *He should. He really should,* she thought as one
of his hands cradled her breast and the other slid slowly
down the front of her gown. Her very thin, supple gown
that molded itself to her body and allowed her to feel every
flex of those strong, elegant fingers.

Her blood sang in her veins. Pinwheel lights whirled
behind her eyes. She felt certain she could hear her heartbeat in her ears, an irregular rushing sound, growing more
and more rapid until something, some foreign noise, intruded.

The door rattled, then squeaked as someone attempted
to force it open. Immediately Jack's hands left her.
"Hurry. This way," he rasped.

Beth allowed him to push her through a nearby door she
had not noticed being there. It opened into the garden and
was obviously for the gardener's access and not meant for
guests. There stood a small toolshed nearby, almost totally
concealed from the rest of the garden by a giant trellis

overgrown with ivy. "In here," he said, keeping his voice low as they ducked inside the small building.

"Can we not get to the terrace?" she murmured, terribly afraid someone had noticed their absence at the party and come looking for them.

"Not without being seen if someone is still in the conservatory," he admitted. "We'll wait a bit, then make our way around and come into the ballroom as if we've been strolling through the gardens."

"How long must we wait?" she asked, her question barely audible.

"Long enough for this," he whispered. He turned her in his arms and his mouth met hers with an urgency that surprised her.

He had stolen kisses before. With the exception of the first one the night he proposed, they had been playful, brief, and not meant to incite. This one, Beth thought as she surrendered with lips parted and seeking, definitely had that intent.

Knowing she might never have another chance to explore a kiss this fully, she poured her very soul into it. She met his questing tongue, returned the query with her own and tasted the absolute fullness of desire. Hot rich spiced wine he was, drugging to the mind and dangerous to a spinster's resolve. Beth breathed in his subtle scent. Too subtle, teasing her to identify it, to fill herself with it. With him. She could not get enough.

She buried her fingers in his hair, holding him as if she feared he would abandon her. Smooth as silk, his dark waves closed over and around her hands, a gentle, warm caress.

The brocade of his waistcoat abraded her bosom through the thin pleated gauze of her gown and the silk of her chemise. She felt the tips of her breasts tingle as they pressed tightly to the hardness of his chest. Another hardness moved sinuously against her lower body. She knew instinctively where it belonged, where she wanted it, though no one had ever told her precisely how man and woman came together. Why had no one ever told her that? Or how powerful the need would be?

His mouth left hers and pressed against her ear. "I cannot take you here," he whispered, his voice rife with longing. "I dare not, but I want you, Beth. I want you more than life."

Her breath shuddered out as his heat continued to sear her everywhere they touched. She knew she should speak. She should shove him away and run. But even if she wanted to, which she did not, Beth knew her legs would fold beneath her. She pictured herself a puddle at his feet. This was madness.

"I need you," he rasped, then his tongue traced the shell of her ear and near the opening. Wet heat flooded her entire being and she groaned. "Come to me," he murmured. "Late in the night, come to me." His palms molded the roundness of her hips and pressed her hard against him. "Please." Fire shot through her.

"How...where?" she demanded, her eager words halting, breathless.

For a long time he said nothing. He remained perfectly still, though she knew what the effort cost him by the way his body tensed, the way he deliberately forced air into and out of his lungs.

When he finally spoke she could hear his frustration. She could feel it, hate it, wish it away. "Forgive me," he said, his voice almost normal, though very sad. "We cannot."

"Why?" she demanded before she thought how it would sound. He must think her the veriest wanton in London. Or anywhere else.

In the moonlight through the window she could just detect his smile, a sad smile, as he pulled away enough to look down at her. "Because it would be mad," he said. "Because it would be wrong. Because there is no way to do this and not ruin you forever."

"Yes, there is," she told him, again without any thought past the desire that urged her on. "Not tonight. Tomorrow," she told him, her words all but tripping over her tongue. "At half past eleven in the morning, wait outside Chez Arnaud milliner's shop in your carriage. I shall be alone and wearing a plain gray cloak and a bonnet that conceals my face. Where we are to go from there, you must arrange. And you must have me home by three."

He appeared reluctant as he expelled a harsh sigh.

"It will be all right," she assured him.

"Only if you agree tonight that you will marry me. Otherwise…"

"No!" she said with a short laugh. "You know my views on marriage, Jack. But even if I am to spend my entire future as a spinster, I need not do so as an old maid! I will meet you."

He brushed a curl off her brow and gently kissed where it had lain. "Suppose you like the physical aspect of marriage, will it change those views of yours perhaps?"

"I cannot let it," she told him frankly. "There are too many other considerations. However, I do admit you have made me curious…about things. And we *are* the best of friends." She brushed against him on purpose.

He made a pained sound in his throat and closed his eyes. Then he moved away from her so that they were no longer touching except for the hand that clutched hers. "Until tomorrow," he agreed, somewhat grudgingly. "For now, I had better return you to the ballroom or neither of us might survive your father's wrath past this evening."

They set out for the terrace, but he turned when they

were halfway through the dark garden. "Beth, I should apologize."

"Do not dare," she whispered. "Remember, half past eleven."

The next morning Colin was still arguing for the liaison while Jack kept voicing second thoughts. All night Jack had worried about it, so much so that his brother had guessed the cause of his turmoil. They had few, if any, secrets, living in each other's pockets since Colin's birth. He provided a good ear if not always sound advice. Jack often accused him of being a conscience whittler. Perhaps that had been what Jack sought in admitting his quandary in the first place, and that troubled him even more.

"I shall have to tell her beforehand," Jack insisted.

"About the title?"

"Yes, and also that I fully intend to change her mind about marrying and that I wish her to marry *me*. And why."

Colin scoffed. "You've already asked her. That's enough, I should think. She will only dig in those pretty heels of hers and become even more adamant about remaining unwed." He smiled slyly and nudged Jack's shoulder with a fist. "Persuade her, man! Make her want it. Make her think it's her idea. You can do it!" He paused a second, then added, "Besides...if there is the possibility of a child..."

Jack frowned. "I swear I can see horns growing out of your head. I do have a bit of honor left, y'know."

Colin laughed. "But you'd toss up her skirts all the same."

"No. No, I shall either tell her the truth—"

"And lose her completely," Colin warned with a firm nod.

"Or I will refuse to compromise her today. Yes, that

would be best in any event. What man wants a woman to succumb to him only to satisfy her curiosity?'' He threw up a hand for emphasis.

"You want her any way you can have her," Colin said with a barely suppressed laugh. "Admit it."

"I *will* have her, too, but not today. You're right about one thing. It's too soon to tell her about the title. Perhaps in a week or so she'll be ready. I do think she's beginning to more than simply *like* me."

"I should jolly well hope so considering what she suggests you do this morning!" Colin exclaimed as he checked the folds of his cravat in the mirror and smiled at himself. "You can bring her here to the house. I'm going to run up some debts for you about town. Won't be back till late this evening."

Jack shook his head. "No need to stay away. I'm not taking her anywhere but for a long ride in the carriage."

"Dashed inconvenient, tupping an untried maid in a bouncing conveyance." Colin shrugged. "However, do what you must."

"As if you would know anything about tupping in carriages," Jack muttered, "or untried maids, for that matter." He left Colin still grinning at his reflection.

Snow started to fall as he began his outing. The pale gray clouds spat large, lazy flakes that melted as they touched the cobblestones. The weather seemed too warm for any great accumulation, though there would be plenty of mud on the unpaved roads and byways. Jack needed to complete his task of acquiring a wife and return to the estate before winter truly set in. There were people there who would be depending upon him and who must be wondering how they would fare with the new master.

All too swiftly his carriage arrived at the appointed place. Chez Arnaud's appeared to be a modest shop, one of many located on Elvin Street and frequented mostly by the merchant class. Sprigs of ivy and holly with red berries festooned most of the windows. Among the greenery were strewn various items to be sold—tins of tobacco, gaily painted toys, woolen scarves, gloves, and, of course, hats. The places of business looked rather cheerful when compared to the more exclusive shops along Pall Mall with their understated displays.

He sat in the carriage peering out the window for some time before he saw her emerge from the milliner's carrying a small striped hatbox. Immediately, he opened the door and stepped down to assist her inside.

Only when they were comfortably settled with the shades covering the windows did she throw off the hood of her cloak and smile up at him. "How did you know it was I instead of some shop girl?" she asked with a laugh.

How had he known? There must be hundreds of such women wearing gray cloaks in this part of London. "I know your gait," he explained as he reasoned it out for himself. "The set of your shoulders, the tilt of your head, the way you move. I never even thought to question whether it was you."

"Hmm. Next you'll declare my every motion fascinates you," she said, pretending amusement, though he could feel her quiver of apprehension.

"Just so. But I might have welcomed anyone who marched up to me since I've been waiting so long," he said, teasing her. "Did you have trouble getting here?"

"Not at all," she assured him. "I only thought a bit of a delay would make you more eager to see me. Did it?"

Jack laughed and kissed her hand through the ostrich-skin glove she wore. "Did I not seem eager enough last evening?"

A pretty frown wrinkled her brow. "In a way, but then you thought better of it, I think. I almost feared you would not meet me." She drew in a deep breath and let it out slowly. "Well then, where are we to go for our tryst?"

He had instructed his driver to seek out streets with little traffic until notified otherwise. Jack slid one arm around her and drew her close. He kissed her forehead. "We must talk about that, Beth."

"Ah, I hear a sharp reluctance in that tone of yours. Have you decided not to, um, enlighten me?"

"Not unless you would make an honest man of me in the near future. You must say you love me," he dared.

"I love you," she replied in a very matter-of-fact tone of voice. "But there's no need to marry."

Jack sighed. This seemed a losing battle, but he was far from surrender. "How can you say you love me and in the same breath deny my proposal?"

All frivolity disappeared from her expression. "Oh, Jack, you are the dearest man I know. But I have told you I cannot marry. There are too many reasons to list."

"Fear of connubial duty is not among those, I take it?"

She shrugged. "No. Actually, that is the only benefit that I can imagine. I have money, which I intend to manage myself. Now tell the truth. If we wed, you would be the master of it all, would you not?"

"Legally," he admitted, "though I would not touch a pence of it. You would be free to do as you like with what you bring to the union."

"There will *be* no union," she stressed. "Suppose I decided to toss my entire fortune away to poor orphans or such, would you consider it good business to allow that?"

"*All* of it?" he asked, certain she was making a jest. Until now, he'd rarely had enough to meet his own needs, much less that of strangers.

Her curt nod told him he had made the wrong answer.

"You see?" she asked, snatching her hand away from his. "You would object. You would believe it your duty to advise and if I did not choose to honor that advice, you'd feel compelled to save me from myself, am I correct?''

Jack knew he was on shaky ground here. He dared not lie about that in the event her example became a reality one day. It would be so like Beth to beggar herself—and perhaps him, too—by giving with open hands until there was nothing left to give. With that kind heart of hers, she would try to save the entire population of poor. But he wanted her, kind heart and all. Most especially her kind heart.

"Beth," he said carefully. "Do you truly believe I would marry you for your money?"

"Heavens no!"

"What if I were wealthy and titled and vowed you could dispense of your funds in any way you chose?"

She shrugged. "But you are not. And if you were, that would only reinforce my resolve. A wealthy man would be even more circumspect than you when it comes to managing me. And a titled one would require too much in the way of social niceties. All my plans would fall by the wayside while I catered to duties as his wife. Meaningless entertainments," she said in a dull voice. "You know what those are like. Even as daughter to a baron, they test my patience and hamper my life. Trust me, if I ever did stoop to marriage, it would not be to a title."

So there it was. Making the admission would make no difference except for the worse, and he might lose her forever on the spot if he confessed. He could not help but wonder about those plans she spoke of that were so dreadfully important to her. "Why not simply tell me what it is you wish to do with your inheritance? I might well agree it needs doing."

"It is no concern of yours. I do not need your advice, or permission or your blessing. If I married you, then I *would* need all of these things,'' she declared. ''So I never will.''

''Never is a very long time,'' he warned as he took her hand again and pressed it to his heart. ''You say you love me.''

She smiled again, almost sadly this time, and caressed his chest affectionately. ''I do, Jack. I have no better friend than you.''

He gazed into her eyes meaningfully. ''I do not wish to be a mere friend, Beth.''

''Then be my lover, too,'' she whispered, and offered him her lips. ''It is what I want, as well.''

He took her, abandoning himself to the delicious feel of his mouth on hers. The swift current of desire enveloped them and carried them away. She felt it as keenly as he, Jack knew, for her breathing quickened and the sound she made was one of want. She meant what she said. She wanted this.

But Colin's last taunt kept him sane. A carriage was no place to make love to the woman he wanted as his wife. And yet, he knew he had to do something greater than he had done thus far to bind her to him.

Need and practicality almost won out over honor, and might have done had the carriage wheel not hit a particularly deep hole in the street that jounced them apart.

Beth laughed, rubbing her nose. It had bumped against his cheekbone. Her bonnet hung askew, its stiff velvet brim badly dented. She had never looked lovelier or more desirable. He was so tempted to knock on the roof of the carriage with his cane and order the driver to take them to the town house. Once there, Jack was certain he could convince her she could not live without their lovemaking.

But suppose she decided she could? Beth knew nothing of intimacy, and the first time for a woman was not entirely pleasant, so he had heard. In this respect, he was as uninitiated as she. He'd had a variety of women, but none who had been new to the experience.

In the end it was this worry, not Jack's dratted honor, that had him persuade her they must abstain. First, he had to convince Beth to marry him. Once he had her word she would, then he could risk it.

"I never thought you were a prude, Jack," she said, teasing him as he tried to repair the bend in her bonnet. "However, perhaps it is just as well."

"What do you mean?" he asked, pretending only slight interest, his gaze firmly fixed on the brim of the hat he was coaxing back into shape.

"I would probably have missed you even more when we part. Father has said we must return to the country tomorrow before the weather worsens and the roads become impassable. That is why I must return by three so I may see to packing."

Jack's hands stilled at their task. She was leaving? Why had she not said so? How could she have thought to give herself to him this afternoon, then simply leave town in the morning as though nothing had happened? Damned if she would!

He hurriedly listed in his mind what was left to be done in London. Not much, but at least another week's worth of errands before he could follow her. There was more paperwork concerning the inheritance, the town house to close, items to order for the people at the manor so they would have enough for the winter.

"Colin and I should leave Friday next," he declared, stating the fact as if he'd made the decision earlier. "We shall call on you and Euphemia a week from Saturday if that is acceptable."

"No!" she exclaimed, then seemed to think better of her too violent protest. "Sunday. Come for supper on Sunday. That would be better. Saturdays are...too busy." Her voice softened as did her expression. "I am happy you won't be far away."

"Are you?" he asked, his tone more clipped than he meant for it to sound. They were nearing her house now and he did not want to leave her on such a curt note. "You'll be glad to see me?" he added.

"Yes, of course," she said, tying the bonnet's ribbons beneath her chin. "Even if you do find me quite resistible, there's no reason we cannot remain friends and neighbors."

Her very calm stirred a fury in Jack he could not suppress. He grasped her face and kissed her as assiduously as he knew how. He drew deeply from her sweetness and stole that complacency of hers straight away. His hand molded her breasts, first one, then the other, caressing them with feverish intent as he aligned her body with his so that she would know what the nearness of her did to him.

Only when she was gasping for breath and shuddering with need for him did he release her and set her away. *There, see if you can find where your serenity went, young lady,* he thought as he struggled to contain the renewed fervor of his own desire.

The carriage stopped. He forced a placid smile, opened the door, got out and offered her his hand to alight.

"Have a lovely trip," he said as if his knees weren't fit to buckle beneath him. As if his arms did not ache from the loss of her in them. As if his trousers fit him as perfectly as they had when he'd donned them this morning.

The sound of her response might have been a word of farewell. He might have understood it if the blood had not been thundering in his ears like a herd of wild horses.

But her eyes were wide, shocked, the pupils dilated with arousal. Two could play at this game and, for more reasons than one, he was infinitely glad he'd had more practice.

Chapter Four

"I wish Father had not insisted we go to the Marstons' this evening," Beth said. She tugged down the skirt of Phemie's hastily pressed gown so that it hung straight. "I had hoped we could leave in the morning as planned." The snowfall had grown heavier during the evening hours and her father had decided to postpone their journey another day.

She did not want to see Jack so soon after their parting this afternoon.

"Well, I am glad to be going," Phemie declared. "Colin hasn't come up to scratch yet, but I almost have him there."

"He and Jack aren't likely to attend," Beth told her. "Any party will be sparsely attended this late in the year. Almost everyone that isn't in permanent residence here will have left for the country for Christmas. And there is the weather to consider."

"Oh, they'll be there," Phemie assured her. "I sent word to Colin that we'll be attending."

"You did not!" Beth exclaimed in shock. "Oh, Phemie, that simply is not done! What will he think of you?"

"That I am hoping to see him tonight. I do swear you

will lose Jack if you insist on playing by society's rules, Beth.''

If Phemie only knew the rules Beth had been so eager to discard, she would be horrified. "For your information, I do not mind *losing Jack,* as you put it. You know very well I am not in the market for a husband. And you will wreck your own chance at Colin if you continue to chase the poor fellow like a hound after a hare.''

Phemie grinned. "Ah, but the hare's slowing these past few days. Methinks he wants to be caught.''

"And the hound is salivating,'' Beth muttered to herself. But who was *she* to throw stones at Phemie after last evening and this afternoon? Beth had done considerably worse than send 'round a note announcing her intention to attend a party.

So Jack would be there tonight after all. What on earth could she say to him after that passionate parting kiss he had given her? Why was she so powerfully drawn to the man? Her good sense flew right out the window every time he so much as looked at her.

Beth admitted her one real fear was that she would begin to entertain hopes that Jack would suit her as a husband after all. When she was apart from him, she could reason well enough and know that it would never work. But when he kissed her, held her and looked into her eyes, Beth's resolve wavered.

Papa was waiting when they descended. He wore a special, tender expression when he looked at her tonight. She wondered why. Had he been maneuvering behind her back again with Lord Harnell? She hoped there would be no more harsh words between them about such things. She loved her father, hard head and all. But he said nothing, only escorted Beth, her mother and Phemie to their waiting conveyance.

The trip took less than a quarter hour since Marston

House was very near their own. They were fashionably late, despite her father's penchant for promptness, because of having to unpack their gowns to wear and have them pressed.

"He's not here," Phemie whispered, her dismay evident after a quick survey of Lord Marston's large drawing room.

It proved to be a rather small gathering, just as Beth had predicted. There were only thirty or forty people, all milling about now while a group of musicians played softly so as not to drown out conversation. There would be no dancing. The weather was too cold to open the huge ballroom required for that.

"We shall likely have games later," Phemie said dully. "I do so hate games."

"So do I," Beth agreed. "I expect the library and the morning room will be open and warm for those who do not wish to participate." She glanced back toward the door leading from the main hall. "I believe I shall go and see. Wait here."

Her main objective was to find a place to sit out the party. The noise within the room had already begun to make her head ache. She did not want to admit her disappointment that Jack had not and probably would not arrive since the party was already well under way.

The library was all but deserted. Only a few people had taken refuge there. Beth was about to return and tell Phemie when one of the servants appeared holding a folded note. "Miss Bethany Goodson?" he queried.

"Yes?"

"A gentleman instructed me to give this to you as soon as you arrived." Once the footman had handed her the note, he left.

The note was written on plain ivory paper. *Crucial that we meet. Hurry upstairs, three doors down from the room set aside for the ladies. Do make haste.* The signature was a large, bold *J*.

Beth refolded the note and stuck it into her reticule. The note had to be from Jack. She knew no one else with that initial, at least not well enough to be the recipient of such a message. Had something terrible happened?

She left the library, but not so hurriedly as to draw attention to herself. The wide staircase led off the end of the hall and curved to the upper floor. The doorway to the first bedroom stood open and Beth could see no ladies inside. She hurried down the hallway to the third door as instructed. It was open only a crack. She slipped inside and quickly closed it.

No matter how dire the reason, she knew she would have no excuse if caught in a bedchamber alone with a man. Too late, she wondered if that was his intention all along. Before she could turn to leave, strong arms grabbed her from behind and a hand closed firmly over her mouth.

''Now try and refuse me,'' a deep voice growled.

The arm around her middle lifted her off her feet and propelled her straight toward the huge tester bed. Beth kicked at his legs, knowing her slippers would do little damage. Her arms flailed, unable to connect with any part of his body or head. Fury at her helplessness blocked out most of her fear.

She bit the flesh of his hand, gaining herself one good breath and a half scream, soon muffled. He cut off all sound then when his hand also covered her nose.

Beth had realized immediately that the man was not Jack. Arthur Harnell pinned her to the bed with his weight. Her head swam dangerously from lack of breath. She continued to struggle, calling soundlessly to the one man who could save her. Then her mind shut down completely and she fell limp.

* * *

Jack felt an unaccountable sensation of urgency as he and Colin approached Euphemia. Her expression of glee annoyed him, but he was used to that. Beth's face kept flitting through his mind, but it was nowhere to be seen in actuality as he scanned the chamber.

"In the library, I believe," Euphemia told him without being asked. Her titter of a laugh grated on his nerves. But that was not the source of uneasiness. Something was wrong; he felt it.

"Excuse me," he mumbled as he stalked back to the hall, ignoring the greetings that came his way. He entered the large comfortable room lined with ornate shelves laden with leather-lined tomes. She was not here. Where the devil was she?

He turned too abruptly and ran headlong into Aurelia Sapps, a friend of Beth's whom he had met several times. "Pardon me," he grunted, then set her gangly body aside to proceed in his search.

"If you are looking for Bethany, she went upstairs," the woman told him with a sly grin that revealed a mouthful of protruding teeth.

"Thank you," he snapped, and went out the door, on his way to the stairs.

"Wait, Mr. Keith," she called as she rushed to catch up. "I can go in the retiring room and see if she's there if you like."

Jack slowed, realizing how ridiculous he must look dashing about the way he was doing. He turned to her and offered his arm as they reached the staircase. "Thank you, Miss Sapps. I would appreciate it. How did you know I was seeking Miss Bethany?"

She laughed, a sort of honking sound that put him in mind of a happy duck. Her beaklike nose and bright yellow gown with its feathery ruffles did nothing to detract from that impression. "Who else? You're so obviously smitten with her," she said. "I saw you kiss her and propose on the Randolph's balcony that night. Verr-rry romantic, sir, I must say." She honked again, more softly this time. Her long, strong fingers bit into his arm in a squeeze of emphasis.

"Yes, well, I'm in love with her, you see." Never hurt to make that abundantly clear when this woman had such a firm grip on him.

"Good for you!" she said merrily. "And her, too. I must say I envy you. Not likely I shall find a man myself, not with my looks. Even the dowry's not enough, Pa says."

Aurelia Sapps was the daughter of a poor baronet married by necessity to an incredibly wealthy heiress. The mother's fortune came directly from trade in whisky, an industry publicly frowned upon by the ton. She hadn't a prayer of making a noble marriage even if she were a great beauty, which she definitely was not.

"I'll just pop in there and find her for you," Aurelia said companionably. Her wide, toothy grin flashed.

Jack smiled back, thinking how he might learn to like the woman for her straightforward ways and friendliness if he had the time. Her eyes were nice, a bottle green that looked well with the color if not the style of her bright red curls. "Thank you, Miss Sapps. I would be eternally grateful."

Jack stood outside in the corridor, arms crossed over his chest, rocking heel to toe impatiently. Then he heard a sound from down the hall, a muted, throaty sound of distress.

His anxiety increased. With no concern for the propriety of what he was doing, Jack threw open the first door, then the next, and yet another. Behind the third, there on the huge bed, he saw Harnell, Bethany trapped beneath him, rucking up the hem of her lavender gown.

Jack flew across the room and dragged Harnell off her by the scruff of his neck. He whirled him away from Beth and landed a solid blow to the man's midsection, then an uppercut to the chin. Harnell dropped to the floor unconscious.

"Beth!" Jack rushed to her and turned her over on her back, coaxing her to come around.

"Oh, my heavens!" came a throaty voice from the doorway.

"Get me a cold cloth!" Jack ordered Aurelia Sapps. "She's fainted."

"That bastard!" Aurelia snapped as she quickly closed the door and hurried to the table where sat a porcelain ewer and basin. She dampened a cloth and brought it to Jack. "Did he hurt her?"

Beth was reviving. Jack sat beside her, holding her close and brushing the hair back from her brow with the cloth. "Are you all right, Beth?" he demanded.

She nodded and grasped his hand. "I'm fine. I think. He...he tricked me up here. I thought the message was from you." Jack felt a shudder run through her as her worried gaze sought his. "He did not...?"

"No, no, he didn't. Take a deep breath now." Harnell had not actually succeeded in his primary intent, but Beth was obviously shaken. Jack cradled her head against his shoulder. "Be calm. Everything's all right now."

Aurelia kicked at the unconscious Harnell. "He needs a lesson, that one. Is he dead?"

"Not yet," Jack admitted. "Killing him here would be in poor taste. I decided to wait until he leaves the house."

"I've a better idea," she announced, one red eyebrow raised and her lips stretched to one side. "My mama's pa can deal with this one. He can toss him overboard when he sails again."

"Never mind. I'll rather enjoy taking care of him myself."

Aurelia shook her head. "Then you'd have to explain it. It will ruin Bethany if this gets out."

Beth was fully alert now and sat up. "Aurelia? What are you doing here?"

"Getting myself a lord to marry," the redhead announced. "If you're quite recovered, you two help me undress him. Well, half undress him. Then we'll put him on the bed."

"What do you have in mind?" Jack asked. He had figured it out, but wondered if the woman was quite sane.

"Obvious, isn't it? Come, get busy! I'm fairly strong. The three of us should be able to lift him, don't you think?"

Jack frowned. "You don't want Harnell. He's cruel, as you can see, up to his neck in debt, and not worth having."

"You're absolutely right, Mr. Keith, and I don't plan to keep him, just wed him. He'll be shipping out soon after the ceremony, and will be glad to go. I only want the freedom a wedding ring will provide. Let's get to this before he wakes."

Jack and Beth helped strip Harnell of his coat and waistcoat while Aurelia squatted and tugged off his shoes and tight white pantaloons. The three of them lifted him onto the bed.

"You two hide in the dressing room if you want to see this," she advised with a quirky grin.

Jack took Beth's arm and guided her to the small room set between the bedchambers and left the door ajar. They watched in awe as the tall, gawky Aurelia Sapps ripped her yellow gown down the front, mussed her tangle of red curls and kicked off her shoes. She clambered up beside the unwitting Harnell, settled herself with a couple of wig-

gles, drew his limp arms around her and screamed the
house down.

Beth laughed nervously and Jack shushed her. It was a
small matter to sneak out through the fourth bedroom that
also adjoined the dressing room in which they hid. The
crowd that rushed upstairs and into the chamber with Aurelia and Harnell had no thoughts for anything other than
the totally shocking compromise that had just occurred.

"Are you steady now?" Jack asked her once they were
headed back down the corridor.

"Not really, but Aurelia's not the only one who can act.
Do I look as disheveled as I feel?"

He stopped in front of the retiring room, tucked an errant
curl behind her ear and allowed his gaze to travel the
length of her. "You look lovely, but you might want to
duck in here and compose yourself. Shall I wait for you?"

"No. Go back and make certain Aurelia is all right. Her
father looked apoplectic. You might be needed to help
manage Harnell."

Jack glanced back down the hallway where people were
beginning to exit the room in question. "I don't like to
leave you," he admitted.

She looked up at him, her eyes swimming with tears
and a grateful and adoring smile on her face. "Thank you,
Jack. Thank you for saving me."

"My pleasure," he said, returning her smile. "I would
do anything for you, Beth. You must know that."

"What an excellent friend you are," she whispered.

He almost told her then that he loved her. But he realized the news might shock her as much as it did him.

When he had seen another man trying to take by force
what Beth had so generously offered him, Jack had fully
understood the sheer depth of his feelings for her. What
he felt went well beyond his conviction that Beth would

be the best choice for a wife, a countess who would help him rebuild and reorder.

Even if she were as silly as Euphemia, as homely as Aurelia or as vapid as her mother, Jack knew he would still love her. Maybe he had loved her all along, even as a child. He had never forgotten her, that was for certain, and admitted now that he had been infinitely glad to find her unwed and available that night at the Randolphs'. He had gone straight for her and never thought to look further afield.

What a tangle he had made of things. The truth would unravel soon now and he had to work quickly to ensure that she loved him, too, at least enough to marry him.

She patted his arm and turned to go into the room where he could not follow. "I shall see you later, downstairs," she said.

Jack hesitated. What he wanted most was to toss her over his shoulder immediately and spirit her away, perhaps to Gretna Green on the border of Scotland and marry her there. But that would make him no better than Harnell who would impose his will on her without a care for her feelings. No. Jack knew he had to make her love him. Somehow.

Beth avoided Jack for the rest of the evening, even though it made her feel guilty to do so. He cast her long looks across the room, which she pretended she did not notice. When he made to approach her, she immersed herself in conversation within groups he dared not interrupt. He would be hurt by her avoidance, she knew, but Beth feared what she would say next if they spoke privately again.

There were the children to think of, her promise to them and to herself. While she thought Jack would be sympathetic to her plans for the future, she could be mistaken.

As mistress or wife, he would demand most of her time and she would be prone to provide it. How could she be a proper mother to four children who weren't even his, and still give him his due?

Phemie took her arm and led her to the morning room that stood deserted now that the crowd had begun to engage in games. Her father was deep into a card game at the moment and would not be budged to leave early.

"Tell me what has you so overset, Beth," Phemie demanded as soon as they were alone.

Beth sank onto the settee and blurted out what had happened abovestairs. Then she confessed her feelings. "I am afraid that I have grown to love him, Phemie, and I cannot afford to do that."

Phemie remained quiet until all was revealed, then asked, "What will you do?"

"I won't see him tomorrow if we remain in London. And if he follows to the country next week and calls as promised, I shall plead the headache and remain in my room. It will only take a few instances of such pretense and he will give up and find someone else."

"Why won't you simply tell him your real reason for refusing to wed? Surely you owe him that much after all he did tonight," Phemie suggested.

"To what purpose? He would agree to accept my terms. I know that. It's the sort of man he is. But I do not believe I could endure it if he began to resent me for what I am bound to do," she added, confirming her own worst fear.

"For love I would endure anything," Phemie declared, her face set with a determination Beth had seldom seen in her. "Even poverty."

"Well, you certainly needn't worry about that," Beth said, sounding acerbic and regretting it immediately. "I am sorry to be blunt, but if Colin weds you, you shall have it all. Dispense with this posturing about the title and living in grandeur before he stops trying to win your regard. Let him know that you want him for himself.''

''I truly do,'' Phemie admitted. ''If he were penniless and without prospect, I would throw myself at his feet even more assiduously than I have already done. However, a drastic change in me at this late date would seem suspect, would it not? He would merely believe it another ploy. Besides, he does not love me as I love him and obviously never will. He finds me amusing, is all. I should abandon the cause as lost, though it breaks my heart even to think of it while there is the least chance.''

Beth embraced her. ''Ah, Phemie, what can we do but go on as best we may? Do you think this will be the saddest Christmas we have yet spent?''

''I do,'' Phemie said with a weary sigh. ''When Jack gives you up and finds another, Colin will not hang about after me. It is just as well we face spinsterhood together. I shall devote myself to your cause, I suppose. My meager stipend might help a bit. You are welcome to it.''

''No!'' Beth said, aghast at this new and unexpected side of her cousin. ''You must not give up on Colin! Not if you love him!''

''As you love Jack,'' Phemie reminded her with a wry smile. ''Perhaps things will not seem so dark once we return to the country. You will resume your responsibility to your children and I shall help you. They must miss you as terribly as you do them, especially the baby, poor little dear.''

Jack offered a hasty, over-the-shoulder apology to Lord Marsten as Colin all but dragged him away from a discussion about parliament.

''That was rude. What's so urgent?'' he demanded. ''Has something happened?''

''God, yes!'' Colin tugged him toward the entrance hall

and motioned a servant to bring their capes and hats. "Let's get out of here."

"No, I want to see Beth before I leave."

"Trust me, Jack. It is imperative you hear what I must tell you before you see her again."

Intrigued, Jack followed suit as Colin donned his cape and left without even a farewell to their hosts.

"Now what's amiss?" Jack demanded once they were settled in the carriage.

"Brace yourself, Jack," Colin warned. "For once, my eavesdropping has proved the adage that says it's unwise."

Jack almost smirked. "Heard ill of yourself, have you?"

Colin sighed and looked away, propping one arm against the window and his chin on his fist. "Actually, no. I was rather heartened in that respect, though the rest of the conversation I could gladly have done without."

"Well, give over. Was it about me?"

"About Bethany." He met Jack's eyes, his own glinting in the carriage light with something akin to outrage. "She has children, Jack."

"That's absurd! Beth's never been married."

"I hope that was a lie. If not, she has bastards, one but a babe in arms! I heard her and Phemie discussing them in the morning room. This is why she's refused you, and probably every other man who had plied a suit for her hand. If she weds, her husband must learn what she has done."

Jack's mouth had dropped open. He clicked it shut and ground his teeth. "I do not believe it," he said finally. "You simply misunderstood."

"No, Jack," Colin declared, shaking his head. "There is no possibility of that."

It would explain everything. Her refusal to wed, as Colin had stated, and also her willingness to make love without benefit of marriage. She had obviously done that before. More than once.

His heart felt like lead in his chest. Broken pieces of lead that weighed so heavily, he could scarcely breathe around them.

"I am so sorry," Colin said as he leaned forward and laid a hand on Jack's shoulder.

"Not half as sorry as I am," Jack muttered as visions of Beth darted through his mind. Beth laughing as she flew along the path in the park on her little brown mare while he gave chase. Beth licking the chocolate from her upper lip in Gaston's Coffeehouse. Beth looking up at him adoringly not an hour ago with unshed tears glazing her eyes.

He wanted to weep himself for what might have been. "I wish I didn't know," he said out loud, more to himself than to Colin. "God, I wish I'd never found out."

"I had no choice but to tell you. What will you do now?" Colin asked, his voice laced with sympathy and regret.

"I don't know." Jack covered his face with one hand and shook his head. "I truly do not know."

Chapter Five

Jack stared down at the invitation Colin had handed him. He almost crushed it in his fist. He had spent a terrible week in London after the Goodsons left, and now had been at Whitfield Manor for an entire fortnight. To say the least, the city had not been the same without her. These past two weeks had proved hell on earth, especially knowing she was but five miles away. And now, to tempt him further, came this stiff bit of vellum requesting the honor of his and his brother's presence at Christmas dinner tomorrow with the baron and his family.

It was already Christmas Eve, a bleak day at Whitfield and they had not even gotten through breakfast yet. The coffee tasted like yesterday's dregs and the food was damned near inedible.

"I am going," Colin announced, grimacing as he set down his cup. "Of course, I shall make your regrets for you."

"Will you answer as Earl Whitworth or shall we dispense with the sham? I doubt Euphemia will welcome you with open arms when we do." Jack tossed the invitation in his direction.

Colin picked it up off the table and placed it beside his

plate. "You might want to peruse the London *Gazette* before you wipe that scowl off your face. No use wasting a bad mood." He pushed the folded newspaper within Jack's reach, tapped idly at a boxed item on the outer fold that he had been reading, then doggedly resumed drinking his coffee.

"God in heaven!" Jack exclaimed when his gaze landed on the article. The Baron and Baroness Goodson announce the betrothal of their daughter, Miss Bethany Goodson, to Lord John Macklin Keith, lately lieutenant of His Majesties Thirteenth Hussars... "Goodson announced the engagement! And it names me, not you! But why now? He's given up hope of the title."

Colin shrugged and sighed. "So he has. You're stuck, old fellow, unless Bethany honors her original agreement with you to cry off publicly. You might want to speak with her about it."

Jack's stomach roiled. His breakfast seemed bent on making a return path up his throat. The very idea of seeing Beth again troubled him. Could he remain cool and detached? Could he go through with the farce they had planned when he wanted her so much he thought he would die of it?

Forcing himself to stay away from her was one thing. Reuniting, then ending it all with the pretense of a squabble might be more than he could handle. His anger was too real. His feelings for her as scrambled as the eggs he'd just eaten.

How could she have lied so abominably?

You lied to her, his conscience reminded him.

That lie of omission hurt no one, he argued.

It will wreck your brother's hopes when the truth comes out, his inner voice declared.

"Do you love Euphemia?" Jack asked Colin.

His brother sat back in his chair and crossed his arms

over his chest. "What a foolish question! Do you take me for an idiot?"

"Damn me, you do love her," Jack said in a near whisper. He saw the answer in Colin's eyes. "I feared as much. I should never have allowed this charade to continue past that first night."

Colin got up and paced over to the window, looking out toward the neighboring estate. Jack knew he could see nothing of Goodson House, of course, for it was well beyond the large copse of trees that lay in between. "Save your worry for your own predicament, brother. I will have Euphemia Meadows." He turned to Jack. "I regret any embarrassment it may cause you in the future, but I plan to marry Phemie. We shall live elsewhere, of course."

"No!" Jack protested. "You will live here, Colin! This is your home now as much as mine. We agreed to share everything! We have always shared."

Colin smiled. "Not this, Jack. Every time you look at Phemie, you will think of Beth and what might have been. I cannot—will not—do that to you."

Jack was still trying to summon up an argument that might work when Colin walked out of the dining room.

The estate was in virtual ruin. Almost all of the household staff had left by the time he and Colin arrived. They had probably gone even before his uncle and cousin had died. As far as he could tell from the books, no one had paid them their wages for some time now. The only ones left were a deaf, half-blind cook and the frail, doddering butler, both far too old to seek employment elsewhere.

Those working the land and living in the cottages feared him as they had the former earl. Jack seemed unable to convince them he meant to improve their lot and that he had sufficient funds to do so. They cowered whenever he came near and refused to answer even the simplest questions.

The accounts were a shambles. The house was unkempt. He was not trained to take charge of an estate. He might have bulled his way through it and succeeded despite that, but his heart was not in the effort. He needed someone.

He needed Beth. As much as he might try to persuade himself he merely required a helpmeet to put the old home-place to rights, Jack knew he needed her more for himself. Much more.

But Beth had said quite clearly she would not have him. And, knowing what he knew about her, he shouldn't want her anyway.

Why not? that small voice inside his head asked him. Why not, indeed? So she had children. What of it? He could scarcely damn her for taking a lover when he'd had more than he could count over the years. But was there more than one? How many children were there? he wondered for the hundredth time. At least two. Speculation on the matter had deviled him constantly these past three weeks. Whose were they? Had she loved and been left in the lurch by some cad? Or more than one cad?

Strong, sensible Beth. Who else had seen that vulnerability she kept so well hidden? Who else had preyed upon her passion as he had almost done? Small wonder she insisted on remaining single. She must be incredibly wary of the entire male gender.

God help him, it suddenly ceased to matter how she had come to motherhood. He still loved her. He still wanted her. Her soft sweetness, her wit, her laughter and her desire for him could not have been feigned. She had been afraid to tell him of her past, that was all.

Perhaps if he told her he knew of her mistakes and that they made no difference in how he felt about her, it might change her mind about marriage. Surely in her desperation to avoid future scandal should she be found out, she would jump at his offer. The baron certainly would once Jack told him about the title.

He passed Colin on the stairs as he hurried up to change into his riding gear. "I'm going to see her."

"Now?" Colin called, turning to follow him up.

"I mean to marry that woman one way or another."

At the top of the stairs Colin caught his arm and whirled him around. "Jack, consider this carefully. Are you certain you—"

Jack shook off his grip and proceeded to the master chamber, not bothering to answer.

"Wait! Let's talk about this!" Colin persisted even as the door slammed in his face.

Hurriedly, Jack pulled on his riding boots and exchanged his morning coat for a tweed jacket. He ran a hand through his hair and slapped on his hat. Best do this before he lost his fervor.

He rushed out to the stables, saddled the gelding, mounted and rode hell-bent for Goodson House.

When he arrived, he was welcomed by the housekeeper, a pleasantly plump woman who greeted him with a questioning smile.

"I—I've come to call on Miss Goodson," he declared.

"She is not here," the woman told him. "I believe she is with the children today. She always spends her Saturdays—"

"Where?" he demanded, ignoring the frown his curt words caused. "Where are they if they aren't here?"

She pressed her fingertips to her lips for so long he thought she would refuse to answer him. Then she looked past him down the road to the village and said, "At the cottage, sir."

"Which cottage?" he snapped, following her line of vision.

"The second after you pass the bridge, sir," she directed. "You will see her blue pony cart there, I expect."

Jack turned swiftly, leaped down the steps and remounted.

He could not countenance why the baron would relegate his grandchildren to a cottage at the edge of the village instead of housing them properly within the manor house. Damn the man for his haughty ways and fear of scandal! Those poor little mites were not to blame for their existence. He would see they never felt themselves in the way of things at Whitfield. Not in the manner Colin and he had believed they were. Children needed acceptance and welcome from those around them. And love. Beth would love them, he knew, but that was not enough.

He spied the blue cart drawn to the side of a quaint little thatch-roofed dwelling. The large gray pony had been unhitched and was tethered nearby, grazing idly. Jack dismounted and wrapped his reins around a small tree.

Now that he was here, his sense of urgency began to abate. Actually, it disappeared altogether. Frantic wailing emanated from inside the closed door while high-pitched voices clamored for attention. "Mama, Mama! Me, me!" he heard. "Mama!" one of the little ones screeched. Good Lord, how many were in there?

He approached the door and barged in, certain she must need assistance. No point in knocking. Thunder could not be heard in such a melee. "Beth?" he called over the cacaphony.

She was crouched beside a cradle where little arms and legs protruded, kicking and flailing above a fat little body. He could hardly see the face of the child with its mouth open that wide.

"Jack!" she exclaimed, barely audible over the noise.

Three other children were assailing her, screaming for attention. The largest looked to be about four years old, the baby in the cradle not more than one, if that. He knew little of children, save for remembering his and Colin's own early years.

But they were people, after all, and he was usually good with people. He scooped up the smallest one that stood outside the cradle and rested the child against his shoulder while he tugged the eldest away from her.

Beth stared at him transfixed, or perhaps worried, even as she slid one arm around the remaining child and patted the screaming one in the cradle.

"What are you doing here?" she asked. He more or less had to read her lips.

"I wanted to tell you that I know about—ouch!" The little wretch he had shouldered bit him right through his shirt collar. Jack shifted it so that it lost purchase with its teeth. "It's of no consequence," he told Beth loudly. "Everyone makes errors in judgment."

The curly topped girl whose hand he was grasping kicked his shin. The solid-soled shoe she wore bounced off his boot. "Stop that!" he ordered, and immediately her faced screwed up and her ear-piercing howl joined that of her cradle mates. "Are all these...."

"Mine, yes!" she confessed. "All *four*."

"Damn!" he muttered.

"You mind your tongue in front of my children!" she shouted, her harried expression turning to one of outrage.

"As if they could hear me over this caterwauling!" he replied, jouncing the one in his arms, hoping the motion would startle the wee bugger into silence. No such luck.

"Let's get them quiet," he shouted to Beth. "I need to talk to you."

"Be my guest!" she shouted as she flung up her hand. "Pour Mary some milk. It's over there." She gestured toward the shelf on the far wall.

He wondered which one Mary was, the kicker or the

biter. Well, something had to be done. He plunked the biter on the well-scrubbed flagstone floor beside its sobbing older sister and located two cups. Just as he picked up the jug to pour, two sturdy little arms grasped him around his knees. Milk flew everywhere, most of it landing squarely on top of the younger of his two charges, the rest on his boots.

The sobbing stopped. The biter sat quivering in a puddle of white, looking up at him with wide blue eyes, lashes dotted with white droplets.

Beth laughed. She grasped her sides and laughed so hard all the children turned to stare at her, their former concerns apparently forgotten.

"Beth, are you quite well?" he asked, his voice entirely too loud in the relative silence that followed the spill. If the poor girl was not mad, it was a flaming wonder.

She managed to contain her mirth long enough to nod. "Wipe off Martha if you will. I'll change her in a moment. Mary, come here, dear."

The kicker trotted over obediently and flung her chubby arms around Beth's neck. The serene maternal smile Beth wore held Jack spellbound for a moment before he remembered his task.

He found a rag hanging on a nail beside the shelf and squatted to mop off the baby's head. It smiled up at him, showing small white evenly spaced teeth as its tongue lapped the milk from around its mouth. Dimpled hands patted at the puddle surrounding it. "So you'd be Martha," he said, apropos of nothing. "Hello, ducky."

Martha giggled, seemingly thrilled to be soaked through and being daubed at by a total stranger. He cleaned off her head and shoulders as best he could and left her sitting there, smacking her palms and swirling her tiny fingers in the milk.

Beth somehow detached herself from the others and

came over to lift the child off the floor. Jack watched, enthralled, as she quickly stripped the baby of its clothing and dunked it into a small wooden tub half filled with water. "Second bath within the hour," she explained. "Our nurse has gone for a bit of rest at her sister's house."

"Much-needed respite, I would think," Jack observed with a wince. "But what of you? Will you manage without her help?"

"I manage very well, thank you, but Darcy will be back within the hour. You need not stay on that account."

The baby in the cradle was silent now except for sucking sounds. Jack glanced across the room where Mary the Kicker and the other one were standing on the bed pointing out the window. "Should they be up there? Might they fall?"

"They have the agility of goats, believe me," she told him without even bothering to look. "Now why are you here?" Her hands seemed to fly, drying the child—Martha, he recalled—and pulling a small, checked garment over the baby's head.

Jack exhaled. He wished he had her full attention for this, but realized that, under the circumstances, he could hardly expect that. "I have known for some time about your children. Colin overheard you and Euphemia discussing them at the Marston party. I have come to the conclusion that you need a husband as badly as I need a wife. Perhaps even more so. The announcement of our betrothal is in the papers, as you must know."

"Yes, I was shocked. Obviously he is more desperate than I thought."

"I believe we should carry through."

"Oh, you do, do you?" she asked. "We did have a clear understanding, Jack. A plan. We shall hold to that. Come tomorrow night and live up to your word."

"Beth, be reasonable. You have four children! How can

you deny they need a father? What happened to him, by the way? Is he still about?''

''I have no idea what has become of him, nor do I care. He abandoned them and has no right to call himself a father!''

Jack felt an urge to kill the bastard who had hurt Beth so. He also had to admit a part of that desire was jealous rage.

Just then a soft thump sounded and a scream ensued. Jack tore across the room and swept the child up in his arms, patting its heaving back and holding it close. ''There, there, you're fine. The rug cushioned you. Hush, hush, sweeting. Did you strike your head on something?'' He ran his palm over the soft dark locks and felt for a bump. ''No, no, see? You had a fright, is all.''

To his great amazement, the child quieted and nestled against him, its small legs wrapping halfway 'round him as it clung like a monkey.

His heart settled back in his chest where it belonged, but felt full now. He was good at this. He could be a father. He *would* be, he realized. If Beth married him, he would be responsible for her children. Mary, blue eyes widened, sat on the bed with her fingers in her pretty bow-shaped mouth. Milky little Martha who liked puddles, clung to Beth's skirts. And this one, whatever its name, embraced him with such trust. He let his eyes stray to the cradle where lay another, barely of an age to stand upright. It slept now, obviously worn out by its struggles.

Beth stood near him, her head cocked to one side and her eyes narrowed as she watched him sway back and forth. After a moment she picked up Martha and plunked her down on the bed beside Mary. Then she reached for the one he was holding. ''You had better go now,'' she said softly. ''It is past time for their naps.''

"Who is this one?" he asked, unable to help running his hand over the child's head once more.

"Diana," she said. "Why?"

Jack shrugged and smiled. "I wanted to know. She has hair like yours."

Beth's expression was unreadable. "And the others? Are they like me, do you think?"

Jack looked at Mary. "She has your mouth. And Martha, your laugh. Her eyes are the same color, too. Yes, they are very like you. Lovely, all of them."

She continued to hold his gaze with hers and still he could not fathom what she was thinking. "Go home, Jack," she said softly. "Leave now. I shall see you tomorrow evening. You and Colin will attend, won't you?"

"Of course." He nodded and backed toward the door. "Until tomorrow then."

"Do not forget our arrangement," she told him.

When he would have argued, she held up a hand. "We can be friends afterward. Close friends, if you like." Her meaning was clear as crystal, but he would not settle for being a mere lover. Taking a lover was precisely how she had acquired four children she had to keep secret. That wicked determination not to marry had served her ill. Well, he would remedy that in short order!

"There is something else I must confess to you," he said, hoping that telling her of his title might make some difference. It certainly couldn't hurt since she was already dead set against marrying him. At least they would have no more lies between them.

The baby stirred and began to fret again. She glanced toward it, then back at him. "Tomorrow, Jack. Please go now."

Yes, tomorrow would do well. "Goodbye, then." He directed a small wave at Mary and Martha who sat perfectly still on the bed, watching him. Mary wriggled her fingers at him, then quickly stuck them back in her mouth. Jack played his last card of the day. ''I love you,'' he said to Beth, and kissed her quickly.

He heard her swift gasp, but she said nothing. In fact, he could swear she had begun holding her breath.

Jack exited the cottage and left her there with her children. Soon to be *their* children if he had any say in it.

Beth clenched her eyes shut and exhaled sharply the moment the door closed. Lord, she could not believe what had just happened. The emotions warring within her exhausted her more than the children's collective tantrum.

She was so angry she could spit. Jack actually believed she had taken a man to her bed and borne his bastards, one after another! Damn Jack Keith and his condescending concern!

But you would willingly have gone to his bed.

''Yes, but I *love* him!'' she argued with herself. However, Jack had not known that. She had not known it herself at the time. How could he think other than what he did, given her eagerness to allow him such liberties?

There, all tangled with the anger, was relief. She had never thought to see him again. He had not called as he'd promised. She'd had no need to feign the headache to avoid him. Small wonder after his finding out about the children. But he had come, after all. He had come, offering to make good their bogus betrothal to protect her good name. Did he believe she could have birthed four children in succession and kept it secret hereabouts? La, but he was naive if he thought that possible.

And dear. He was so dear to say he loved her. She knew he did not, of course. Perhaps he loved her as a friend, but if he loved her as a woman, he would surely have taken her when she offered herself in London. But he had not.

No, Jack was simply a dear, sweet man who would go well out of his way to save her.

Had he not done so when he rid her of Harnell? Now he felt obliged to save her again, a needless sacrifice on his part.

Everyone in the county knew Beth had taken responsibility for the children of poor Lily Nesmith whose worthless husband had abandoned her during the last pregnancy. Lily had pleaded on her deathbed after birthing little Deborah. Beth was already so attached to the children, she could never have said no.

If Beth believed for a moment that Jack loved her half as much as she loved him, she might consider relenting. She might turn over her entire fortune when she inherited next week and trust that he would do right by the girls she claimed as hers.

He had seemed quite taken with them, despite their crankiness today. What a tender way he had with little ones. Who would have thought it of a former soldier?

Phemie burst into the cottage. "I saw Jack ride past the house on the way from the village. Has he been here?"

"Yes, he was here," Beth admitted, unwilling to relate what had happened or her feelings about it at the moment. She distracted Phemie with a question. "Have you seen Colin?"

"No," Phemie admitted, wringing her hands. "They've been in residence at Whitfield House for two whole weeks, Beth. I cannot understand why he has not called. I know I said I would give him up, but I miss him so dreadfully! Haven't you missed Jack?"

Beth sighed. "Of course, but that's neither here nor there. Well, you shall see Colin when he comes for Christmas dinner tomorrow."

"They are coming?" Phemie fairly danced with excitement. "Jack has promised they will be there?"

"He said they would. So run home and decide what to wear. I shall be along shortly."

Beth needed time alone to plan how she was to break her betrothal to Jack and sound convincing. Would the vicar, the mayor, the squire and their wives find it entertaining? And would she ever be able to make her father understand?

He had recently taken to the notion of having Jack as a son-in-law, despite Jack's lack of consequence. Papa had sent the announcement to the London papers before she knew he had written it. She supposed he had grown truly desperate on her behalf after Lord Harnell's betrothal to Aurelia Sapps had been announced.

Beth had no heart for the chore of devising a confrontation. It appeared Jack had stolen that heart while she wasn't looking.

Chapter Six

Christmas day had dawned with a cold drizzle of rain, reflecting Beth's mood precisely. She wanted to weep with frustration. All through a sleepless night, she had tried to imagine a dialogue that would serve to end her betrothal to Jack. Yet each attempt proved fruitless, ending only with him taking her in his arms and forgiving her supposed transgressions that, by anyone's lights, should be unforgivable.

Preparation for the Christmas dinner had not served to distract her. Even the children's excitement over being brought to the manor house had not done so. Her father's insistence that they occupy the unused nursery had come closest to taking her mind from her most immediate problem. At last, after a full half year, he had accepted that her attachment to them was no passing fancy. Even her mother had bestirred herself to welcome them.

The other guests had been here nearly an hour now and had spent the time exclaiming over the warmth and welcome of Goodson House dressed in its Christmas finery. Holly, ivy and various other greenery festooned the mantels, wound around the stair rail and graced the clutches of candles spaced about the parlor. A huge yule log burned

within the fireplace and the scents of cinnamon and nut-
meg filled the rooms. It was almost time to eat and still
the Keiths had not arrived.

"Finally! They are here!" Phemie exclaimed as she
peered out the window at the circular drive. She nudged
Beth's shoulder with her elbow. "I feared they had decided not to come, they are so late. Should we wait here
or go and greet them at the door?"

"Wait," Beth declared, not about to move from her seat
at the pianoforte. She fixed her fingers on the keys and
began playing a carol softly as she looked up at her cousin.
"You mustn't seem so eager, Phemie. And for goodness'
sake, exhale, would you? You look fit to burst right out of
that dress."

"Says she who rarely fills one out," Phemie sniped
playfully. "Shoulders back, here they come."

The men entered, barely taking time to acknowledge the
other guests as they made their way through the room.
Colin approached first, nodded in greeting to Beth, and
then turned his full attention to Phemie. The two moved
far enough away to speak privately, leaving her to deal
with Jack.

"You play beautifully," he said, lounging comfortably
with one elbow on the instrument. "Do you sing?"

"Not well," Beth admitted. "Do you?"

"Like the finest frog in your pond. Shall I?"

Beth laughed and stopped playing at the end of the first
verse. "No thank you. We've precious few guests as it is.
I would hate to drive them back out into this weather before we've fortified them with food."

As if on cue, dinner was announced.

She stood and he reached for her hand. Bowing low over
it, he actually touched it with his lips. No one would think
a thing of it, she realized. Everyone believed them be-

trothed. In fact, they were. It was up to her to break the contract.

"How are the children?" he asked as they strolled toward the dining room. "Are they here?"

Beth looked away. "They are upstairs with Darcy. Father decided the cottage is scarcely warm enough since the weather's turning off quite cold."

"I'm glad to know he's that compassionate, especially since they *are* his grandchildren. Is the nurse to bring them down into company this afternoon?"

What a strange question for him to ask. "No, of course not. Whyever would she do that?"

"Whyever not? I for one should like to wish them happy Christmas. I've brought trinkets and sweets."

What was he up to? "Kind of you, I'm sure, but young as they are, they will be more comfortable in the nursery."

"Especially when these neighbors you've invited might object. I suppose they know nothing of the children." He glanced around at the other guests, Vicar Dunn, Squire McFaddin, Sheriff Tanner and their respective wives.

Beth granted Jack patience since he did not know the full truth concerning the births of her daughters. "Of course they do. Everyone knows of them."

"Then why not show them off? They are handsome children." It sounded like a dare.

"And so well behaved," Beth said with a quirk of her brow.

He did not laugh as she expected, but looked quite serious. "Bring them down, Beth. I recall how Colin and I were hidden away like pesky rodents when Uncle and Aunt had guests. You saw how we turned out."

She frowned up at him, realizing suddenly just how unhappy his childhood must have been. The best Beth could recall, old Whitworth had not been a pleasant fellow and his lady had done nothing but whine.

"Please do not worry, Jack. They are far too young to be affected by exclusion."

He said nothing, but his sensuous lips firmed into a straight line and he refused to look at her.

"Oh, very well," she conceded. "I shall send word to have Darcy dress them and bring them in for a few moments after dessert. But only if they are still awake, mind you. You have seen for yourself how need of a nap can wreak havoc." She stopped long enough to give the order to one of the footmen and watched him hurry away to relay her message to Darcy.

Jack squeezed her hand and the look on his face was reward enough for any inconvenience this might cause. Despite the oddity of his request, it caused a warm and giddy sensation that felt as cozy as Christmas itself.

What a fine father Jack would make. If only he truly did love her. Could he have meant it? Was it possible?

Dinner was pleasant enough though Beth barely tasted any of it. No one intruded on the conversation Jack kept up with her during the meal. Not until dessert was served, when her father tapped his glass with a fork to gain everyone's attention.

"A toast!" he announced as he stood. "To my daughter, Bethany, and her intended, Lord John of Whitfield. Happy life!"

"Here, here!" everyone commented as they stood and raised their glasses high.

Bethany cast a meaningful look at Jack, leaned close and whispered, "Our denouement must be put into effect very soon. Are you prepared?" He merely smiled at her.

Her father continued. "If there is no objection, we shall join you ladies in the withdrawing room shortly."

Her mother murmured her assent and led the way. There would be time for the women to refresh themselves upstairs and for the gentlemen to smoke or do whatever they must. Then the play she and Jack had planned to end their betrothal must commence.

Lord, how she dreaded it. Could she feign a temper and give him a setdown? Would he reciprocate or bow out gracefully? What excuse would she use? She could not think of a single reason why she should not marry him. Except that he did not really love her and she could hardly use that. She much doubted there was a couple within this company who had wed for love. She and Jack should have discussed this in more detail, Beth thought as a galloping case of nerves assailed her.

She rushed upstairs, tried to calm herself, checked her appearance and hurried back down. Long before she was ready, the men filed in, obviously having foregone their cigars for the pleasure of feminine company.

Jack joined her immediately. "Your father mentioned he would like us to have a Christmas wedding," he said, appearing amused by the suggestion.

"Ah, a year-long engagement," she said with relief, knowing that would give them plenty of time to stage their breaking of the betrothal.

He chuckled softly and brushed her ear with his lips. "No. I believe he would like the vicar to perform it *today*."

She drew back and looked up at him in horror. "Today? But…but that's not possible, even if we wished it so. There are banns—"

"Already called. We should have attended church."

"I was afraid you would be…" Beth clamped her mouth shut, but saw that he understood her despite the fact that she didn't finish. She had not gone to church in the village because she feared she would see him there.

"Your father is quite efficient. Announcement in the papers, banns called in our home county. He has thought of everything, even having a houseful of guests to witness the event.''

"There's no license," she argued.

"Easily obtained since he *is* the local magistrate, Beth."

"Oh."

Jack trailed his fingers up the underside of her arm, the backs of them grazed the side of her breast. No one could see the gesture, but Beth's breathing grew rapid and her face heated.

"Stop!" she whispered. "What are you doing? Do you wish me to slap you and end it here and now?"

"That's up to you, of course. I would as soon you didn't. Marry me, Beth. Today."

She huffed impatiently. "You are only offering because you think I need saving, and I assure you I do not! Leave off this teasing!"

He slid his arm around her and squeezed her waist. She jumped away. "Sir! You forget yourself!" The words came out more loudly than she'd intended. Conversation halted.

It was now or never. "I shall not wed a man who has so little regard for my wishes!" she announced, not altogether certain what she would follow that announcement with. Everyone was watching them now.

"Beth, my darling," he replied, also raising his voice so that all could hear. "You know your slightest wish is my command. You have but to name it."

"B-but I..." She stuttered for a moment, then grasped words at random. "I have no desire to live in London, I have *told* you! I detest the city and I shall *not* reside there no matter what you say! If that is what you require, then we must call off our agreement!"

He inclined his head and his smile grew wider as he replied, "It was but a suggestion, my dear. We shall live wherever you choose. In fact, I prefer the country myself. Here, it is, then.''

She cast about for something, anything, to counter his concession. ''You…you…you will not want the…the children to live with us and I shall not give them up!''

He laughed. ''Whatever gave you such a notion! Of course they shall live with us. Where else would they live?''

Beth saw Darcy and the children standing in the doorway to the withdrawing room, as entranced as everyone else by the one-sided argument between herself and Jack. Little Mary pulled away from the young maid and darted across the room.

Jack scooped her up and chucked her under the chin. He beckoned Darcy and the tweenie assigned to assist her with the little ones.

He looked at Beth. ''You fear I won't claim these darlings? Why, look at Mary's brows. How could I deny her? She is the image of me, don't you think? And, Martha,'' he added, brushing his free hand over the child's head. ''I see both of us in her.''

''Jack,'' Beth said, hardly able to contain her laughter. Mouths were hanging open all over the room. He was actually attempting to make everyone believe they were *his!* Borne of *her!* God love him, she should make matters clear. ''You do not understand…''

He brushed aside her protest. ''It is time you let go this aversion to marriage, Beth, and grant me the opportunity to get acquainted with my children. If for no other reason, you must honor our engagement and marry me as soon as possible. Please.''

She decided it would serve him right if she agreed. ''Very well,'' she said with a curt nod of her head. ''If the vicar is prepared.''

A gasp went up from those assembled, and then whispers and chuckles abounded as the excitement spread. Her father beamed. Her mother rolled her eyes. Phemie slid onto the stool of the pianoforte and began playing a gay little tune totally inappropriate for the occasion. Colin began to sing off-key.

Mary clapped her hands and chimed in, making up her own lyrics while the other little ones noisily vied for their part of the attention.

It was not a solemn ceremony. The vicar had to shout to be heard. Jack laughed out loud when Beth purposely omitted the word *obey* from her vows. His *I will* resounded like a shout when an unexpected lull occurred.

Beth might have thought the entire ceremony a mockery had Jack's kiss not been the one brazenly serious act of the afternoon. Her own sigh blended with that of numerous other ladies present. A shameless romantic, her Jack.

And suddenly as that, Beth felt married in truth. She belonged to Jack Keith and he belonged to her. For better or worse, the deed was done. There was no undoing it.

Hours later Phemie locked her arm through Colin's as they headed for the stairs. Everyone was leaving now that the bride and groom had departed. The wedding festivities had lasted well into the evening.

How good it was to have Colin under the same roof. He had remained so that Beth and Jack would have more privacy for their wedding night at Whitfield Manor.

"I'll just show you where you are to sleep," she told him.

"How kind you are to trouble yourself," he replied, his smile as devilish as could be.

"Well, our scheme worked well, did it not?" she asked, supremely proud of herself. "Beth never suspected a thing."

"A tribute to your talents and mine, my dear. Neither

did Jack. All that was needed really was for him to be
without her for a while. He was so miserable!''

Phemie offered him her most adoring gaze. ''I am so
happy you came to me that next day for an explanation of
Beth's children instead of asking Beth herself. If you had
not confessed how much Jack loved her, I should never
have confided in you. You must take full credit for their
happiness.''

''You had as great a hand in it. If you had not informed
your uncle that Jack was the true heir after I confessed it,
he might never have gone along with the plan to cook up
this hasty wedding.''

''Oh, he knew all along,'' Phemie told him. ''At least
after that first week. He always made it a point to inves-
tigate each of our suitors quite thoroughly.'' She shrugged
and dimpled. ''He had only put forth that dastardly Arthur
Harnell to encourage Beth to choose another. You must
admit it worked.''

Colin's look of surprise tickled her. ''So you knew from
the start I wasn't the heir?'' he asked. ''And still you allowed—''

''Uncle is not the only one with a need for all the facts,''
she admitted. ''He investigates. I snoop.''

Phemie watched as he shook his head in wonder as if
unable to think of a comment. Men needed prodding at
times to speak their mind. And if their minds were not yet
made up, prodding was even more essential.

''So, is your proposal forthcoming or shall I be forced
to persuade you?'' she asked prettily.

He blew out a breath of frustration. ''At the moment,
sweetheart, I fear I have little to offer you.''

''You have yourself,'' she argued, ''and that is *all* I
require.'' And it was, of course, but he also would inherit
a tidy sum from his maternal grandmother, according to

Uncle's findings. No point in her giving away the surprise now, however.

His gaze softened as he stopped on the stairs and cradled her face in his hands. "How could I ever have thought you a fortune seeker? Why did you pretend?"

"Perhaps I feared exposing my heart?" She blinked up at him, letting her eyes fill with unshed tears.

"Oh, love, we play too many games to conceal what we feel," he said. "That serves no purpose, does it?"

"None at all that I can see!" she said with a brightness to rival all the candles in Auntie's huge chandelier. "Come, let's celebrate with a tot of Uncle's Christmas cheer. I had a decanter delivered to your chamber when I ordered the room prepared."

He frowned. "Are you certain that's prudent, Phemie? We could be discovered. Remember what happened to Harnell and Aurelia Sapps."

"Yes, I remember," she said with a shrug and a daring smile.

He smiled back, looking as wicked as he ever had. "You're about to *persuade* me, aren't you, Phemie?"

On the way home to Whitfield, Jack struggled to keep his desire banked. Beth went out of her way to tempt him just as she had all afternoon and evening. He had been hard put to keep his hands off her even in company.

The moment they entered the drafty old manor, he regretted not whisking her away to somewhere grander, more in keeping with a honeymoon. But had he done so, it would necessitate traveling, and the five miles they had come provided quite enough of that.

He lifted her in his arms the moment old Carnes opened the door. "Meet my wife, Carnes," Jack shouted to the butler.

"I'm too old to beat anyone, milord," the deaf old fellow assured him in a crackled monotone.

Beth giggled as Jack carried her all the way upstairs, her arms around his neck, toying with his hair, sending flames licking through his veins.

"You are a troublemaker," he said as he tossed her onto his bed. "And a horrible tease!"

She laughed gaily and kicked off her slippers as she peeled off her gloves. "Who's teasing?"

"You might have waited until we were home to begin the seduction," he said in mock accusation as he sat beside her. He tossed off one boot and then looked at her. "I sincerely hope you won't regret this."

"So do I," she agreed, suddenly serious. "Were we too impulsive, Jack? Will you be sorry?"

He leaned back and embraced her. "Never in a million years." To prove it, he kissed her slowly and thoroughly, tasting her passion, her joy and her fears, as well. "Don't be afraid," he whispered against her ear. "Living without you is the worst fate I could imagine. Living with you is all I want in life."

She snuggled closer, returning his kisses, hampering his efforts to undress them both. Somehow, together they managed and soon lay as God had made them.

"You steal my breath, you are so beautiful," he told her as he feasted his eyes on her loveliness. "You smell so sweet, of jasmine and woman." His lips trailed down her throat to the ripe, small breasts already peaked and awaiting his kisses.

"And you, of spices and adventures in faraway places," she replied breathlessly.

"You are my grandest adventure by far." He fought the need to consume her on the instant, hoping to draw out their lovemaking, to make their first time memorable. He caressed her every curve, her slender waist, the gentle flare of her hip, a firm thigh and the sweet turn of her calf. How glorious was the smooth, warm skin that was his alone to touch. When his hand trailed up her inner thigh, she shuddered. Her sweet moan almost undid him completely.

"The sounds you make incite me," he said, his lips against her ear as his fingers sought her heat. "You want this," he murmured, his mind drugged with need at discovering how ready she was for him. "I want you, Beth. Only you."

She answered with a soft and wordless plea as he covered her and positioned himself to take all she offered. He might not be her first, but he vowed he would be her last.

"I am beyond waiting," he warned as he thrust inside her, claiming her with more aggression than he'd intended.

Her sharp intake of breath occurred the instant he realized his mistake and he stilled, unable to breath for the space of a second. "Oh, Beth," he groaned finally. "You *lied*." But what a marvelous lie it was. He *was* her first. Her first and only.

"You assumed," she murmured, now moving beneath him, urging him with her body to complete what he had begun.

With the greatest effort of his life, Jack gentled his passion and spent it slowly, allowing her time to adjust to his invasion, drawing each foray out with almost excruciating delays.

"Exquisite," he breathed as he loved her. "Incomparable. Without equal." She proved all that and more.

Her body responded with an eagerness that tested his resolve to its limit. The instant he felt control desert him, she surrendered herself completely, driving him over an edge of pleasure he had never even dreamed existed.

His mind blanked of everything but soaring sensation, a breath-stealing explosion that left him unable to move. Their bodies seemed fused with a oneness he knew would remain in spirit long after they arose from this bed. She was his. Only his.

Her voice dragged him back to reality. "I suppose you must be wondering."

"I suppose. I am beyond guessing at the moment," he confessed, almost wishing she would simply lie there and let him feel. Thinking proved difficult in his present state. Reluctantly he made himself move to her side so that she could breathe comfortably. "Are you all right?" he remembered to ask.

"Mmm," she hummed, and he could hear the smile in it. "Better than that. I knew you would be excellent at this, but I must say you quite exceeded my expectations." She shivered and burrowed even closer.

He wanted to take her again, but figured he should wait until his heartbeat regained some sort of normalcy. Besides, his curiosity deviled him now that she had brought the matter up. "How did you get the children?" he asked. The question sounded rather lackadaisical considering the importance of it.

"Adopted," she explained. "Do you mind?"

"That must be why they don't resemble us much," he said lazily as he stroked her back.

"Could be."

"What is the little fellow's name, by the way?" he asked. "You never said."

"You never asked. *Her* name is Deborah. They are all girls."

Jack smiled as he buried his nose in the curve of her neck. "They'll need brothers then. And there must be an heir to the title. Shall we?" He slid his hand down to her hip and coaxed her to lie on top. He loved the way her breasts pressed against him and her body seemed to seek his with unerring accuracy.

"An heir?" she questioned, bracing her arms on his

chest to look down at him. "Oh, I see. You are heir to Colin now. But surely he will have sons."

The moment of truth. "I am Whitworth, Beth. Not Colin."

Her brows drew together and she tugged a tuft of his chest hair. "You lied, Jack!"

"You assumed," he said, repeating her excuse for their former misunderstanding. "Do you mind?"

She thrust out her chin and looked away, taking a moment to decide whether she should be angry. Then she faced him again. "In the spirit of Christmas, I suppose I must forgive you. But there can be no more secrets, Jack. No more charades. Not ever."

"Then you should admit that last secret you would keep from me." He sighed when she did not reply. "Well, I'm waiting."

"What secret?" she demanded.

"That you love me, you silly widgeon. There's no need to prevaricate about it now. It's clear as day and you'll never convince me otherwise."

She laughed merrily and propped her chin in one hand while she drummed her fingers against his chest with the other. "You'll have to torture that one out of me. Make me confess."

"Before this night is over," he warned as he moved beneath her suggestively. "I shall have you singing the words, see if I don't."

She brushed her fingers over his brow and bestowed the sweetest kiss of peace. "Happy Christmas, Jack."

"A day to remember," he assured her, "and a night to repeat forever."

* * * * *

Dear Reader,

Did you know that many of our Christmas traditions, such as the Christmas tree, Christmas cards and gift giving, date from *after* the Regency period? The most important things, however, were the same—Christmas as a time for family and children and friends, for church, for feasting and celebration, for memories and for going home....

But what if you are an isolated young widow, with no money for feasting, no friends to celebrate with and no family except a small, beloved daughter? A daughter whose greatest wish is for a father... Or what if you are a man with no memories, no money and no name?

Christmas is also a time for new beginnings, for the rebirth of hopes and dreams, for joy in the midst of bitter winter cold....

So surely Christmas would be the most beautiful time of all for a wedding....

Anne Gracie

www.annegracie.com

THE VIRTUOUS WIDOW
Anne Gracie

For my parents, Jack and Betty Dunn,
who met and fell in love on a flight of stairs many years
ago, and who have remained very much in love ever since.

And for Zoë, who, as an imperious tot,
instructed me in the pleasures of dollhouses.

Chapter One

Northumberland, England
December, 1816

"Is my wishing candle still burning, Mama?"

Ellie kissed her small daughter tenderly. "Yes, darling. It hasn't gone out. Now, stop your worrying and go to sleep. The candle is downstairs in the window where you put it."

"Shining out into the darkness so Papa will see it and know where we are."

Ellie hesitated. Her voice was husky as she replied, "Yes, my darling. Papa will know that we are here, safe and warm."

Amy snuggled down under the threadbare blankets and the faded patchwork quilt that covered them. "And in the morning he will be with us for breakfast."

A lump caught in Ellie's throat. "No, darling. Papa will not be there. You *know* that."

Amy frowned. "But tomorrow is my birthday and you said Papa would come."

Tears blurred her eyes as Ellie passed a gentle work-worn hand over her daughter's soft cheek. "No, darling, that was last year. And you know why Papa did not come then.''

There was a long silence. "Because I didn't put a candle in the window last year?''

Ellie was horrified. "Oh, no! No, my darling, it had nothing to do with you, I promise you.'' She gathered the little girl into her arms and hugged her for a long moment, stroking the child's glossy curls, waiting until the lump had gone from her throat and she could speak again. "Darling, your papa died, that's why he never came home.''

"Because he couldn't see the way, because I didn't put a candle out for him.''

The misery in her daughter's voice pierced Ellie's heart to the core. "No, sweetheart, It wasn't the candle. Papa's death was nobody's fault.'' It wasn't true. Hart's death had been by his own hand, but gambling and suicide was too ugly a tale for a child.

"Now stop this at once,'' said Ellie as firmly as she could. "Tomorrow is your birthday and you will be a big girl of four. And do you know what? Because you've been such a good girl and such a help to Mama, there will be a lovely surprise waiting for you in the morning. But only if you go to sleep immediately.''

"A surprise? What surprise?'' asked the little girl eagerly.

"It wouldn't be a surprise if I told you. Now go to sleep.'' She began to hum a lullaby, to soothe the anxieties from her daughter's mind.

"I know what the surprise is,'' murmured her daughter sleepily. "Papa will be here for breakfast.''

Ellie sighed. "No, Amy, he won't. Papa has been dead for more than a year. You know he is, so why do you persist with this?''

"It's a special candle, Mama. The lady said so. A wishing candle. It will bring Papa, you'll see.'' She smiled and snuggled down under the bedclothes, curling up like a little cat.

Ellie frowned. That wretched gypsy woman with her false tales! Unbeknown to her mother, Amy had traded half a dozen eggs and some milk for a thick red candle. A wishing candle, indeed! More like a rather expensive Christmas candle. And a hurtful candle, if the old woman had put the notion in Amy's head that it could bring her father back.

Amy's few memories of her father were idealised fairy tales. The truth was too painful for a little girl. Hart had never been an attentive father or husband. Sir Hartley Carmichael, Baronet, had wanted a son—an heir. A small, spirited girl with tumbled dark curls and bright blue eyes held no interest for him. Was quite useless, in fact, and he'd said so on many occasions—in front of Amy herself.

Ellie looked at her sleeping daughter and her heart filled. There was nothing more precious in the world than this child of hers. She picked up the candle and went into her own room. Shivering in the bitter December cold, she hurriedly slipped into her thick, flannel nightgown and climbed into bed.

She was about to blow the candle out when she recalled the one burning in the downstairs window. Candles were expensive. She couldn't afford to let one burn down to a stub for no purpose. No practical purpose, that is. She recalled her daughter's face, freshly washed for bed and luminous with hope as she placed the candle in the window. A lump filled Ellie's throat. She got out of bed, slipped her shoes back on and flung a shawl around her for warmth. She could not afford the happy dreams that came so easily to children.

She was halfway down the steep, narrow staircase, when suddenly a loud thump rattled the door of her cottage. She froze and waited. Bitter cold crept around her, insidious drafts of freezing air nibbling at her bare legs. She scarcely noticed.

The thump came again. It sounded like a fist hitting the door. Ellie did not move. She hardly dared to breathe. There was a swirl of air behind her and a small, frightened voice behind her whispered, "Is it the squire?"

"No, darling, it isn't. Go back to bed," said Ellie in a low, calm voice.

A small warm paw slipped into her hand, gripping it tightly. "Your hand's cold, Mama." The thump came again, twice this time. Ellie felt her daughter jump in fright.

"It *is* the squire," Amy whispered.

"No, it's not," Ellie said firmly. "He always shouts when I don't open the door to him. Doesn't he?" She felt her daughter's tight grip on her hand relax slightly as the truth of her words sank in. "Wait here, darling, and I shall see who it is."

She crept down another six steps, to where she could see the front door, the sturdy wooden bar she'd put across it looking reassuringly strong. Ellie had soon learned that the cottage keys counted for little against her landlord.

Light flickered and danced intermittently across the dark room from Amy's wishing candle.

Someone banged again, not as loud as before. A deep voice called, "Help!"

"It must be Papa," squeaked Amy suddenly, from close behind her. "He's seen my candle and he's come at last." She slipped past Ellie and raced towards the door.

"No, Amy. Wait!" Ellie followed her, almost falling down the stairs in her rush to prevent her daughter from letting in who-knew-what.

"But it's Papa, Mama. It's Papa," said Amy, trying to lift the heavy bar.

"Hush!" Ellie snatched her daughter to her. "It isn't Papa, Amy. Papa is dead."

Their cottage was isolated, situated a little off the main road and hidden behind a birch spinney. But further along the road was the Angel, an isolated inn which attracted the most disreputable customers. Ellie had twice been followed home... With that den of villains down the road, there was no way she would open her door to a stranger at night.

The deep voice called again, "Help." It sounded weaker this time. He hit the door a couple of times, almost half-heartedly. Or as if he was running out of strength, Ellie thought suddenly. She bit her lip, holding her daughter against her. It might be a ruse to trick her.

"Who is it?" she called. There was no reply, just the sound of something falling. Then silence. Ellie waited for a moment, hopping from one foot to the other in indecision. Then she made up her mind. "Stand on the stairs, darling," she ordered Amy. "If it's a bad man, run to your room and put the bar across your door, as I showed you—understand?"

Amy nodded, her heart-shaped little face pale and frightened. Ellie picked up the heaviest pan she had. She turned the key and lifted the bar. Raising the pan, she took a deep breath and flung open the door.

A flurry of sleet blew in, causing her to shiver. She peered out into the darkness. Nobody. Not a sound. Still holding the pan high, she took a tentative step forward to look properly and encountered something large and cold huddled on her doorstep.

It was a man, lying very, very, still. She bent and touched his face. Cold. Insensible. Her fingers touched something wet, warm and sticky. Blood. He was bleeding from the head. There was life still in him, but not if she left him outside in the freezing weather for much longer.

Dropping the pan she grabbed him by the shoulders and tugged. He was very heavy.

"Is he dead, Mama?" Amy had crept back down the stairs.

"No, darling, but he's hurt. We need to bring him inside to get warm. Run and fetch the rug from in front of the fire, there's a good girl."

Amy scampered off and returned in a moment dragging the square, threadbare cloth. Ellie placed it as close as she could to the man's prone body, then pushed and pushed until finally he rolled over onto the rug. Then she pulled with all her might. Amy pulled too. Inch by inch the man slid into the cottage. Ellie subsided on the floor, gasping.

She barred the door again and lit a lantern. Their unexpected guest wore no jacket or coat—only a shirt and breeches. And no shoes, just a pair of filthy, muddied stockings. And yet it was December, and outside there was sleet and ice.

Blood flowed copiously from a nasty gash at the back of his head. Hit from behind; a cowardly blow. He'd been stripped of his belongings, even his coat and boots, and left to die in the bitter cold. Ellie knew what it felt like to lose everything. She laid a hand on his chest, suddenly possessive. She could not help his being robbed, but she would *not* let him die.

His shirt was sopping wet and freezing to the touch, the flesh beneath it ominously cold. Quickly she made a pad of clean cloth and bound it around his forehead as tight as she dared to staunch the blood.

"We'll have to get these wet clothes off him," she told Amy. "Else he'll catch his death of cold. Can you bring me some more towels from the cupboard under the stairs?" The child ran off as Ellie stripped the man's shirt, undershirt and wet, filthy stockings off.

He had been severely beaten. His flesh was abraded and

beginning to show bruises. There were several livid, dark red, curved marks as if he'd been kicked and one clear imprint of a boot heel on his right shoulder. She felt his ribs carefully and gave a prayer of thanks that they seemed to have been spared. His head injury was the worst, she thought. He would live, she thought, as long as he didn't catch a chill and sicken of the cold.

Carefully, she rubbed a rough-textured towel over the broad planes of his chest and stomach and down his arms. Her mouth dried. She had only ever seen one man's naked torso before. But this man was not like her husband.

Hart's chest had been narrow and bony, white and hairless, his stomach soft, his arms pale, smooth and elegant. This man's chest was broad and hard, but not bony. Thick bands of muscles lay relaxed now in his unconscious state, but firm and solid, nevertheless. A light dusting of soft, curly dark hair formed a wedge over the golden skin, arrowing into a faint line of hair trailing down his stomach and disappearing into his breeches. She tried not to notice it as she scrubbed him with the towel, forcing warmth and life back into his chilled skin.

He was surprisingly clean, she thought. His flesh did not have that sour odour she associated with Hart's flesh. This man smelt of nothing—perhaps a faint smell of soap, and of fresh sweat and…was it leather? Horses? Whatever it was, Ellie decided, it was no hardship to be so close to him.

Despite his muscles, he was thin. She could count each of his ribs. And his stomach above the waistband of his breeches was flat, even slightly concave. His skin carried numerous small scars, not recent injuries. A man who had spent his life fighting, perhaps. She glanced at his hands. They were not the soft white hands of a gentleman. They were strong and brown and battered, the knuckles skinned and swollen. He was probably a farm labourer or something like that. That would explain his muscles and his thinness. He was not a rich man, that was certain. His clothes, though once of good quality, were old and well worn. The shirt had been inexpertly patched a number of times. As had his breeches.

His breeches. They clung cold and sodden to his form. They would have to come off. She swallowed as she reached for his waistband, then hesitated, as her daughter arrived with a bundle of towels. "Good girl. Now run upstairs, my love, and fetch me a blanket from my bed and also the warm brick that's in it."

Amy trotted off and Ellie took a deep breath. She was not unacquainted with the male form, she told herself firmly, as she unbuttoned the stranger's drenched breeches. She had been married. But this man was not her husband. He was much bigger, for a start.

She grasped the breeches and tugged them over his hips, rolling him from side to side as she worked them downwards. The heavy wet fabric clung stubbornly to his chilled flesh. Finally she had them off him. Panting, she sat back on her heels. He was naked. She stared, unable to look away.

"Is Papa all right?" Amy came down the stairs, carefully lugging a bundled-up blanket.

Hastily, Ellie tucked a towel over the stranger's groin. "He's *not* your papa."

Amy gave her an odd look, then raced back upstairs. Ellie dragged the man as close as she could to the fire. When Amy returned with the brick, Ellie placed it in the hearth. She heated some soup, then strained it through a piece of muslin into the teapot.

"Soup in the *teapot?*" Amy giggled at something so silly.

Ellie smiled, relieved that her daughter found something

to laugh at. "This is going to take some time, so it's back to bed for you, young lady."

"Oh, but, Mama—"

"The man will still be here in the morning," Ellie said firmly. "We already have one sick person here—I don't want you to catch a chill as well. So, miss, off to bed at once." She kissed her daughter and pushed her gently towards the door. Reluctantly, Amy went. Ellie hid a smile. Her curious little puss would stay up all night if she could.

She cleaned his head wound thoroughly, then laid a pad of hot, steaming herbs on it, to draw out any remaining impurities. He groaned and tried to move his head.

"Hush." She smoothed a hand over his skin, keeping the hot poultice steady with her hand. "It stings a little, but it's doing you good." He subsided, but Ellie felt tension in his body as if part of him was awake. Defensive. She soothed him gently, murmuring, "Rest quietly. Nobody will harm you here." Slowly his big body relaxed.

His eyelids flickered, then his eyes slowly opened. Ellie bent over him earnestly, still supporting his head in her hand. "How do you feel?" she asked softly.

The stranger said nothing, just stared at her out of blue, blue eyes.

How did he feel? Like his head was about to split open. He blinked at her, trying to focus on her face. Pretty face, he thought vaguely. Soft, smooth skin. His eyes followed the fall of shining dark hair from her smooth creamy brow, down to a tumble of soft curls around her shoulders.

Who was she? And where the devil were they? With an effort he glanced away from her for a second, taking in the room. Small…a cottage? Had he been billeted in some nearby cottage? They did that sometimes with the wounded. Left them to the dubious care of some peasant woman while the fighting moved on… He frowned, trying to recall. Had they won the battle or lost it? Or was it still raging? He listened. No, there was no sound of guns.

His gaze returned to the woman. The cottage told him nothing. But the woman... He couldn't take his eyes off her. Soft, worried eyes. Soft worried mouth. Pretty mouth. Worried? Or frightened? He had no idea.

He tried to move and heard himself groan. His head was killing him. Like someone had taken an axe to it. How had that happened? Was he bleeding? He tried to feel his head. And found he could not move. Trapped, dammit! He could not move his hands and legs. Someone had tied him up. He'd been taken prisoner. He began to struggle.

"Hush," the woman said soothingly. She began to loosen the bindings around his arms as she spoke. "It's all right. I just wrapped you tight in my blanket because you were all wet and I feared you would take a chill."

He blinked up at her. His head throbbed unbearably. The rest of his body ached as well, but his head was the worst. Dizziness and confusion washed over him.

And then it hit him. She had spoken in English. Not Portuguese, or Spanish or French. English—not foreigners' English, either—proper English. His sort of English. So where were they? He tried to speak, to ask her. He felt his mouth move, but it was as if someone had cut out his tongue. Or severed it from his brain. He felt his lips moving, but no words came out. He fixed his gaze on her face and tried to muster the energy to ask her the question. Questions. They crowded his splitting head.

The woman sat down on the floor beside him again and smoothed his hair gently back from his forehead. It felt so good, he closed his eyes for a moment to savour it.

"I don't have any brandy," she said apologetically. "All I have is hot soup. Now, drink a little. It will give you strength and warmth."

Warmth? Did he need warmth? He realised that he was

shivering. She lifted his head up and though he knew she
was being as gentle as she could be, his brain thundered
and swirled and he felt consciousness slipping from him.
But then she tucked him against her shoulder and held him
there, still and secure and somehow…cared for. He
gripped her thigh and clung stubbornly to his senses and
gradually felt the black swirling subside.

He recoiled as something clunked against his teeth. "It
is only the teapot," she murmured in his ear. "It contains
warm broth. Now, drink. It will help."

He wanted to tell her that he was a man, that he would
drink it himself, out of a cup, not a teapot, like some helpless infant, but the words would not come. She tipped the
teapot up and he had to swallow or have it spill down him.
He swallowed. It was good broth. Warm. Tasty. It warmed
his insides. And she felt so soft and good, her breasts
against him, her arm around him, holding him upright
against her. Weakly, he closed his eyes and allowed himself to be fed like a baby.

He drank the broth slowly, in small mouthfuls. The
woman's breath was warm against his face. She seemed
to know how much to give him and when he needed to
wait between mouthfuls. He could smell her hair. He
wanted to turn his head and bury his face in it. He drank
the broth instead. The fire crackled in the grate. Outside
the wind whistled and howled, rattling at the doors and
windows. It was chilly inside the cottage, and the floor
underneath him was hard and cold, but oddly, he felt warm
and cosy and at peace.

He finished the broth and half-sat, half-lay against her,
allowing her to wipe his mouth, like a child. They sat for
a moment or two, in companionable silence, with the wind
swirling outside the cottage and the questions swirling inside his head.

Beneath the blanket he was stark naked, he suddenly

realised. He stared at her, another question on his unmoving lips. Who was she, to strip him of his clothes?

As if she knew what he wanted, she murmured gently in his ear, "You arrived at my cottage almost an hour ago. I don't know what happened to you before that. You were half-dressed and sopping wet. Frozen from the sleet and the rain. I don't know how long you'd been outside, or how you managed to find the cottage, but you collapsed at the door—"

"Is Papa awake now?" a little voice said, like the piping of a bird.

Papa? He opened his eyes and saw a vivid little face staring at him with bright, inquisitive eyes. A child. A little girl.

"Go back to bed this instant, Amy," said the woman sharply.

He winced and jerked his head and the blackness swirled again. When he reopened his eyes, he wasn't sure how much time had passed. He was no longer leaning against the woman's shoulder and the little face of the child was gone. And he was shivering. Hard.

The woman bent over him, her eyes dark with worry. "I'm sorry," she murmured. "I didn't mean to bump you like that. My daughter gave me a fright, that was all. Are you all right?" A faint frown crumpled the smoothness of her brow. "The bleeding has stopped and I have bandaged your head."

He barely took in her words. All he could think of was that his head hurt like the devil and she was worried. He lifted a hand and stroked down her cheek slowly with the back of his fingers. It was like touching fine, cool, soft satin.

She sighed. And then she pulled back. "I'm afraid you will freeze if I leave you down here on the stone floor. Even with the fire going all night—and I don't have the fucl for that—the stone floor will draw all the warmth from your body.''

He could only stare at her and try to control the shivering.

''The only place to keep you warm is in bed.'' She blushed and did not meet his eye. ''There…there is only one bed.''

He frowned, trying to absorb what she was telling him, but unable to understand why it would distress her. He still couldn't recall who she was—the blow had knocked all sense from his head—but the child had called him 'Papa.' He tried to think, but the effort only made the pain worse.

''It is upstairs. The bed. I cannot carry you up there.''

His confusion cleared. She was worried about his ability to get up the stairs. He nodded and gritted his teeth over the subsequent waves of swirling blackness. He could do that much for her. He would climb her stairs. He did not like to see her worried. He held out his hand to her and braced himself to stand. He wished he could remember her name.

Ellie took his arm and heaved until he was upright—shaky and looking appallingly pale, but standing and still conscious. She tucked the blanket tight under his armpits and knotted it over his shoulder, like a toga. She hoped it was warm enough. His feet and his long brawny calves were bare and probably cold, but it was better than having him trip. Or naked.

She wedged her shoulder under his armpit and steered him towards the stairs. The first step was in a narrow doorway with a very low lintel, for the cottage had not been designed for such tall men as he.

''Bend your head,'' she told him. Obediently, he bent, but lost his balance and lurched forward. Ellie clung to him, pulling him back against the doorway, to keep him upright. Fearful that he would straighten and hit his injury on the low beam, she cupped one hand protectively around his head and drew it down against her own forehead for safety. He leaned on her, half-unconscious, breathing heavily, one arm around her, one hand clutching the wooden stair-rail, his face against hers. White lines of pain bracketed his mouth.

There were only fourteen steep and narrow stairs, but it took a superhuman effort to get him up them. He seemed barely conscious, except for the grim frown of concentration on his face and the slow determined putting of one foot in front of the other. He gripped the stair-rail with fists of stone and hauled himself up, pausing at each step achieved, reeling with faintness. Ellie held him tightly, supporting him with all the strength she could muster. He was a big man; if he collapsed, she could not stop him falling. And if he fell, he might never regain consciousness.

There was little conversation between them, only the grim, silent battle. One painful step at a time. From time to time, she would murmur encouragement—"we are past the halfway mark," "only four steps left"—but she had no idea if he understood. The only sound he made was a grunt of exertion, or the raw harsh panting of a man in pain, at the end of his tether. He hung on to consciousness by willpower alone. She had never seen such stubbornness, or such courage.

At last they reached the top of the stairs. Straight ahead of them was the tiny room where Amy's bed was tucked—no more than a narrow cupboard it was, really, but cosy enough and warm for her daughter. On the right was Ellie's bedroom.

"Bend your head again." This time she was ready when he lurched forward and stumbled into her room. She managed to steer him to the small curtained-off alcove where her bed stood. He sprawled across it with a groan and lay there, unmoving. She collapsed beside him, gasping for breath, weak with relief. Her breath clouded visibly in the icy air. She had to get him covered, while he was still warm from the exertion of the climb.

She had no nightshirt for him to wear. He was too broad in the shoulders and chest for any of her clothing and she had long ago sold anything of Hart's that remained. The few thin blankets she had did not look warm enough to keep an unconscious man from catching a chill. The thickest, warmest coverings were on Amy's bed.

She wrapped him in a sheet and tugged the covers over him. She took all the clothes she possessed and spread them out over the bed—dresses, shawls, a faded pelisse, a threadbare cloak—any layer of cloth which would help keep out the cold. She fetched the hot brick and set it at his feet. Then she stood back. She could do no more. She was shivering herself, she realised. And her feet were frozen. She normally got into bed to keep warm.

But tonight there was a strange man in her bed.

Amy's bed was only a narrow bench, as long and as wide as a child. No room for Ellie there. Downstairs, the fire was dying. Ellie sat on the wooden stool, drew her knees against her chest and wrapped her shawl even tighter around herself in an illusion of warmth. She had used up all her extra clothes to make the bed warm for the stranger. She stared across at him. He lay there, warm, relaxed, comfortable while she hugged herself against the cold. He had collapsed. He was insensible. He wouldn't know she was there.

She crept to the edge of the bed on frozen toes and looked at him. He lay on his back, his breathing deep and regular. In the frail light of the candle the bandage glimmered white against his tanned skin and the thick, dark, tousled hair. There was a shadow of dark bristle on his lean, angular jaw. He seemed so big and dark and menacing in her bed. He took up much more of it than she did. And what if he woke?

She couldn't do this. She crept back to her stool. The chill settled. Drafts whispered up at her, insinuating themselves against her skin, nibbling at her like rats. Her chattering teeth echoed a crazed counterpoint to his deep, even breaths.

She had no choice. It was her bed, after all. It would do nobody any good if she froze to death out here. What mattered propriety when it came to her very health? She ran downstairs again and fetched her frying pan. She took a deep breath, wrapped the sheet more tightly around herself and stepped into the sleeping alcove, frying pan in hand. Feeling as if she were burning her bridges, she closed the curtains which kept the cold drafts out. In the tiny, enclosed space, she felt even more alone with the stranger than ever...

Outside, pellets of hail beat against her window.

Carefully, stealthily, Ellie tucked the pan under the edge of the mattress, comfortingly to hand, then crept under the bedclothes. He wasn't just in her bed, he took up most of the space. And almost all of the bedclothes. Without warning, she found herself lying hard against him, full length, his big body touching hers from shoulder to ankle. Threadbare sheets were all that lay between them. Ellie went rigid with anxiety. She poked him. "Hsst! Are you awake?" Her hand hovered, ready to snatch up the pan.

He didn't move; he just lay there, breathing slowly and evenly as he had for the last fifteen minutes. She tried to move away from him, but his weight had caused the mattress to sag. Her body could not help but roll downhill towards him. Against him. It was a most unsettling sensation. She wriggled a little, trying to reduce the contact between them. Her frozen toes slipped from their sheet and touched his long legs…and she sighed with pleasure. He was warm, like a furnace.

Fever? She put out a hand in the darkness and felt his forehead. It seemed cool enough. But that could be the effect of the cold night air. She slipped a hand under the bedclothes and felt his chest. The skin was warm and dry, the muscles beneath it firm. He didn't feel feverish at all. He felt…nice.

She snatched her hand away and tucked herself back in her own cocoon of bedclothes. She closed her eyes firmly, trying to shut out the awareness of the man in her bed. Of course, she would not get a wink of sleep—she was braced against the possibility that he was awake, shamming unconsciousness, but at least she would be warm.

She had never actually slept with a man before. Hart had not cared to stay with her longer than necessary. After coitus he had immediately left her, and once she had quickened with child he had never returned to her bed. So the very sensation of having a man sleep beside her was most…unsettling.

She could smell him, smell the very masculine smell of his body, the scent of the herbal poultice she had made for his injury. His big, hard body seemed to fill the bed. It lifted the bedclothes so that there was a gap between him and her smaller frame, a gap for cold drafts to creep into. She wriggled closer, to close the gap a little, still lying rigid, apart from him, straining against the dip in the mattress.

Slowly, insidiously, his body heat warmed her and gradually her defences relaxed. The combination of his reassuring stillness and the regularity of his deep breathing eased her anxious mind until finally she slept.

And as she slept, her body curled against his, closing the gap seamlessly. Her cold toes slipped from their cool linen cocoon and rested on the hard warmth of his long

bare calves. And her hand crept out and snuggled itself
between the layers that wrapped him, until it was resting
on that warm, firm, broad masculine chest…

Weak winter sun woke her, lighting the small, spare
room, setting a golden glow through the faded curtains that
covered her sleeping alcove. Feeling cosy, relaxed and
contented, Ellie yawned sleepily and stretched…and found
herself snuggled hard against a man's ribs, her feet curled
around his leg, her arm across his prone body.

She shot out of bed like a stone from a catapult and
stood there shivering in the sudden cold, staring at the
stranger, blinking as it all came back to her. She snatched
some of her clothes and hurried downstairs to get the fire
going again.

The man slept on through the day. Apart from him
sleeping like the dead, Ellie could find nothing wrong with
him. She checked his head wound several times. It was no
longer bleeding and showed no sign of infection. His
breathing was deep and even. He wasn't feverish and he
didn't toss and turn. He muttered occasionally, and each
time, Amy came running to tell.

Amy was fascinated by him. Ellie had managed to stop
her daughter referring to the stranger as Papa, but she
couldn't seem to keep her away from his bedside. The
weather was too bitter for her to play outside and the size
of the cottage meant that if Amy wasn't with Ellie downstairs, she was upstairs watching the man.

It was harmless, Ellie told herself. And rather sweet.
While Amy played with her dolls upstairs, she told him
long, rambling stories and sang him songs, a little off-key.
She told him of her special red wishing candle, that had
brought him home. The child seemed quite unperturbed
that he never responded to her prattle, that he just slept on.

It would be a different story when he woke. If he ever did wake...

She probably should have fetched Dr. Geddes. But she disliked him intensely. Dr. Geddes dressed fashionably, yet his tools of trade were filthy. He would bleed the man, give him a horrid-tasting potion of his own invention and charge a large fee. Ellie had little money and even less faith in him. Besides, Dr. Geddes was a friend of the squire...

She folded the shirt, now clean and dry, and set it with his buckskin breeches on the chest in her room. Both garments had once been of good quality, but had seen hard wear and tear. There was nothing incongruous about a poor labourer wearing such clothes, however. In the last year she had been amazed to learn of the thriving trade in used clothing—second-, third-, even fourth-hand clothing. Even things she'd thought at the time were total rags she knew now could have been sold for a few pennies, or a farthing.

She'd sold everything too cheaply, she realised in retrospect. Her jewellery, her furniture, treasured possessions, Amy's clothes, her beautiful dolls' house, with its exquisitely made furnishings, the tiny, perfect dolls with their lovely clothes and charming miniature knick-knacks—she could have sold them to far more purpose now. She had been ignorant, then, of the true value of things.

Still, they were neither starving nor frozen, and her daughter derived just as much pleasure from her current dolls' house, made from an old cheese box, with homemade dolls and furnishings made from odds and ends.

Ellie examined the stranger's other belongings. There were precious few—just the clothes he stood up in. His stockings were thick and coarse but walking on the bare ground in them had made holes, which she had yet to darn. She had found no other belongings to give a clue to his identity, only one item found wadded in his breeches pocket, a delicate cambric handkerchief, stiff with dried blood. An incongruous thing for such a man to be carrying. It did not go with the rest of him, his strong hands and his bruised knuckles.

She recalled the way those big, battered knuckles had slipped so gently across her cheek and sighed. Such a small, unthinking gesture…it had unravelled all her resolve to keep him at a distance.

He was a stranger, she told herself sternly. A brawler and possibly a thief as well. She hoped he had not stolen the handkerchief. It was bad enough having a strange man sleeping in her bed, let alone a thief.

Rat-tat-tat! Ellie jumped at the sound.

Amy's eyes were big with fright. "Someone at the door, Mama," she whispered.

"Miz Carmichael?" a thick voice shouted.

"It's all right, darling. It's only Ned. Just wait here." Ellie put aside her mending and went to answer the door. She hesitated, then turned to her daughter. "You mustn't tell Ned, or anyone else, about the man upstairs, all right? It's a secret, darling."

Her daughter gazed at her with solemn blue eyes and nodded. "'Coz of the squire," she said, and went back to playing with her dolls' house.

Ellie closed her eyes in silent anguish, wishing she could have protected her daughter from such grim realities. But there was nothing she could do about it. She opened the door.

"Brought your milk and the curds you wanted, Miz Carmichael," said the man at the door and added, "Thought you might like these 'uns, too." He handed her a brace of hares. "Make a nice stew, they will. No need to tell the squire, eh?" He winked and made to move off.

"Ned, you shouldn't have!" Ellie was horrified, and yet she couldn't help clutching the dead animals to her. It was a long time since she and Amy had eaten any meat, and yet Ned could hang or be transported for poaching. "I wouldn't for the world get you into troub—"

Ned chuckled. "Lord love ye, missus, don't ye worry about me—I bin takin' care o' Squire's extra livestock all me life, and me father and granfer before me."

"But—"

The grizzled man waved a hand dismissively. "A gift for little missie's birthday."

There was nothing Ellie could say. To argue would be to diminish Ned's gift, and she could never do that. "Then I thank you, Ned. Amy and I will very much enjoy them." She smiled and gestured back into the cottage. "Would you care to come in, then, and have a cup of soup? I have some hot on the fire."

"Oh, no, no, thank ye, missus. I'd not presume." He shuffled his feet awkwardly, touched his forehead and stomped off into the forest before she could say another word.

Ellie watched him go, touched by the man's awkwardness, his pride and the risky, generous gift. The hares hung heavy in her arms. They would be a feast. And the sooner they were in the pot, the safer it would be for all concerned. She had planned to make curd cakes for Amy's birthday surprise. Now they would both enjoy a good, thick meaty stew as well—it would almost be a proper birthday celebration. And if the man upstairs ever woke up, she would have something substantial to feed him, too.

She smiled to herself as she struggled to strip the skin from the first hare. She'd thought him a thief because of the handkerchief. Who was she to point her finger, Ellie Carmichael, proud possessor of two fat illegal hares...?

He had slept like the dead now, for a night and a day. Ellie stared at his shape and wished she could do something. She wanted him awake. She wanted him up and out of her bed. She wanted him gone. It was unsettling, having him there, asleep in her bedclothes. It was not so difficult to get used to it during the day, to assume he was harmless, to allow her daughter to sit beside him, treating an unconscious man—a complete stranger—as if he was one of her playthings. During the day he didn't seem so intimidating. Now...

She hugged her wrapper tighter around her, trying to summon the courage to climb into the bed beside him once more. In the shadows of the night he seemed to grow bigger, darker, more menacing, the virile-looking body sprawled relaxed in her bed more threatening.

But he hadn't stirred for a night and a day. Another night of sharing would do no harm, surely. Besides, she didn't have any choice... No, she'd made a choice, her conscience corrected her. She could have called for help. He would have been taken "on the parish." But he wouldn't have received proper care—not with the poor clothing he wore. An injured gentleman, yes, the doctor or even the squire would see to his care. But there were too many poor and injured men in England since the war against Napoleon had been won. They'd returned as brief heroes. Now, months later, as they searched for work or begged in the streets, they'd come to be regarded as a blight on the land. It wouldn't matter if one more died.

There were too many indigent widows and little girls, too.

She could not abandon him. Somehow, with no exchange of words between them, she had made herself responsible for this man—stranger or not, thief or not. He was helpless and in need. Ellie knew what it felt like to be helpless and in need. And she would help him.

Without further debate, Ellie wrapped herself in her separate sheet—she hadn't lost all sense of propriety—and slipped into the bed beside him. She sighed with pleasure. He was better than a hot brick on a cold winter's night.

This time there was little sense of strangeness. She was used to his masculine smell, she even found it appealing. The sag of the bed felt right, and she didn't struggle too hard against it. After all, if there was too much of a gap between them, icy drafts would get in. But recalling the immodest position she had woken in, she determinedly turned her back to him. It was not so intimate, having one's back against a stranger, she thought sleepily, as she snuggled her backside against his hip.

And once again, in the warmth of his body heat and the calm steady rhythm of his deep, even breathing, Ellie forgot her fears of the stranger and went to sleep. And her toes reached out and curled contentedly against his calves…

Ellie came awake slowly to a delicious sense of…pleasure. She had been having the most delectable dream. She kept her eyes closed, prolonging the delightful sensation of being…loved. Hart was caressing her in the way she had always dreamed of… His big, warm hands smoothing, kneading, loving her skin. She felt beautiful, loved, desired in a way she had never before felt. Warm, sleepy, smiling, she stretched and moved sensually, squirming pleasurably in the grip of the marvellous dream. Her skin felt alive as his hands moved over, across, around, between…sending delicious shivers through her body, shivers which had nothing to do with the cold and everything to do with…desire.

Hands slipped up her thighs and caressed her hips and she moved restlessly, her legs trembling. She felt a big, warm hand cup one breast, felt her flesh move silkily against the rougher skin of his hand. Her breasts seemed to swell under the caress and when she felt warm breath against her naked skin she clenched her eyes shut and felt her body arch with pleasure. A hot mouth closed over her breast and his tongue rubbed gently back and forth across her turgid nipple. She shuddered uncontrollably, waves of pleasure and excitement juddering through her with a force she had never experienced. He sucked, hard, and she almost came off the bed in shock as hot spears of ecstasy drove though her body. She could barely think, only feel. Her hands gripped his shoulders and gloried in the feel of his power and the smooth, naked skin under her palms.

Still creating those glorious sensations at her breast, she felt a large, calloused hand smooth down over her belly, caressing, smoothing, exciting... Her legs fell apart, trembling with need.

His mouth came down over hers, softly, tenderly, possessively, nipping gently at her lips. ''Open,'' he murmured huskily, and their mouths merged as his tongue tasted her, learned her, possessed her, and she tasted him and learned him in response.

And froze...

It wasn't Hart! Ellie jerked her head back and opened her eyes. *It wasn't Hart!*

He smiled at her early morning bewilderment. ''Morning, love.''

It was the stranger! It hadn't been a harmless, delicious dream of her husband. She had been lying with a stranger! Allowing him intimacies even her husband had never taken. Her breast still throbbed with want. And his hand was still creating the most incredible sensations between her—

With a small scream, Ellie shoved him away from her and shot out of bed. There was a thud as his head connected with a bedpost and he swore. She stood shivering in the middle of the room, staring at him, outraged, dragging her nightgown down over her flushed and trembling nakedness.

"Who are you? How—how dare you! Get out—get out of my bed!"

"You didn't need to shove so hard," he grumbled. "My head was bad enough when I woke. Now it feels like—"

"I don't care what your head feels like! I said, get out!" Ellie almost screeched it.

He blinked at her in puzzlement, rubbing his head absently. "What's the matter, love?"

"As if you don't know, you—you ravisher! Get out of my bed!"

He frowned in vague confusion, then shrugged, climbed out and walked towards her. Stark naked. Acres of naked masculine skin, bared to her shocked gaze. With not a shred of shame.

"Stop! Get back!" She felt her whole body blushing in response.

He gave her a very male look, as if to say, make up your mind, but he stopped his movement towards her and sat back down on the bed, rubbing his head. Still naked. Making no attempt to cover himself. Even though he was still shamefully, powerfully aroused.

As, even more shamefully, was she. Her knees trembled, so she sat on the stool, half-turned away from the beautiful, shocking sight of him. "Cover yourself!" Ellie snapped.

She heard a slither of fabric, and turning back to face him, she felt herself blush again. He had picked up one of her stockings and draped it carefully across himself. Across the part which had most shocked her. The rest of him sat there in shameless naked glory. His body was glorious, too. She tried not to notice how much.

His blue, blue eyes were twinkling roguishly. "Is that better, love?"

"Don't call me that!" she snapped. "And cover your-self properly. My daughter could come in at any moment."

At her words he glanced towards the door and drew one of the blankets around his shoulders, covering his chest and torso and...the rest. It didn't seem to make him any less naked. His long legs, bare, brawny and boldly mas-culine, were braced apart on the edge of the bed. She tried not to think about what the blanket concealed.

"You'll have to leave," Ellie said firmly. "I shall go downstairs and make you some breakfast while you dress yourself. And then you will have to leave."

He frowned. "Where do you want me to go?"

Ellie stared in astonishment. "Where do *I* want you to go? Go wherever you want. It's nothing to do with me."

"Are you so angry with me, then?" His voice was soft, deep and filled with concern.

Ellie recalled the shocking things he had done to her. It seemed even worse that she had enjoyed them so much. "Of course I am angry. What did you expect when you attacked me in that appalling way?"

His brow furrowed. "Attacked?" His brow cleared after a minute and he looked incredulous. "You mean just now, in bed? But you were enjoying it as much as I was."

Ellie went scarlet. "Oh, you are shameless! I want you out of my house this instant!" As she spoke, his stomach rumbled. "As soon as you have eaten," she amended gruffly, feeling foolish. It was ridiculous to care whether he was hungry or not. She had taken in a stranger and cared for him for several days and how had he repaid her? With near-ravishment, that's how! The scoundrel! She wanted him out!

There was a short silence. "Did we have a quarrel, love?"

"Quarrel!" Ellie said wrathfully. "I'll give you quarrel! And I *told* you not to call me that!"

"Call you what?" He frowned. "Love?"

Ellie flushed and nodded curtly.

He rubbed his head and then said in an embarrassed voice. "I'm sorry if it makes you cross, but the truth is, I have the devil of a head on me and cannot seem to recall your name."

"It is Ellie. Mrs. Ellie Carmichael," she added for emphasis. Better he think she was married, not a widow. He might leave faster if he thought she expected a husband home any minute. It was Lady Carmichael, in truth, but it seemed ludicrous for a pauper to be titled.

"Ellie," he said softly. "I like it…Carmichael, eh?" He frowned, as if suddenly confused. "Then—"

"What you think of my name is immaterial to me." Ellie tossed him his clothes. "Have the goodness to dress yourself at once and leave this house!"

"Why do you want me to leave?"

Ellie narrowed her eyes at him. "Because this is my home and I say who can stay here! And you, sir, have outstayed your welcome!"

He looked at her seriously. "And have I no rights?"

She gasped at his audacity. "*Rights!* And what rights, pray, do you think you may have here, sirrah!" Did he think a few stolen caresses gave him rights? She was no doxy!

He hesitated, looking oddly uncertain. "Is this property not in my name?"

"*Your* name? Why should it be?" Ellie glared at him, but could not help feeling suddenly frightened at this talk of rights. What if the squire had sold the cottage without telling her? He had threatened to do so, often enough. Nor would she be surprised to learn he would imply that Ellie was part of the sale. The squire was a vindictive man.

"Women do not commonly own property. It is generally held in the husband's name."

The squire *had* sold the cottage. And this man had bought it for his wife and himself. And had been set upon by thieves while on his way to inspect his new property. Fear wrapped itself around Ellie's throat but she drew herself up proudly. "I am not for sale. My daughter and I will leave this place as soon as possible. You will give us a week or two, I presume, out of simple decency."

"Dammit, woman, you don't have to go anywhere!" he roared. "What sort of man do you think I am?"

"I have not the slightest idea," said Ellie frostily. "Nor do I care. But I am *not* for sale!"

"Who the devil suggested you were, for heaven's sake!" he said, exasperated, and clutched his head again. "Blast this head of mine. What the deuce is the matter with it?"

"Someone hit you," said Ellie. He gave her a look, which she ignored. "I do not know what the squire told you, but I am a virtuous woman and I will not be bought! Not by the squire, not by you or any other man, no matter what straits of desperation you try to bring me to." Her voice quavered a little and broke.

There was a long silence in the upstairs room. The wind whistled around the eaves, rattling the window panes. Ellie sat on the hard stool, her shawl wrapped around her defensively, staring defiantly across the room at him. She swallowed. She had no idea of what she might be forced to do to keep Amy safe, but she had not reached that point. Yet.

He stared back at her, an unreadable expression on his face. Finally he spoke. "I have no idea what this conversation is about... I think whoever hit me over the head—was it you?"

She shook her head.

"That's a relief, then," he said wryly. "But whoever it was made a good job of it. My brain is quite scrambled. I have no idea what you are talking of. I cannot think straight at all. And my head feels as if it's about to split open.'' He stood and made to take a step, then swayed and went suddenly pale.

Without thinking she jumped up and hurried to help. ''Put your head down between your knees.'' She pushed him gently into position. ''It will help the dizziness.''

After a few moments he recovered enough to lie back on the bed. He was still as pale as paper. Ellie tucked blankets around him, all thought of throwing him out forgotten. Whether he owned the cottage or not, whether he thought her a doxy or not, she could not push a sick man out into such weather. She could, however, send for his relatives.

''Who are you?'' she said when he was settled against the pillows. ''What's your name?''

He looked blank for a moment, then his eyes narrowed. ''You tell me,'' he said slowly. ''I told you my brain was all scrambled.''

''Don't be silly. Who are you?'' She leaned forward intently, awaiting his reply.

He stared at her, his blue eyes dark and intense against his stark white pallor. There was a long silence as his gaze bored into her. And then he answered.

''I am your husband.''

Chapter Two

Ellie stirred the porridge angrily. The cheek of him! *I am your husband.* Why would he say such an outlandish thing? To her, of all people! He'd sounded quite sure of it, too, even a little surprised, as if wondering why she had asked him. And then he'd lain back on the bed as if too exhausted to speak any further.

She spooned the thick oatmeal porridge into two bowls and set one before Amy.

"Sugar?" the little girl asked hopefully.

"Sorry, darling. There's no sugar left." Ellie poured milk on to her daughter's bowl, and watched her daughter make islands and oceans out of porridge and milk. Gone were the days of silver dishes on the sideboard, containing every imaginable delicacy.

She picked up the other bowl. "I'll take this to the man upstairs." She took a deep breath and mounted the stairs. *I am your husband.* Indeed!

He was awake when she entered the room, his blue eyes sombre.

"How is your head?" She kept her tone brusque, impersonal.

He grimaced.

"I have brought you some porridge. Can you sit up?"
She made no move to help him. She would have no truck
with his nonsense. He had disturbed her quite enough as
it was.

He sat up slowly. She could see from the sharp white
lines around his mouth that he was in pain. She said nothing, set the bowl down with something of a snap and
helped him to arrange the pillows behind him. She tried
to remain indifferent, but it was not possible to avoid
touching him. Each time her hand came in contact with
his skin, or brushed across his warm, naked torso, she felt
it, clear through to the soles of her feet. And in less acceptable regions.

He knew it, too, the devil! He'd looked up at her in such
an intimate, knowing way! How dare he embarrass her any
further! She ripped a blanket off the bed and flung it
around his naked back and chest, then she thrust the bowl
and spoon at him. "Eat."

"Yes, Mrs. Carmichael," he said in a tone of crushed
obedience.

She glanced at him in suspicion. His blue, blue eyes
caressed her boldly. She glared at him, then began to tidy
the room briskly.

"You're gorgeous when you're angry," he said in a
deep, low voice and as her breath hissed in fury, he applied
himself in a leisurely manner to the porridge.

By the time she went up again to fetch his empty bowl,
her wrath had dissipated. She was now more puzzled than
angry. His behaviour made little sense. Why lie to her,
when she was the one person in the world who would
know it was a lie? And though he was teasing her now,
he hadn't been teasing when he'd claimed to be her husband. It was all very odd. She decided to ask him, straight
out.

"What is your name—no nonsense now. I want the

truth, if you please." She took his bowl and stood looking down at him.

There was a long pause. Finally he said, "I don't know."

He said it with no inflexion at all. Ellie stared at him, and suddenly she knew he was telling the truth. "You mean you cannot remember who you are?"

"No."

Ellie was stunned. She sat down beside him on the edge of the bed, quite forgetting her resolve to keep her distance. She had heard tales of people who had lost their memories, but she had never thought to meet one. "You cannot remember *anything* about yourself?"

"No. All morning I have tried and tried, but I cannot think straight. I have no idea what my name is, nor anything about my family, or what I do for a living, or even how I came to be here." He smiled, a little sheepishly. "So you will have to tell me everything."

"But I don't know myself!"

He patted her knee and she skittered away. "No, not how I came to be hurt, but the rest. My name and all the rest."

"If you cannot remember anything, then why did you say you were my husband?"

He frowned at the accusing note in her voice and said teasingly, "Am I not your husband, then?"

"You *know* you are not."

He blinked at her in amazement. "You cannot mean it! But I thought——"

Ellie shook her head.

He considered her words for a moment and his frown grew. "But if Amy is my daughter..."

"She is no such thing!" Ellie gasped, and jumped up, horrified. "I just said you were not my husband. How dare you suggest——?"

"Then why does she call me Papa?"

"You mean—? Oh…" She sank back down on the bed. "That explains a good deal." She turned to him and said slowly, "Amy's papa, my husband, Hartley Carmichael, died a year ago. She was just a little girl and she doesn't quite remember him…" It was too difficult to explain, she realised. She finished lamely, "You have blue eyes, like her papa. And her."

"That doesn't explain how you and I came to be sharing a b—"

She knew what he was thinking and interrupted, "I never saw you before in my life until two nights ago when you arrived at my door, bleeding and frozen half-solid."

"What!"

She stood up and added in a wooden little voice, "There is only one bed big enough for an adult. It was a bitter night, one of the coldest I can recall. You were hurt and in danger of freezing to death. I could not leave you on the floor." She was unable to meet his eyes. "And as I did not want to freeze to death myself, I shared my bed with a stranger."

She flushed, recalling how the stranger had found her in his bed this morning. She had responded wantonly to his caresses. She did not blame him for thinking her a fallen woman. Her voice shook. She did not expect him to believe her, but forced herself to add, "You are the only man I have ever shared a bed with. Except for my husband, of course."

She could stay in the room no longer, with those eyes boring into her. She couldn't meet their icy blaze, couldn't bear to see the look in them. She snatched up the bowl and ran downstairs.

He watched her go, his head splitting, his mind a whirl. They were strangers? Then why would he feel this ease in her company, this sense of belonging? She didn't feel like

a stranger. He'd never felt so right, so much at home as
he had in bed that morning, bringing Ellie to sweet, sensual
wakefulness…as if she were a part of him.

Unanswered questions gnawed at his vitals like rats.
What the devil was his name? It seemed to be floating
somewhere just beyond him…hovering there, on the tip of
his tongue…but each time he tried for it, it drifted out of
reach. He tried some names, hoping one would leap out at
him, bringing the rest of his identity tumbling with him.
Abraham…Allan…Adam… Was he an Adam, perhaps?
He tasted it on his tongue. Familiar, yet also strange.

Bruce…David…Daniel… Was he trapped in the lion's
den? He smiled and wriggled lower in the bed. His Ellie
could be a little lioness when roused… She'd certainly
roused him. Edward…Gilbert…James… He pulled the
bedclothes around him. He could smell Ellie on them. He
inhaled deeply and felt his body respond instantly.
Walter…William… He dozed.

"Hello, Papa." A little voice pulled him back from the
brink of sleep. He opened his eyes. A pair of big blue eyes
regarded him seriously across an old cheese box.

"Hello, Amy." He sat up, drawing the sheets up with
him, across his chest.

"Does your head hurt a lot?"

The headache had dwindled to a dull thump. "No, it
feels a lot better, thank you."

"Mama says you don't know who you are."

He grimaced ruefully. "That's right. I can't even remember my name. I don't suppose you know my name,
do you?" He tensed when the child unexpectedly nodded
her head. Had Ellie not told him the truth after all? He'd
had a feeling she was hiding something.

The little girl carefully put the cheese box on to the bed
and then climbed up after it. She sat cross-legged and regarded him solemnly. "I think your name might be…"

Her big blue eyes skimmed his chin, the top of his chest and along his arms.

He had not the faintest notion of what she found so interesting.

"Your name is…" She leaned forward and hesitantly touched his jaw and giggled. She sat back, her eyes full of mischief and said, "I think your name is…Mr. Bruin."

"Mr. Bruin?" He frowned. Bruin meant bear. "Mr. Bear?"

"Yes, because you are big and even your face is hairy." The little girl chortled in glee. "Just like a bear!"

He had to laugh at her neat trick. So, he looked like a big hairy bear to a little girl, did he? He ran a hand over his jaw. Maybe she was right. He did need a shave.

"If you think I'm a bear, then why did you call me Papa?"

She glanced guilty at the doorway. "Mama says I'm not s'posed to call you that. You won't tell, will you?"

"No, I won't tell." Again he wondered what Mama was trying to hide.

She beamed at him.

"But if your mama does not like you to call me Papa, maybe you could call me Mr. Bruin instead." It was better than having no name at all.

Her face screwed in thought, then she nodded. "Yes, that will be a good game. And you can call me Princess Amy. Do you like dolls, Mr. Bruin? I hope you don't eat them."

He resigned himself to being a little girl's playmate for the afternoon. It was better than cudgelling his aching brain for information which would not come, he supposed.

"Oh, no," he said firmly. "We bears never eat dolls."

She looked at him suspiciously. "Bears might eat *my* dolls—my dolls are very special dolls. The type which are delicious to bears."

He heaved a huge regretful sigh. "Oh, very well, you have caught me there. I solemnly promise never to eat Princess Amy's Very Special Dolls."

"Good." She snuggled closer to him, pulled the box on to his knees and began to introduce her dolls to him.

The cheese box was a home-made dolls' house, he realised. Everything in it was made by clumsy small fingers or her mother's neat touch. And some of her dolls were made of acorns, with cradles and all sorts of miniature items made of acorn caps and walnut shells.

He smiled to himself. Delicious to bears, indeed. She was a delightful child. Her eyes were such a bright blue...almost the exact same colour as his. It was a most discomforting thought. He hoped Ellie had not lied about Amy's parentage. If he had created this charming child with Ellie...and left her to grow up without his name, in what looked to him a lot like poverty...then he didn't much like himself.

All thoughts led to the same question—who the devil was he? And was he already married?

"He was so badly hurt he now cannot remember a thing," explained Ellie to the one person who could be trusted not to tell the squire of her unexpected houseguest.

"It's an absolute disgrace!" The vicar paced the floor in agitation. "That gang of robbers is getting bolder and bolder and will the squire do a thing about it? No—he is much too indolent to bother! He ought to close down the Angel. I'm sure that den of iniquity is their headquarters. Can your fellow identify any of the miscreants?"

"No, he doesn't even know his own name, let alone anything that happened."

The elderly vicar pursed his lips thoughtfully. "And there was nothing on his person to indicate his identity?"

Ellie shook her head. "Nothing. Whoever robbed him

had stripped him of even his coat and shoes. I thought you may have heard something.''

"No. No one has made enquiries. Er...he is not causing you any, er, difficulty?''

"No, he has been a gentleman the entire time...'' Except for where his hands had roamed this morning, she thought, fighting the blush. The vicar had no idea of the sleeping arrangements at her cottage, otherwise he wouldn't have countenanced it for a moment.

The vicar frowned suddenly and glanced around. "Where is little Miss Amy?''

"I left her at the cottage. It is very bitter out and she had a bad cold which she has only just recovered from. It...it was only for a few minutes...'' Her voice trailed off.

"You left her alone with this stranger?'' He sounded incredulous.

Ellie felt suddenly foolish. Criminally foolish. "I didn't think...I don't *feel* as though he would hurt Amy—or me.'' She bit her lip in distress. "But...you're right. He could be a murderer, for all I know.''

The vicar said doubtfully. "I'm sure there's nothing to worry about. If you'd had doubts about this fellow, you'd have brought Amy with you. You have good instincts.''

With every comforting word, Ellie's doubts grew. As did her anxiety.

He nodded. "You are having second thoughts. Leave this matter in my hands. If a man has gone missing, we shall eventually hear something. Go home, my dear. See to your child.''

"Oh, yes. Yes, I will. Thank you for the loan of these items, Vicar.'' She lifted the small packet in her hand. "I shall return them shortly.''

Ellie ran most of the way home, her fears growing by the minute. How could she have let her...her feelings, outweigh her common sense! Leaving Amy behind, just because it was cold and damp outside! Taking a man's word for it that he recalled nothing. Assuming that simply because she liked him—liked him far too much, in fact— that he was therefore trustworthy. For all she knew, he could be the veriest villain!

It was all very well for the vicar to talk of her instincts being sound, but he didn't know of the mess she had made of her life. She trusted her instincts and her feelings as far as she could throw them. Which was not at all! Dear Lord, she had left her daughter with a complete stranger! If anything happened to Amy, she couldn't bear it.

She raced to the cottage and flung open the door. The downstairs room was empty. No sign of her daughter. She heard voices above her. She could not make out what was being said. Then she heard a small anxious squeak.

"No, no! Stop that!" Amy shrieked.

Ellie raced up the steep stairs, taking them two at a time, almost tripping on her skirts as she did. She hurtled into the room and stood there, gasping for breath, staring at the sight which greeted her.

The murderer she had left her daughter with was sitting in her bed where she had left him. He had found his shirt, thank goodness, and wore it now, covering that broad, disturbing chest. He was also wearing one of her shawls and her best bonnet, albeit crookedly, its ribbons tied in a clumsy bow across his stubble-roughened jaw. His arms were full of dolls. Across his lap, over the bedclothes, a tea towel had been laid and on it, a diminutive tea party was set out, with pretend food and drink in acorn-cap bowls.

He met Ellie's gaze rather sheepishly, his blue eyes twinkling in wry humour.

"Oh, Mama, Mr. Bruin keeps moving and spilling my dolls' picnic. Look!" Amy crossly displayed several tipped-over bowls. "Bad Mr. Bruin!" the little girl said severely.

"I'm sorry, Princess Amy, but I did warn you that we bears are great clumsy beasts and not fit company for a picnic with ladies," responded Ellie's murderer apologetically.

Ellie burst into tears.

There was a shocked silence. "Mama, what is it? What's the matter?" Amy scrambled off the bed and threw her arms around her mother's legs tightly.

Ellie sat down on the stool, pulled Amy into her arms and hugged her tightly, tucking the child into her body, rocking her. The sobs kept coming. Hard, painful, from deep in her chest. She couldn't stop them.

She heard movement from the direction of the bed, but the weeping had taken hold of her. She could do nothing but hold her daughter and let the tears come. She knew it was weak, knew it was spineless of her, that she was supposed to be strong and look after Amy...Amy, who was now sobbing in fright because she had never seen her mother cry before...

But Ellie could not control the harsh sobs. They came from somewhere deep inside her, wrenching painfully out of her body, almost choking her. She had never cried like this before. It was terrifying.

In a vague way, she sensed him standing beside her. She thought she felt a few awkward pats on her shoulder and back, but she couldn't be sure. Suddenly she felt powerful arms scoop her up. He lifted both her and Amy and carried them back to the bed and sat down, holding them on his lap, in the circle of his arms, hard against his big, warm chest. Ellie tried to resist, but feebly and after a moment or two, something inside her, some barrier, just...dissolved and she relaxed against him, letting herself be held in a way she had never in her life been held. The sobs came even harder then.

He asked no questions, just held them, nuzzling Ellie's hair with his jaw and cheek, making soothing sounds. Amy stopped crying almost immediately. After a moment, Ellie heard him whisper to her daughter to go and wash her face, that Mama would be all right soon, that she was just tired. She felt her daughter slip out of her grasp. Amy leaned against his knee and waited anxiously, patting and stroking her mother's heaving shoulders.

Ellie forced herself to smile in a way she hoped would reassure the little girl. She tried desperately to get control of her emotions, but she couldn't yet speak—she was breathing in jerky gasps, gulping and snuffling in an ugly fashion. Sobs welled up intermittently; dry, painful shuddery eruptions. She heard Amy tiptoe downstairs.

Finally, the last of the frightful, frightening outburst passed. Ellie was exhausted, with as much energy as a wet rag—and feeling about as attractive.

"I...I'm sorry about that," she said gruffly. "I...I don't know what came over me."

"Hush, now. It doesn't matter." His arms were warm and steady around her. He smoothed a damp curl back from her face.

"I'm not usually such a dreadful watering pot, really I'm not."

"I know." His voice was deep and soft in her ear.

"It was just...I suddenly got the idea—I mean, I thought..." How could she tell him what she'd thought? What could she say? *I thought you were going to hurt my daughter and when I found you hadn't, I burst into tears all over you instead.* How ridiculous was that? He would think she belonged in Bedlam. She wasn't sure herself that she didn't belong there!

"I've never cried like that in my life. Not even when my husband died."

"Then you were well overdue for it. Don't refine too much on it," he said in a matter-of-fact voice. "No doubt you were at the end of your tether and things had built up inside you until there was no bearing it. When that happens, you have to let it out somehow."

She made a small gesture of repudiation of his words and he went on, "Women cry, men usually get into a fight, or—" she felt the smile in his voice "—take to the bedchamber. But I have seen men weep and weep, just like you did when things have got too much to bear. There is no shame in it."

There was a small silence. "Have you wept like that?"

She felt him tense. He said nothing for a long moment and then shook his head. "No, blast it! I still cannot recall. I thought I had it for a minute." He sighed and she felt his warm breath in her hair. "It is so frustrating, as if it's all there, waiting. Like something half glimpsed in the corner of my eye and when I turn my head to look at it directly, it is gone…"

She laid her hand on his. "It will come soon, I am certain of it."

"That's as may be. Now, do you want to talk about it?"

"About what?"

He turned her in his arms so that she could see his face properly. "Don't prevaricate. What was it that so upset you? Tell me. I might not be able to remember anything, but I'll help you in any way I can. Did someone try to hurt you?" His voice was deep and sincere.

Ellie couldn't bring herself to confess the ugly suspicion that had crept over her at the vicarage. She looked at him, trying to think of how she could explain…

Her face must have shown more than she realised.

"It's me, isn't it?" he said softly. "I'm your problem."

She said nothing for a moment, but he knew it anyway. His hands dropped away and suddenly she felt cold. He gently lifted her off his lap and placed her on the bed beside him.

"No, no," she said hurriedly. "It's—there are so many problems and difficulties, but I don't want to burden—"

"Just tell me this—I...I need to know it." His voice was a little hoarse. "Do you *truly* not know me, or do you know me and...and fear me for some reason?"

There was a short silence, then he reached down beneath the mattress and drew out the frying pan she had placed there on the first night.

Ellie reddened. She didn't know where to look.

"I found it this morning, as I was getting dressed. This was for me, wasn't it? In case I attacked you in the night."

Ellie nodded, embarrassed.

"And when you came rushing in here just now, having run a mile or more...I was the reason. You were worried about Amy, weren't you? About leaving her alone with me. And when you found her safe and...untouched, you burst into tears of relief..."

Ellie was miserably silent.

His fist curled into a knot of tension at her unspoken confirmation of his theory. "I cannot blame you for it. We neither of us have any notion of the sort of man I am. I do not *believe* I would harm a child...but until I get my memory back, I cannot *know* what sort of man I am...or have been." Frustration and distress were evident in his voice.

Ellie tried to think of what to say. He was a good man, she felt it in her bones. But he was right. They didn't know anything about him.

"I suppose I made the situation worse, grabbing you like that," he said bitterly. "I didn't know what to do. I just needed to hold you... I see now it was presumptuous of me.''

Ellie wanted to cry out, No! She wanted to tell him that he had done exactly the right thing, that she had derived such comfort from being held that it was too embarrassing to admit. She couldn't explain how in his embrace she had discovered the release of being weak for once...even for a short while. All her life she had had to be the strong one.

She wanted to tell him how wonderful it had been to be held by a strong man as if she were precious, as if he cherished her...despite her weakness.

But she could not expose such vulnerability to him. Men exploited a woman's vulnerability. And God help her, she was coming to care for him—much more than was reasonable—a nameless stranger she had known two nights and two days, and most of that with him insensible. She could not let him know that about her.

''And for this morning...in bed...I also apologise.''

Ellie's face flamed. She scrambled to her feet. ''There's nothing to apologise for,'' she said huskily. ''We were both half-asleep and you cannot be held responsible for...for what you did. You did not know what you were—''

''Yes, I did,'' he interrupted her in a deep voice. ''I knew exactly what I was doing. And I give you fair warning, Mrs. Carmichael. While my memory is impaired, your virtue is safe with me. But the moment I discover who I am, and whether I am married or not...''

She waited for him to finish his sentence and, when he did not, looked up at him anxiously.

He smiled at her in a possessive, wolfish manner and said with soft deliberation. ''If I am not married, then be warned, Mrs. Ellie Carmichael...I plan to have you naked in bed with me again, doing all of those things we were doing and more." It was a vow.

Ellie's face was scarlet, but she managed to say with some composure. "I think I may have some say in that matter, sir."

"You liked it well enough this morning..."

"You have no idea what I thought!" she snapped. "And we will discuss this foolishness no further! Now, I have brought some slippers for you. The vicar's feet are too small to borrow his boots, but the slippers will do at a pinch. And there is a razor, too."

He ran a rueful hand over his jaw. "So you don't like my bristles, eh? Your daughter didn't, but I thought you may have rather enjoyed the...stimulation." He grinned at her, a thoroughly wicked twinkle in those impossibly blue eyes.

"Enough!" said Ellie briskly, thinking her whole body must have turned scarlet by now. "I shall fetch hot water for you to shave and then we shall dine. There is hare stew in the pot."

"Yes, the smell has been tantalising me for some time." His eyes were warm upon her. "There are so many tantalising things in this cottage, a hungry fellow like me has no chance..." His eyes told her exactly what he meant by "hungry." And it wasn't about stew.

She fled.

"Mama sent me up with her looking glass," announced Amy from the doorway. "She says you will need it to shave."

He grinned. A few minutes earlier, Mama had poked her head in the room, dumped a pot of hot water just inside the doorway and disappeared again, muttering things about having work to do. He probably shouldn't have taken off his shirt, but he was damned if he was going to shave in the only shirt he apparently owned.

Amy handed him the small, square looking glass and he took it gingerly, suddenly unnerved by the prospect of his own reflection. Would he recognise himself?

He lifted the glass slowly and grimaced. No wonder she didn't trust him an inch! He was a bloody pirate! All that was missing was the gold earring and the eyepatch! His skin was dark—tanned by weather, he decided, comparing it with other parts of his body. So he lived a lot out of doors. Gentlemen didn't do that. Pirates, however...

His eyes were blue, but then he knew that earlier from the little girl watching him so solemnly. No wonder she'd thought him a bear, though—he didn't just need a shave, he needed a haircut as well. Under the bandage, his hair was thick and dark and unruly. His brows were thick and black and frowning like the devil. His nose was long and—he turned his head slightly—not quite straight. He'd broken his nose at some time. And his skin carried several small scars as well as the remains of recent bruises. All in all, not a pretty sight. He'd found old scars on his body, too. He'd been in more than his share of fights.

A fine fellow for a woman to take in and care for—a brawling, hairy, black-bearded pirate! He wouldn't have blamed anyone for leaving such a villainous creature out in the cold, let alone an unprotected woman with a small daughter. He reached for the hot water and soap. At least he could take care of the beard.

"Will you hold the looking glass for me, please, Princess?"

Eagerly Amy took it and watched, fascinated, as he soaped up his skin and then carefully shaved the soap and beard off.

"Better?" he asked when he'd finished.

She reached out and passed a small soft palm over the

newly shaven skin. "Nice," she said consideringly, "but I liked Mr. Bruin's prickles, too."

He chuckled. "Prickly bears don't belong in cottages. Now, I'm going to finish washing, so you pop downstairs, Princess, and help your mother. I'll be down shortly."

Ellie's throat went dry. She tried to swallow as he bent his head under the low beam and came down the last few steps. He suddenly looked so…different. Freshly shaved, he had removed the bandage and combed his hair neatly back with water. His skin glowed with health, his eyes were bright and lit with a lurking devilish gleam. His clean white shirt seemed to shine against his tanned skin; the sleeves were rolled back almost to his elbow. The shirt was tucked into buckskin breeches, not quite skin-tight, but nevertheless…

It was foolish, she told herself severely. They must have been tight when he arrived, too—in fact, tighter, because he was drenched. It was knowing the body beneath the buckskins, knowing it had been pressed against her, naked, only this morning, which was creating this unwanted heat in the pit of her stomach.

"Sit down. The table is set." She gestured and turned back to the fire to lift off the heavy pot of bubbling stew.

A brawny arm wrapped itself around her waist, while with his other hand, he whisked the cloth pad from her hand and used it to lift the black cast-iron pot off its hook.

"I can do that," she muttered, wriggling out of his light clasp.

"I know. But I've caused you enough work. While I'm here, I'll lighten your load as much as possible." He carried the pot carefully to the table.

While I'm here… The words echoed in her head. Yes, as soon as he recovered his memory, he would be off, no doubt, back to his wife and children. All twelve of them, she thought glumly.

They ate in silence. He ate neatly and without fuss. He passed her the bread and the salt and refilled her cup of water without being asked. Ellie pondered as she ate. His manners and his accent suggested he was gently bred, but his body bore the signs of one who had led a very physically challenging existence. He was also familiar with the workings of a cottage hearth; he deftly swapped the stewing pot with the large water kettle, rebuilt the fire in a manner which revealed he knew not to squander her precious fuel and generally showed himself to be at home in her meagre surroundings—as no gentleman would be. A servant might acquire table manners and an accent, but he showed none of the servility of a man who had been in service. On the contrary, he was rather arrogant in the way he simply did what he wished, whether she wanted to be helped or not.

He fixed a loose shutter. The banging had driven her mad most of the year, but somehow, his fixing it—without saying a word to her—annoyed her. He went outside into the cold, despite his lack of coat, and chopped her a huge pile of wood, stacking it under the eaves at the back door which was much more convenient than where she had stored her wood before. He swung the axe with ease and familiarity. And his muscles rippled beneath the loose, soft shirt in a way that dried her mouth. Her eyes clung to his form like ivy to a rock...until she remembered to go on with what she had been doing. She should have been grateful for his help. She was grateful...only...

Any minute now he would remember his name and that he had a wife who had a right to command these services from him! And twelve children. How dare he make himself indispensable...making her and Amy feel like they were part of a family... It wasn't fair.

* * *

In the afternoon she'd seen Amy standing outside looking up, her little face pale and stiff with fear. Ellie had rushed out to see what was happening, only to rival her daughter in fear as she watched the wretched man clambering about on her steep roof, replacing and adjusting slates as if he hadn't a care in the world. She stood there, twisting a tea-towel helplessly in her hands, watching. Several times his foot slipped and her heart leapt right out of her chest and lodged as a hard lump in her throat as she realised he was fixing her leaking roof. He must have noticed the pot she placed in the corner of her room to catch the drips.

She hadn't breathed a scrap of air the whole time he was up there, and how he'd got up there without a ladder she didn't even want to think about! But when he'd come down finally in a rush which left her gasping in fright, and then he'd stood there, with that…that *look* in his eye, as if she should be pleased he'd risked his fool neck for such a trivial matter, well!

She'd wanted to throttle him there and then. Or jump on him and kiss him senseless.

But of course, she couldn't do any of that, because he wasn't hers to kiss or throttle and he probably never would be. She couldn't even yell at him, because how could she possibly yell at him for helping her? For scaring her silly? For making her realise that she loved him? The wretch!

She loved him.

The triumphant grin died slowly from his face and a light came into his eyes that made Ellie wonder whether she had said the words aloud. He stared at her, burning with intensity, his blue eyes blazing at whatever he read in her face. He strode towards her purposefully. She knew he was going to gather her up in his arms and kiss her like he had in the morning, in that way that melted her very bones.

But she could not, oh, she could not. For if she let him love her she could not bear it if she had to let him go... She held a shaking hand up to stop him and he came to a halt a scant pace away. His eyes devoured her, his chest heaving. Her eyes clung to him, even as her hands warded him off. They stood there, unmoving.

"Mr. Bruin!" said a cross little voice.

He ignored it, staring at Ellie, eating her up with his eyes.

"Mr. Bruin!" Amy tugged furiously at his buckskin breeches.

With a visible effort, he finally tore his gaze from Ellie and squatted down in front of her daughter. "What is it, Princess?"

"You are *not* allowed to climb up on the roof without askin' Mama! It's very dangerous. You could've fallen down and broken your head again. You're a bad bear!" Her voice quivered as she added, "And you frightened me and Mama terrible bad."

His voice softened. "Did I, Princess? I'm very sorry, then." And he gathered the little girl into his arms and hugged her gently. His eyes met Ellie's across the little girl's head, filled with contrition and some nameless emotion.

Ellie's eyes misted. What was she to do with a man like this? How could any woman not love him? She turned back to the cottage. He probably had half a dozen adoring wives.

Ellie was jumpy. The night was closing in on her. They sat by the fire in companionable silence. She was mending, he was whittling at a stick. Amy had gone to bed some time before. It was long past Ellie's bedtime too, but she had been putting off the moment. They would share a bed again soon. There was no choice. Of course, they had shared a bed for the last two nights, but he had been mostly unconscious. Mostly...

She kept trying not to think about the feeling of waking up in his embrace. She could not allow it to happen again. It was unseemly behaviour in a respectable widow and she would have no part of it. Besides, she feared if she allowed him to touch her like that again, there could be no stopping. She had already fallen more than halfway in love with him. If she gave herself to him she knew she would be letting him into her heart as well as her body...

She'd lost almost everything in her life as it was, but she had survived the loss. If she let herself love him and then lost him, it might be the loss she could not bear. For Amy's sake, if not for her own, she had to keep herself strong. She could not afford to break her heart. She would not *let* him break her heart.

She cleared her throat. "Mr. Bruin." She had taken to using Amy's name for him.

He looked up. "Mrs. Carmichael?" A slow smile crinkled across his face, white teeth gleaming wolfishly in the firelight. He had that look in his eye again. She felt her pulse flutter.

"It is about the sleeping arrangements," she said in an attempt to sound brisk and matter of fact. It came out as something of a squeak.

"Yes?" His voice deepened.

"I am a virtuous widow," she began.

He raised an eyebrow.

"I am—" she repeated indignantly.

"It's all right, love," he said. "I am not doubting your virtue."

"Don't call me lo—"

He held up his hand pacifically. "Mrs. Carmichael...

Ellie…your virtue is safe with me. On my honour as a gentleman, I will do nothing to cause you distress.''

Ellie looked troubled. It was all very well for him to make a noble-sounding promise, but how did either of them know he *was* a gentleman? And what did causing her distress mean? His leaving would cause her distress, but would he stay, once he recovered his wits? She doubted it. Why would a handsome man in the peak of health and fitness want to stay in a small cottage in the middle of nowhere with a poverty-stricken widow and a small girl?

"There is no choice but to…" she swallowed convulsively "…share a bed, but that is as far as it goes. I will wrap myself entirely in a sheet and you shall do the same. And thus we may share a bed and blankets, but remain chaste. Are you agreed?" Her voice squeaked again.

He bowed ironically. "I am agreed. Now, shall I go up and disrobe while you do the same down here with the fire?"

Ellie felt herself go hot. "Very well." She fetched down her thickest nightgown and, the moment she heard his footstep overhead, began to unbutton her dress. She undressed in the firelight, glancing once or twice at the window, at the black, opaque night outside, feeling exposed. Wrapping her thickest shawl around her, she took a candle and hurried upstairs. On the threshold she paused.

"Did you find your sheet?" she whispered. "I put it on the bed for you."

A deep chuckle answered her. The sound shivered through her bones deliciously.

"Did you?" she repeated, lifting the candle to peer into the sleeping alcove.

"Yes, love. I gave my word, remember. I'm as chaste as a bug in a rug." His bare upper chest and shoulders glowed dark against the white sheet. His eyes were deep shadows of mystery, and his white teeth gleamed briefly. He didn't look chaste. He looked handsome and powerful and altogether far too appealing for a virtuous widow's peace of mind.

She swallowed and turning her back, sat down to remove her shoes and stockings. Then she picked up her own sheet and wrapped herself tightly in it, feeling his eyes watching her every movement. Finally she blew out the candle, set it on the floor next to the bed, took a deep breath and slipped in beside him.

She lay stiffly on her back, huddled beneath the blankets in the cocoon of her sheet, trying not to touch him. All she could hear was the wind in the trees and the breathing of the man beside her. It was worse than the first time she had slept with him. Then she'd feared him as a stranger. Now the danger he represented was not the sort that a frying pan could fix.

Before, he had been a stranger to her, nothing more than a wounded, beautiful body. Now she knew how his eyes could dance, what he tasted like, how his hands felt moving over her skin, caressing her as if she was beautiful to him, precious. Before her marriage, men had only wanted her for her inheritance. Now she had nothing to offer a man except herself. And yet this man in her bed wanted her. And when he touched her she felt...cherished.

It was dangerously seductive. He had already found his way under her skin, if not her skirts. Now, all she had was a thin cotton sheet to protect her virtue—and her heart. She lay rigid, hardly daring to breathe.

"Oh, for heaven's sake!" With a surge of bedclothes he turned, flipped her on her side and pulled her into the curve of his body.

"Stop it! You promised—"

"And I do not break my promises! This is as chaste as I can manage it. Now stop fussing, Ellie. There is a sheet wrapped around each of us—it is perfectly decorous. But I cannot possibly sleep while you lie there as stiff as a board…'' He chuckled awkwardly. ''That's my problem, too, if you want to know.''

Ellie buried her hot cheek in her cool pillow. No, she didn't want to know that. It was bad enough that she could feel his problem, even through the sheets. The feel of him set off all sorts of reactions in her own body.

''I'm sorry, I shouldn't have said that. Now, stop worrying, love, and go to sleep. We'll both rest better like this, you know it.''

Ellie did not know it, but she allowed herself to remain in the curve of his body, enjoying the warmth of him and the feeling of strength and protection which emanated from him. It was a strange and seductive sensation, this feeling of being…cherished.

They lay in silence for a long time, listening to the wind in the trees. And finally, Ellie slept.

He lay in the dark, holding Ellie against the length of his body. Even through the sheets wound around them, he could feel her soft curves, curled trustfully against him. Her feet had kicked free of their cotton shroud and tucked themselves between his calves, like two cold little stones. He smiled in the dark. He was happy to be her personal hot brick.

She sighed in her sleep and snuggled closer to him. He buried his face in the nape of her neck. He laid his mouth on her skin and tasted her gently with his tongue. Her scent was unique, like fresh harvested wheat…like bread dough, before it was baked…and hay as it was scythed. Fresh and good. He felt as if the fragrance of her skin had become a part of him.

Who the devil was he? It was unbearable to be so helpless, to be imprisoned in the dark, unable to make deci-

sions about his life. How the hell could he plan any sort
of a future when his past was a blank slate?

And what if his memory failed to return? Would he be
forever hamstrung by self-ignorance? And if his memory
didn't come back, how long could he stay here with Ellie?
He couldn't ask her to support him. Yet he couldn't continue to live with her—a few days in winter they might
get away with, but much more and her reputation would
be compromised. And Ellie was a woman who valued her
reputation. He inhaled the scent of her. He must not damage her. Must not let her be hurt by his situation. But how?

Questions continued to rattle fruitlessly in his head, until
at last he fell asleep.

When he awoke Ellie was wrapped around him. They
were lying face to face. Or rather her face to his chest.
She was using him as a pillow. Warm little puffs of air
warmed his chest as she breathed. Her hair, loosened from
its braid, flowed in waves over his skin. One of her hands
was curled around his neck, the other was draped across
his chest. The sheets they had been wrapped so chastely
in were now bundled ineffectively around their middles,
leaving them uncovered above and below. There was nothing chaste about their current positions.

The warm soft weight of her against his naked skin was
irresistibly appealing. He stifled a moan. He was rock hard
and aching from wanting her. Her legs were twined around
his, one leg over his hip. She was open to him. One small
movement and he could be inside her. He had never
wanted anything so much. She was his woman, his heart-
mate and she was soft, sleepy and open to him.

He swallowed hard. He wanted so badly, needed so
much, to be inside her. His entire body throbbed with the
need. He fought it. He had given his word. She trusted

him. He might be a nameless pirate, but he had given his word and she'd believed him.

He would not take her, but that didn't mean he had to be a saint. He ran his hand down her body. The sheets were bunched around her middle, riding up over her thighs. He ran his hand along the leg she'd thrown across his hip, caressed her sweetly rounded backside, hesitated, then stroked the silken skin of her belly and thighs. She was warm, sweet and more than ready for him. A hard shudder rocked his body. He closed his eyes, willing the need back down.

He must have awoken her. Eyes still closed, she stretched languidly and the need rocked through him, almost shattering his fragile self-control. She moved her legs against his and he tried unsuccessfully to close his mind against the delicious friction of her soft skin rubbing against his.

Sleepily, she opened her eyes and looked at him, blinking drowsily. Still barely awake, she smiled at him. Her skin was flushed a soft pink, her lips were parted and damp and smiling in welcome. His hand moved again, caressing her intimately and her eyes widened in shock, even as her body arched towards him. He had not broken his word, but he was perilously close to it. He removed his hand.

She moved back in sudden caution, only to find her legs were gripping him.

"Oh!" she exclaimed and tried to untangle herself from him. He watched her sweet embarrassment as she discovered her sheet and nightgown pushed up to her middle, and the extremely intimate position they were in. She struggled to pull the sheet and nightgown down and in the process her hand brushed against his arousal.

She froze as she realised what she'd done and he gritted his teeth, willing control. Her face flamed adorably and she avoided his eyes in sudden shyness. It was odd for a married woman with a child to be so shy, but he had no time to explore that question. His focus was on the battle between his body and his mind. His body wanted nothing more than to make love to her. His mind also wanted it, heart and soul.

But for a man who had no memories, one single extremely inconvenient memory remained: *"your virtue is safe with me. On my honour as a gentleman, I will do nothing to cause you distress..."*

Again, she tugged surreptitiously at the hem of her nightgown, and again, she brushed up against him. Another encounter and he would not be answerable for the consequences. He reached down and lifted her hands away from the danger zone.

"Don't worry about it, Ellie. These things happen," he said softly. "I haven't forgotten my promise. Good morning," he added, and kissed her.

Recalling her earlier shyness, he planned to make it a gentle, tender, unthreatening kiss, but as her mouth opened under his and he tasted her sweet, tart, sleepy mouth, he was lost.

Their second kiss was more passionate.

He kissed her a third time and felt at the end of it that his body was about to explode. He raised his head, like a drowning man going down for the last time, and said softly, "Three is my limit, Mrs. Carmichael."

She blinked at him, her eyes wide and dazed looking, her lips slightly swollen from his kisses. She gazed into his eyes, as if reading his soul. He wondered what she saw in him but was distracted when her eyes dropped.

"Three?" she whispered vaguely. Staring hungrily at his mouth, she licked her lips.

He groaned. She didn't understand. He was poised on the brink. If she didn't get out of bed now, he would be lost. "Three kisses. If I kiss you again, I fear I will forget

my promise to you.'' She frowned, so he reminded her.
''My promise that your virtue would be safe with me,''
and added ironically, ''*on my honour as a gentleman.* If
you are not out of this bed in one minute, I will not be
answerable for the consequences.''

It took a moment for her to comprehend what he was
saying and he had to smile. She was even more befuddled
by passion than he was. But once his meaning percolated
to her brain, she gasped and scrambled hurriedly out of
the bed. She stood there on the bare floor, staring, her chest
heaving as if she had run a race. His own breathing was
just as ragged.

''I…I am sorry,'' she said in a low voice and, snatching
her clothes from the hook behind the door, left the room.

A moment later she was back, in the doorway, clutching
her clothes against her chest, looking uncomfortable. ''I…I
wish…we could have…you know.'' She blushed rosily.
''I'm sorry.'' She turned to go then paused and turned
back, resolutely. ''It was the loveliest awakening I have
ever had, thank you,'' she said in a gruff little voice and
hurried down the stairs.

He lay back in the bed, his body throbbing with unsatisfied need, a wry smile on his face. *''It was the loveliest
awakening I have ever had, thank you.''* It took courage
for Mrs. ''I-am-a-Virtuous-Widow'' to admit that; courage
and a kind of shy, sensual honesty that made him want to
leap down the stairs after her and drag her back to bed. It
would be an awakening in more ways than one, he suspected.

It would be wise to spend the day in making a straw
pallet for him to sleep on during the coming night…but
he had no intention of being wise. Tonight he would retract
his gentlemanly promise. It didn't matter that he didn't
know who he was. Whoever he was, he would make it
right for her.

Tonight she would be his.

Chapter Three

Ellie swept out the ash and charcoal from last night's fire and began to set a new one, her hands moving mechanically, her mind reliving the wondrously delicious sensations she had experienced at his hands a few moments earlier. His hands… She felt herself blush, again, thinking of where his hands had been, so big and capable…touching her with such tenderness…and creating such sensations. She had never felt anything so…so…

It made her want to weep again, at the beauty of it…and the frustration.

The wood shavings which remained from his whittling smouldered, then smoked. She blew on them gently and flames licked at the wood. He'd built a fire inside her, a fire which still smouldered within her. She watched curl after curl of wood smoulder, then burst into brilliant flame. A moment of splendour, then each one crumbled into grey ash. Was that what it would be like to be possessed by him? One moment of glory, followed by a lifetime of regret? Or would it build into a more permanent fire, one with deep hot coals?

She filled the big black kettle with water and swung it on to the lowest hook. Hastily, because he might come down at any minute, she washed herself with soap and cold water and dressed before the fire. The kettle soon began to steam and she set the porridge to cook, stirring it rhythmically, her mind dreamily recalling the sensation of waking up in his arms.

Rat-tat-tat!

Ellie jumped. Someone at the door at this hour of the morning? Her eye fell on the hare skins hung up to dry on a hook near the door. Of course. Ned with the milk. She flung open the door, a smile of welcome on her face.

It froze there. "Sq...Squire Hammet."

A large burly man dressed more to suit a London afternoon promenade than a rural Northumberland morning pushed past her. His gaze raked her intimately.

Ellie shrivelled inside and braced herself. "To what do I owe this unexpected visit?"

"You've had a man here, missy!" The squire's angry gaze probed the small room.

"Why do you say that?" Ellie prayed that the floorboards overhead would not squeak.

"A man was seen on your roof yesterday." The squire thrust his red face at her. The scent of expensive pomade emanated from him, as did the faint scent of soiled linen. Like his friend, her late husband, the squire favoured expensive clothing, but disdained bathing.

Ellie turned away, trying to hide her fear and disgust. "There was a man here yesterday. He fixed the leaking roof for me."

"It's my blasted cottage! I say who fixes the roof or not! So, you have a secret fancy man do you, Miss-Prim-and-Proper?" His face was mottled with anger. "Too high and mighty to give the time of day to me, who lent you this house out of the kindness of my heart, and now I find you've let some filthy peasant come sniffing around your skirts."

"You are disgusting!"

"Who was it, dammit—I want to know the fellow's name!"

Ellie turned angrily. "I have no idea of his name or anything about him. He merely fixed my roof for me and I gave him some food in return! I've been asking you to fix those broken slates for months now and you have done nothing!"

"Only because you have refused your part of the bargain." Small, hot eyes ran over her body lasciviously.

Ellie shuddered and forced herself to ignore it. "There was no bargain. There never will be. I pay rent on this cottage and that is the end of it."

"Pah, a peppercorn rent!"

"The rent you offered me on the day of Hart's funeral! If it was lower than usual, I did not know it at the time. I thought you were being kind because you were my husband's friend. I should have known better," she finished bitterly and turned to stir the porridge.

"You should have indeed. There's no such thing as something for nothing." The squire's voice thickened and Ellie jumped as thick, meaty hands slid around her, groping for her breasts.

"Take your hands off me!" She jerked her elbow into his stomach, hard and he gasped and released her. She whirled and pushed him hard. Off balance, he staggered back and banged his head on the shelf behind him.

She flung open the door and stood there, holding it. "You are not welcome in this cottage, sir. If I've told you once, I've told you a hundred times, I am—and shall be— no man's mistress. And even if I was so inclined, I would *never* be yours, Squire Hammet!"

The squire stood there, breathing heavily and rubbed his head. "You little vixen! I'll punish you for that, see if I don't. His eyes ran over her again. "I don't mean to leave here unsatisfied again. I had a good eyeful of you this morning and I liked what I saw.''

Ellie felt ill. She never got dressed downstairs, usually. Of all the days to do it, when Squire Hammet was outside the window, watching. She glanced at the fire, to where her cast-iron poker was propped. If only she could get hold of it...

"No, you don't, vixen." The squire put his big burly body between her and the poker.

Ellie was beside the open door. She could run away into the forest and hide, but she couldn't leave Amy in the house.

The squire seemed to read her mind. "Where's that brat of yours?" He glanced around the room and his eyes came to rest on the cheese-box dolls' house. "You would not want her to...have an accident, would you?" With no warning his shiny boots stamped down on the child's toy, smashing it to bits. He kicked the shattered remains into the fire.

Ellie gasped with fright and rage. She watched the flames devour a little girl's dream world. Amy was upstairs, still asleep, she hoped. She did not want her daughter to witness what would come next. She would kill the squire before she let him touch her.

"Mama, Mama!" In bare feet and nightgown, Amy came hurtling down the stairs. She flew across the room to her mother, but in a flash the squire reached out and grabbed the child by the arm. Amy shrieked with fear and pain.

"Let go of her!" screamed Ellie.

Amy squirmed in the squire's grasp, then, unable to break free, the little girl suddenly turned and fastened her teeth in the hand of the man who held her. The squire let out a bellow of rage and Amy wriggled out of his grasp and fled.

Ellie darted forward and grabbed the poker. She lifted it, but before she could bring it down on the man's elegantly curled and pomaded head, a strong hand grabbed the squire by the collar, whirled him around and flung him across the room.

It was Mr. Bruin, dressed in nothing but a shirt and breeches, thick, dark stubble covering his jaw, blue eyes blazing with fury.

"Get out!" he said. "And if I ever find you bothering this lady again—"

"Lady!" the squire spat. "Some lady! You've obviously spent the night in her bed, but don't assume it's anything special! Half the men in the county have been under those skirts—and she's not fussy about class—in fact, she enjoys a bit of the rough—"

A big, powerful fist cut off the rest of the sentence. "Enjoy a bit of the rough, yourself, do you, Squire?" said Mr. Bruin softly, punctuating each word with a punch.

The squire was a big man, thicker and more solid in build than Mr. Bruin, but he was no match for Ellie's barefoot avenger. She winced at the sound of flesh punishing flesh, even as part of her was cheering.

"Now get out, you piece of carrion!"

The squire wheezed, sagged and scuttled out the door, looking much smaller than when he had arrived. His nose was bleeding and from the crack she'd heard, it was probably broken. His face bore numerous marks from the fight and his eyes were swollen half-closed. They would probably be black by the afternoon.

Mr. Bruin, on the other hand, was unmarked and not even winded.

"I'll have you for this!" the squire swore from a safe distance. "I'm the magistrate around here. I'll have you transported, you ruffian!"

"I'm sure the court will enjoy hearing how a lone virtuous widow and child were forced to defend themselves with a poker from the unwanted attentions of a prancing, pomaded, middle-aged Lothario. Yes, I can just see you admitting to the world you were bested by a woman, a poker and a little girl,'' said Ellie's defender in a deep, amused voice.

The squire swore vilely.

"Need another lesson in manners, do you, louse?" Mr. Bruin bunched his fists. "Or shall I leave you to the tender mercies of Mrs. Carmichael and her poker?"

Ellie watched as the squire fled, still cursing and muttering threats. He had made her life almost unbearable before: after this humiliation he would make it impossible. She would have to leave this place, but she didn't regret it one iota.

"That saw him off!" she said with satisfaction.

"You've dealt with this before," he said slowly.

She nodded. "He was one of my husband's closest friends, you know. When the magnitude of Hart's indebtedness became known, he offered me help." She laughed, bitterly. "I was an heiress when Hart married me. I was a pauperess when he died. I knew nothing—then—about the cost of living. None of our friends wanted to know me, so when the squire offered to help his dear friend's widow and child...I believed him. It seemed all perfectly above board." She shrugged. "I was stupid."

"A little naïve, perhaps," he corrected her, his gaze intense.

"Stupid," she repeated in a flat voice. "He said he'd keep an eye on me." She shuddered. "I didn't realise exactly what he meant by that."

"And that's why you feared for Amy that day when you left her with me. You thought you'd been 'stupid' again. Trusted another wrong 'un."

She nodded. They fell silent. It was too silent, she sud-

denly realised. *"Amy!"* Had she been hurt in the scuffle?
Ellie raced into the cottage.

Her daughter was squatting before the fire, earnestly stirring the porridge. "It nearly burned, Mama," she said,
"an' it was too heavy to lift and you said I wasn't to touch
the fire things, so I just kept stirring it. Was that right?"
She gave them an odd, guilty look.

Relieved, Ellie hugged her daughter. "Yes, darling, it
was very right. Mr. Bruin has saved us and you have saved
our breakfast."

He chuckled. "Nonsense, you were both well on the
way to saving yourselves. Princess, I never would have
expected it of you!" His laughter died as Amy's gaze
dropped in shame.

"It's wicked to bite people, isn't it, Mama?" she whispered.

"Oh, my darling," Ellie's eyes misted. "You're not
wicked at all. I thought you were very brave and clever to
do what you did."

"You mean you're not vexed with me, Mama?"

"No, indeed."

"And it's all right to bite the squire again?"

Before Ellie could reply, she and Amy were swept into
Mr. Bruin's arms and whirled around the room in a mad,
impromptu waltz. "Yes, indeed, Princess," he said. "You
may bite the nasty old squire as often as you want. And
your mama may hit him with a poker. And then when my
two little Amazons are finished with him, I will toss him
out the door."

Laughing, he set them down, then knelt down and said,
"Princess Amy, you are one of the bravest, cleverest
young ladies I know. Not only did you bite the evil Squire-
dragon and rescue yourself, you saved the porridge from
burning! I would fain be your knight."

The little girl laughed delightedly, seized a wooden

spoon and tapped him lightly on each shoulder. "Arise, Sir Bruin!"

Ellie laughed, even as her eyes filled. His nonsense had transformed the ugly incident into a bold adventure. He understood children so well... Too well for a bachelor?

"Are knights and princesses interested in porridge?" She forced a light-hearted note.

"Oh, yes, indee—"

Rat-tat-tat!

Everyone froze for a moment as the knock echoed through the small cottage.

"The squire," whispered Amy. "He's come back to put us in prison!"

"Blast him for his impudence! I'll see to this!" He strode to the door and flung it open. "What the devil do you—?"

He stopped. A small, spare, neatly dressed man stood at the door.

"Gawd be praised, Capt'n!" said the man, beaming up at him. "When your horse came home without you, we all thought you was dead! Only I know'd better. I told 'em you was a survivor."

There was a sudden silence in the small cottage. The stranger's words seemed to echo. Ellie wondered whether anyone else could hear her heart thudding the way she could.

It was over, then, their brief idyll. He had been found.

"Capt'n? What's the matter?" The small man frowned at the tall, silent man in the doorway and then glanced behind him, to where Ellie and Amy stood, watchful and apprehensive. His bright bird-like gaze ran over Ellie and the little girl and his eyes narrowed.

The man he called Capt'n finally spoke. "Since I gather you know who I am, you'd better come in out of the cold."

The small man's head snapped back at that. "Know who

you are? Are you bammin' me, Capt'n? Course I know who you are!''

"Come in, then."

He ushered the stranger inside and closed the door. He turned and met Ellie's gaze briefly. She couldn't read his expression. He began to offer a chair, then stopped in mid-movement. It was as if he was suddenly unsure of anything, she thought. Ellie filled the gap.

"Please, have a seat," she said to the stranger. "We were about to break our fast. It is only porridge and some milk, but you are very welcome to join us."

The man didn't respond. He continued to stare at "the Capt'n" with a puzzled expression.

"It's all right, the porridge isn't burnt," a little voice assured him. "I stopped it from getting burnt, didn't I, Mama?"

It broke the ice. Ellie couldn't help but smile and the stranger glanced down at Amy, smiled and said to Ellie, "I thank you for the offer, ma'am—and little miss—but I ate earlier. I wouldn't mind a drink to whet me whistle, though."

Ellie grimaced. "I'm sorry. There is only milk or water."

"Adam's ale will do me nicely, ma'am."

As Ellie fetched him a cup of water she glanced surreptitiously at Mr. Bruin. He was standing stiff and silent, a frown on his face. His body was braced, as if for a blow.

"Eat your porridge while it's hot," she said quietly. He sat down at the table and began to spoon porridge into his mouth.

They ate in silence, unanswered questions hovering over them, like the spectre at the feast. Even Amy was silent and anxious. The stranger watched the tableau, his eyes narrowed, going from one to the other, taking in everything.

Finally the porridge was finished, though Ellie doubted if anyone had enjoyed it. She began to collect the bowls, but Mr. Bruin stopped her with a gesture. He was nervous, Ellie knew. She sat down beside him again and took his hand.

The stranger noticed. She felt his disapproval and a sliver of ice slipped into her heart. It meant something, that look. It meant he thought she had no right to be holding this man's hand, this dear, battered hand, beloved in such a short time. He knew who her Mr. Bruin truly was. She hung on to the hand tighter, knowing it might be the last time.

She felt him squeeze her hard in response. He was as worried as she was. Amy came around the table and leaned against him. He put an arm around the little girl. Ellie felt a half-hysterical bubble of emotion rise in her throat. It was as if the three of them were a family, ranged defensively against the stranger, when, in fact, the opposite was true. This small spare man had come to take their beloved Mr. Bruin back to his true family.

"So, you say you know me. Then who am I?"

The stranger stared disbelievingly back at him.

Ellie explained in a flat voice, "He arrived here having been robbed and injured. His head was bleeding profusely and he slept like the dead for a night and a day. When he awoke, he had no recollection of anything—who he was, where he lived—nothing."

"Head injury, eh? That explains a lot."

At Ellie's look, he explained, "I've seen it before ma'am, in the army. Man gets hit on the head and loses it all for a time. Knew one bloke what never recovered all the memories, but most of 'em does." He turned. "You'll be all right, Capt'n Ambrose. Soon as I get you home, it'll all come back to you."

"Captain Ambrose? It doesn't sound the least bit familiar. What is my full name?"

"Capt'n Daniel Matthew Bramford Ambrose, late of the 5th Regiment."

Daniel. Ellie thought. It suited him.

"And you are?" said Daniel.

The small man leapt to his feet and saluted. "Sergeant William Aloysius Tomkins, sir!" He waited a moment, then shrugged and sat down again. "Thought it might bring something back, sir. I was your sergeant for nigh on seven years. You call me Tomkins when you're with the nobs and Tommy when we're on our own."

Daniel smiled faintly. "So, I am...I was a soldier..."

The sergeant grinned. "Indeed you was, Capt'n, for the last seven years—all but a month or two—and a mighty good one, at that. Best man in a scrap anyone could ask for."

Daniel glanced down at his big battle-scarred hands and glanced up at Ellie, a rueful look in his eyes. She thought he'd been a fighter and he was, just not the sort of fighter she'd imagined. He wasn't a gutter brawler—he was possibly a hero.

Ellie found herself fighting a battle between wanting to hear more about him—and wanting to know nothing more, for with every word the sergeant spoke, her Mr. Bruin and the fragile dreams she'd built around him drifted further away from her...

"Where do I live?"

"Until recently, all over the Peninsula, fighting Boney, sir, but when your brother died a few months back, you sold out and came home. To Rothbury. Ring a bell, sir?"

Ellie knew it. It was a town about a half-day's travel to the north-west of her.

Daniel shook his head.

"No? Oh, well, it'll come, don't you worry." The sergeant paused, then said deliberately, "You have family responsibilities at Rothbury, Capt'n."

Family responsibilities. Ellie felt the sliver of ice slide deeper in her heart.

"Family responsibilities?" Daniel said at last. He was squeezing Ellie's hand so tightly it was painful, but she couldn't bear to have him let go of her. It would happen all too soon.

"I have a wife, then?"

Say no, say no, say no! Ellie prayed silently. She could not breathe.

The stranger took an age to answer. He glanced at Ellie, then at Amy and then back at Daniel. And then said in the most ordinary of voices, "Yes, Capt'n, of course you have a wife. And a fine, beautiful lady she is, too."

Ellie could not breathe. Something was blocking her throat. *Of course he had a wife.* She had known it from the start. Stupid, stupid Ellie, to have let herself fall in love in a matter of days with a mysterious stranger.

He was strong and rugged and handsome, he was honourable, he was protective of women, he loved children. Of course he had a wife. He was altogether lovable.

And of course, his wife would be a fine, beautiful lady and probably sweet-natured and intelligent as well. She certainly wouldn't be a poverty-stricken, shabbily dressed widow. Stupid, stupid Ellie, thinking she had found love at last. Foolish, woolly-headed widgeon for forgetting that even when she had been a carefree young lady, passably pretty and very well dressed, she hadn't found love. She had needed her late father's money to buy her a husband. And not a very good one at that.

She'd long ago learned that fate was not her friend. She'd just forgotten the lesson.

The sergeant continued, "And, of course, your, um…

Mrs. Ambrose has been terribly distressed by your disappearance.''

Daniel nodded vaguely. He was still gripping her hand so hard Ellie knew it would come up in a bruise later. Even so, she hung on to his hand for all she was worth. If a bruise was all she was going to have of him, then a bruise was what she would have. She could take that to bed with her instead. That and her dreams and memories. And regrets.

Regrets.

How she wished he hadn't been such a gentleman this morning.

''Mr. Bruin, you're squeezin' me too hard,'' complained Amy.

''Sorry, Princess,'' he murmured and gave her a gentle hug. ''You run and play with your dolls while your mother and I talk to Sergeant Tomkins, here.''

''I can't. The squire smashed them up and kicked them in the fire.'' Amy touched him, hesitantly. ''Are you going to leave Mama and me, Mr. Bruin?'' Her voice quavered.

That was Ellie's signal. Amy needed her mother to be strong. She wasn't going to fall apart. She wasn't going to be ruled by her instincts, those instincts which shrieked inside her to weep and cling and rage at fate, the instincts which had made her fall in love with a married man. He wasn't her Mr. Bruin; he was a Mr. Daniel Ambrose, with a loving wife awaiting his return. She had pride. She had her daughter to think of. She refused to disgrace herself.

Ellie wrenched her hand out of Daniel's, jumped to her feet and said brightly. ''Yes, darling, isn't that wonderful for Mr. Bruin? Although he isn't Mr. Bruin anymore, he's Mr. Ambrose. And Sergeant Tomkins is his friend and has come to take him home to his family, who is waiting for him and who love him very much and miss him terribly. Isn't that exciting? Now come and help Mama wash these dishes and let the gentlemen talk.'' She gathered up the bowls, knowing she was babbling, smiling so hard she thought her face would split.

But Amy didn't move. She fixed big blue eyes on Daniel and asked in a tragic little voice, ''Have you already got a little girl of your own, Mr. Bruin?''

He stroked her curly head with a big, gentle hand. His voice was deep and husky and it seemed to catch in his throat as he said, ''I don't know, Princess. Have I got a little girl, Sergeant? Or any children at all?''

The sergeant tugged at the neatly tied stock around his stiff collar. He cleared his throat. ''Er...not yet, sir. Though...er, hrrumph, your mother has...er, expectations of...of being made a grandmother...soon. She speaks of it often.''

Oh mercy, his wife must be expecting a child. Ellie closed her eyes and swished the bowls and water frantically, appearing busy. ''Oh! So you are anticipating a happy event! How splendid! No wonder your wife is so anxious about you, Mr. Ambrose. A woman is always more emotional at that...delicate time. What delightful anticipation for your mother. To be a grandmother must be marvellous. A child has a special relationship with a grandmother. If she has one, that is. Amy never had a grandmother. They both died before she was born.''

Foolish, babbling Ellie. She forced herself to take a deep breath and added brightly, ''It's so amazingly lucky that Sergeant Tomkins managed to find you in such an out-of-the-way place. How did you find him, Sergeant? Tell us the whole story.''

The sergeant regarded her thoughtfully for a moment and then explained to Daniel, ''You'd decided to go to Newcastle to order some new clothes, them that you'd come home from the wars with bein' unfit for company, so your mother said, an' nothing in the house to fit you, your late brother bein' a smaller man than you, sir.''

That explained the worn and shabby clothes, thought Ellie sadly as she rubbed apathetically at the dishes. They'd been to war with him.

"You'd decided to stay for a few weeks, to get out of your m—" The sergeant stopped and cleared his throat. "You were feeling a little restless at Rothbury, sir. So you sent me on ahead to find lodgings and set up a few appointments. But when you didn't arrive in the lodgings I got worried—you being a man what keeps to your word, sir.''

Oh, yes, he kept to his word, thought Ellie regretfully, thinking of those few glorious moments when she'd woken in his arms. And he'd told her to go. On his honour.

"So then when they sent word that your horse had been found but no sign of you, I came a'lookin'. I asked in every village between here and town, lookin' in every ditch and gully and clump of trees, headin' for Rothbury. And then I saw a pair of boots, sir, on sale in the market place, and I thinks to myself, I've seen them boots before.''

There was a pause and the sergeant said a little throatily. "I don't mind saying the sight of them boots gave me a right nasty turn, Capt'n, because I figured the only way you'd give up your boots was if you was dead.''

He loved Daniel, too, thought Ellie sadly. And he'd grieved when he thought him dead.

"So then I went to the church, to see if the minister had buried anyone lately. He told me you were alive and in the care of a local widow…'' He glanced at Ellie and then back at Daniel. "I bought back your boots. And there's a change of clothes for you, sir, in the bag there.''

An awkward silence fell in the cottage.

"Ah, right," Daniel finally said. "Good thinking, Sergeant."

Ellie forced herself to say it. To get it over with. "So, Mr. Daniel Ambrose, you'd better put on your boots and change your clothes. With any luck this mild weather will hold and you will be home to your wife by this evening." She smiled, a wide, desperate smile that stretched her lips and made her jaw ache. Could a smile shatter a person? She hoped not.

"Oh, Ellie," he said softly and put out a hand.

She wanted to grab it, to cling and never let him go, but she turned away instead. "Hurry up, then." She felt her eyes fill and blinked furiously to keep them from spilling down her cheeks. "You don't want to keep the sergeant waiting. Your wi—" Her voice cracked. "Your family is waiting to hear the news that you are alive."

Daniel watched her turn away. He felt ill. *He had a wife!* Dammit! How could he have forgotten that? The sergeant seemed to think this wife loved him, too. Had he loved her, this unknown beautiful lady who was expecting his child?

And if he had, how could he go on loving her, now that he had found Ellie?

Because he didn't believe it was possible to love anyone more than he loved Ellie. He might not remember any details of his life, but right at this moment he knew, deep within himself, in his bones and his blood, that he loved Ellie with every shred of his being.

Had he loved another woman in this same way, with this intensity of feeling, before he was hit on the head by footpads?

This wife meant nothing to him now. Would Ellie mean nothing to him once his memory was regained? The thought terrified him. He didn't want his memories. He wanted Ellie.

He looked at her. She turned away, her mouth stretched in a travesty of a smile, her eyes brimming with tears. She was trying so hard to be brave and cheerful, not to make him feel bad. Oh Ellie, Ellie... How was it possible to love someone so much in such a short time? How was it possible to lose so much with one blow?

And how was he ever going to leave her?

The sergeant handed him his boots.

Ellie watched Daniel trudge up the stairs to her bedroom for the last time. Her hands were busy wiping the table down, but her mind was with him, imagining every move he made. The way he pulled off his shirt, the look and feel of the broad, hard chest underneath, his beautiful sculpted shoulders, the way he bent his head when—

"Here y'are, Mrs. Carmichael. This should cover everything."

Ellie blinked. The sergeant was holding something out to her. Without thinking she extended her hand and took it. Then she glanced down. It was a small leather pouch. It was heavy and the contents clinked. "What is this?"

"Payment."

"Payment? For what?"

"For looking after Capt'n Ambrose, of course. What else?"

It was as if he had slapped her. She gathered her dignity together and laid the pouch gently on the table. "No, thank you."

The sergeant frowned. "Ain't it enough?"

Ellie stared at the man incredulously. Her heart was breaking and he thought she wanted to haggle over a few coins? "No payment is necessary, Sergeant."

The sergeant jutted his chin mulishly. "Capt'n Ambrose always pays his shot."

Ellie just looked at him. He shifted, uneasy under her gaze.

"Ellie, could you help me with this for a moment?" Daniel called from upstairs.

"Coming," she called. "Put your money away, Sergeant Tomkins," she said wearily. "It's not wanted here."

The moment she entered the upstairs room he pulled her into his arms. He hugged her hard against his body and she could feel his need and his pain. "I don't want to leave you," he groaned and covered her mouth with his, tasting her hungrily, devouring her.

It was nothing like the gentle, teasing, warmly passionate kisses of the morning. This was need, pure and simple. Heat. Desperation. Fear and desire. Urgency.

Ellie returned every kiss, each caress in equal urgency, knowing she might never see him again. Oh, why had they not made love this morning? Her foolish scruples seemed meaningless, now she was faced with the probability of a life without Daniel.

She shook with the force of the knowledge.

He took her head in his hands, his palms framing her face. His eyes burned into her soul. "Ellie, I *promise* you, this isn't the end. I'll sort something out." His voice was ragged. "I'll try to come back and see—"

Ellie shook her head. "No, Daniel. It must be a clean break. I could not bear to live on crumbs." She kissed him fiercely. "I want all of you. Crumbs would be the worst form of torture. As it is, I will have my memories. Only I wish we had…you know…this morning."

"Made love," he corrected her, in a low, husky voice. "Not *you know*. You mean you wish we had made love."

Tears spilled down her cheeks and she said in a broken voice, "No, Daniel, even without the…the consummation, we have already made…created love. Can you not feel it all around us? I hope we made enough, for it's going to have to last me the rest of my life..."

"Oh, Ellie, my sweet, lovely Ellie." He groaned and held her tighter, "How can I bear to leave you?"

"You must, Daniel. You have a wife. There is no choice for either of us."

"Ready, Capt'n?" called the sergeant from downstairs. "Need a hand with anything?"

"Blast him," muttered Daniel. He clung to her, burying his face in her hair, inhaling the scent of her, the scent of life, of love. He wished they had celebrated their love physically, for it would add a dimension he thought she was unaware of. But she was right; even without that consummation, they had already created so much love.

He desperately hoped it was enough to survive the return of his memories.

Finally, reluctantly, they pulled apart and went downstairs. Ellie felt the sergeant's shrewd gaze run over her, and knew that she looked like a woman who had just kissed and been well kissed in return. She raised her chin. She did not care what he thought of her.

The sergeant had brought two horses. They were saddled. Ready. Waiting.

"What about the squire?" said Daniel in a rough undervoice. "I canno—"

Ellie put her hands over his lips. "Hush. Don't worry about it. I've been dealing with him for months. Nothing has changed." His mouth twisted under her fingers. He touched them with his tongue and she pulled them away, unable to take much more.

"Mr. Bruin, Mr. Bruin, you're not goin', are you?"

Daniel picked up the distressed little girl and hugged her. "I have to, Princess. Now, be a good girl and look after your mother for me, won't you?" He kissed her goodbye.

Amy wept and clung to his neck. "No, no, Mr. Bruin, you have to stay. The wishing candle brought you…"

His face rigid with the effort of staying in control, Daniel unhooked the small, desperate hands and passed Amy over to her mother.

"I *will* sort something out, I promise you," he said in a low, ragged voice.

"Don't make promises you cannot keep."

"I always keep my promises. Always." His eyes were damp. They clung to her, but he didn't kiss or touch Ellie again. She was relieved. Neither of them could have borne it.

The best way to perform drastic surgery was fast. He turned and strode to the horses, mounting his in one fluid movement. He turned in the saddle, looked across the clearing at Ellie and her daughter with burning blue eyes and said, *"Always."* And he galloped away.

Always, thought Ellie miserably. Did he mean he always kept his promises? Or that he would always love her? Whichever it was, it didn't matter. He was gone. She had the rest of the day to get through somehow, a sunset to await, a daughter to feed and tuck into bed and watch over until she fell asleep. Only then could she seek her own bed and find the release she needed.

The release she needed. Tears and sleep. Not the release she craved…

She carried Amy into the cottage. Making a drink for them both, she found the small pouch of money the sergeant had offered her hidden away behind the milk jug. She looked inside it. Twenty pounds. A fortune, enough to keep her and Amy fed for a long time yet.

Capt'n Ambrose always pays his shot. The sergeant had prevailed yet again.

Somehow, she got through the rest of the day.

When it came time to go up to bed, Amy trotted ahead

of her mother, up the stairs.

"Mama." Amy turned, her freshly washed little face lit up. "Look what I found on my bed." She held up a tiny wooden doll, carved, a little clumsily, out of birchwood. "It's got blue eyes, just like me. An' Mr. Bruin, too." Amy's eyes shone.

A thick lump formed in Ellie's throat. Daniel's whittling. She'd thought he'd been simply killing time, making wood shavings, but he'd made her daughter a doll.

"It's lovely, darling. I'll make her some clothes tomorrow."

"Not her. This is a boy doll," said Amy firmly. "I'll call him Daniel, after Mr. Bruin."

"L…lovely." Ellie managed a smile, though she feared it wobbled a bit.

Later, when Amy was asleep, and the cold descended around her so that she could delay the moment no more, Ellie stepped reluctantly into her own room. Her eyes were drawn inevitably to the sleeping alcove, to the bed.

And then, finally, the tears came, for of course there was nothing there. Not even a small wooden doll. There was never going to be a Daniel there for her again.

He was gone.

Chapter Four

"No, darling, I cannot make you a new dolls' house yet. Not until we find a new house of our own. Houses for people come before houses for dolls."

Amy nodded. "The squire doesn't like us anymore, does he, Mama?"

"No, darling he doesn't. Now help Mama pack by bringing all your clothes down here. I'm going to bundle them all up in a sheet, so we can put them on Ned's cart."

"Don't worry, Mama. If the squire comes back again, Daniel will hit him for us again, won't you Daniel?" Amy gestured fiercely with her small wooden Daniel.

"Nobody is hitting anybody," snapped Ellie. "Now fetch your things down here at once."

Ellie bit her lip as, chastened, Amy did her bidding. She had no idea where they were going to live. The vicar had offered them a room in the vicarage until after Christmas, but then his pupils would return for their lessons and there would be no room. But she was sure she would find something soon.

She had to.

Rat-tat-tat!

She froze. The squire had been back twice already since

Daniel had left. Ellie remembered her daughter's words and her temper suddenly flared. She didn't need a Daniel to protect her; a wooden Daniel would do no good and the real Daniel...well, the real Daniel was back where he belonged, with his loving wife who was expecting their child. Daniel would be there to protect that woman and that child, not the woman and child he had stumbled across in a storm, brought by the light of a gypsy candle.

His memory would no doubt have returned by now. He probably didn't even remember Ellie. Whereas, she...she remembered everything. Too much, in fact. She couldn't forget a thing. He was there, in her mind and her heart, every time she slipped into a cold and empty bed. And she woke with the thought of Daniel every morning, missing his warm caresses, the low rumble of his voice... Bitter regret choked her as she recalled how she had fended him off. If only they had made love...just once.

It wasn't only in bed that he haunted her. He was there, in every corner of her cottage, in the stories her daughter prattled, in the doll he'd made for her. Ellie stoked the fire, morning, noon and night, with wood that Daniel had chopped, and her mouth still dried as she remembered the way his shoulder muscles bunched and flowed with each fall of the axe.

He was there each time it rained and her roof didn't leak. Her heart still caught in her throat when she recalled the way he'd come down off the roof in such a rush, giving her such a fright. The moment she realised she loved him...

It had rained most days since Daniel had left.

The knocker banged again. Ellie forced the bitter lump from her throat. She lifted the poker, strode to the door and flung it open, weapon brandished belligerently.

There was no one there. The rain had stopped and a heavy mist had fallen. It swirled and ebbed, making the cottage surroundings eerily fluid. Poker held high, Ellie stepped out on to the wet ground.

"Hello, Ellie." The deep voice seeped into her frozen bones like heat.

She whirled around, stared, could say nothing. The fog eddied around a tall silhouette, wrapped in a dark cloak, but the cloak was no disguise to Ellie. She knew every plane of that body, had been living with it in her mind and her heart for weeks.

"What are you doing here, Daniel?" she managed to croak.

He moved towards her. "I've come for you, Ellie. I want you with me."

Pain streaked through Ellie. The words she had so wanted, but now it was all wrong. She held up the poker, as if to ward him off, and shook her head. "No, Daniel. I can't. I won't. I have Amy to think of."

He stood stock-still, shocked, his brow furrowed. "But of course I want Amy as well."

Ellie shook her head, more frantically. "No, I can't do that. I won't. Go back home, Daniel. No matter what my feelings for you are, I won't come with you. I won't ruin Amy's life that way."

There was a long silence. Behind her Ellie could hear the slow plop, plop of water dripping off the roof...the roof he had fixed for her.

"And what *are* your feelings for me?"

Ellie's face crumpled with anguish. "You know what they are," she whispered.

He shook his head. His eyes blazed with intensity. "No, I thought I did, but now...I'm only sure of my own feelings." He took a deep breath and said in a voice vibrating with emotion, "I love you, Ellie. I have my memory back and I know I have never loved anyone and will never love anyone again as much as I love you. You are my heart, Ellie.''

Tears blurred Ellie's vision at his words. All she'd ever dreamed of was in those few words... *You are my heart, Ellie.* But it was too late.

''Go back to your wife, Daniel,'' she said miserably and turned away.

There was a short, fraught silence. Then Daniel swore. Then he laughed. ''I'd forgotten that.''

Ellie turned. ''Forgotten your wife?'' she said, shocked.

Daniel's blue eyes blazed into her. ''I don't have a wife. I've never had a wife. It was all a stupid misunderstanding.'' He laid his hand over his heart and declared, ''I am a single man, in possession of all my wits and I'm able to support a wife in relative comfort. I love you most desperately, Mrs. Ellie Carmichael, and I've come to ask you to be my wife.''

There was a long silence. Ellie just stared. The raised poker wavered. A strong masculine hand took it gently out of her slackened grasp.

''Well, Ellie-love, aren't you going to answer me?''

Ellie couldn't see him for tears, but she could feel him and she flung herself into his arms and kissed him fiercely. ''Oh, Daniel, Daniel, yes, of course I'll marry you! I love you so much it hurts!''

''The sergeant lied,'' Daniel explained some time later, an arm around both Ellie and Amy. ''The silly clunch thought he was rescuing me from a designing hussy. He'd started to wonder if he'd made a mistake—apparently you just about gave him frostbite when he offered you money—but he thought it would be better to get me out of your clutches and recover my memory before I made any decisions.''

He grinned and kissed Ellie again. ''So, having regained

my memory, I've brought myself straight back to your clutches. And what very nice clutches they are, too, my dear," he leered in a growly voice and both Ellie and Amy giggled.

"So you remember everything, now?"

"Indeed I do. The moment I arrived back at Rothbury, it all came back to me. Most peculiar how the mind works—or doesn't, as the case may be. Rothbury is a house as well as a village," he explained. "I was born there."

"And, er, what do you do there?" Ellie enquired delicately.

"I oversee the farm. I've found a position for you, too. You will be in charge of the house. After we're married, of course." He looked at her. "You're sure, Ellie? Knowing nothing about me, you'll marry me and come and keep house with me?"

She smiled mistily and nodded happily. "Oh, yes, please. I could think of nothing more wonderful. I would be a good housekeeper, I think. In fact, I did try to find a position like that after Hart died and we found there was no money left, but having no references...and also a daughter..." She hesitated. "You know I bring nothing to this marriage."

He looked affronted. "You bring yourself, don't you? You're all I want, love. Just you. Oh, and a small bonus called Princess Amy."

"Oh, Daniel..." She kissed him again. It was that or weep all over him.

He had brought a special licence. "I've arranged everything, my love. The vicar has agreed to marry us this afternoon—no need to wait for the banns to be called. Then Tommy—Sergeant Tomkins to you—will take Amy to stay the night at the vicarage."

"But why—"

He looked at her and his blue eyes were suddenly burning with intensity. "We have a wedding night ahead of us, love...and this is a small cottage. Amy is better off at the vicarage. Don't worry, she already has Tommy eating out of her hand. He loves a bossy woman! And the vicar is delighted, too. He loves Christmas weddings."

Christmas. They were only a few days away from Christmas. She'd been trying to forget about it, expecting this to be her worst Christmas ever. But now...

Daniel continued, "We'll stay one night here and then I'll take you home to Rothbury. I thought it would be nice if we celebrated Christmas there, with my poor old mother."

Ellie smiled. "Oh, yes, that would be lovely. But...a wedding, today...I have noth—" She glanced down at the shabby dress she wore. "I don't suppose my old blue dress—"

"You look beautiful in anything, my love, but I brought you a dress...and some other things." He gestured to a portmanteau, which the sergeant had carried in earlier.

Hesitantly Ellie opened the lid. Inside, wrapped in tissue, was a beautiful heavy cream satin dress. She lifted it out and held it against herself. The dress was exquisite, long-sleeved and high-waisted, embroidered over the bodice and around the hem in the most delicate and lovely green-and-gold silk embroidery. It was utterly beautiful... Totally unsuitable for a housekeeper, of course, but did she care?

"Is it all right?"

She turned, clutching the dress to her breasts and whispered, "It's beautiful, Daniel."

"The colour is all right, is it?"

She smiled. "It's lovely, though I'm not exactly a maiden, Daniel."

"You are to me," he said. "Anyway, that wasn't why

I chose it. It reminded me of when I first saw you—you were dressed in that white night-thingummy.''

Ellie thought of her much-patched, thick flannel night-gown and laughed. ''Only a man could see any similarity between my shapeless old nightgown and this beautiful thing.'' She laid the dress carefully over the chair and flew across the room to hug and kiss him.

''A man in love,'' he corrected her. ''And that night-gown did have shape—your shape, and a delectable shape it is too.'' He ran his hands over her lovingly and kissed her deeply. Ellie kissed him back, shivering with pleasur-able anticipation.

''Enough of that, my love. We'll be churched before long. We can wait until tonight.''

''I don't know if I can,'' she whispered.

He laughed, lifted her in his arms and swung her around exuberantly, then kissed her again and pushed her towards the table. ''There's more stuff in the portmanteau.''

She looked and drew out a lovely green merino pelisse, trimmed with white fur at the collar and cuffs and a pair of pretty white boots which even looked to be the right size. Beneath it was a miniature pelisse identical to the first, but in blue. With it was a dainty little blue dress with a charming lace collar. And the sweetest pair of tiny fur-lined red kid boots, perfect winter wear for a little girl. Ellie's eyes misted. He'd brought a wedding outfit for Amy, too. And of the finest quality. She wondered how he could afford it, but it didn't matter.

She smiled a wobbly smile and hugged him. How did she ever deserve such a dear, kind thoughtful man? ''Thank you, Daniel. I don't know how—''

''Come on, love, let's get you to that church, or we'll be anticipating our vows. The sergeant shall escort you and Amy. I shall meet you there, as is proper.'' He pulled out a fob-watch and consulted it. "Shall we say one hour?"

"One hour!" gasped Ellie. "Two, at least. Amy and I need to wash our hair and—"

"Very well, two hours it is," he said briskly and kissed her mouth, a swift, hard, possessive promise of a kiss. "And not a moment longer, mind! I have waited long enough!"

Freshly prepared for Christmas, the church looked beautiful. Small and built of sombre grey stone, it glowed inside as the soft winter sunshine pierced the stained-glass windows, flooding the inside with rainbows of delicate colour and making the brass and silver gleam. It smelt of beeswax and fresh-cut pinewood. Greenery decorated the softly shining oak pews and the two huge brass urns on either side of the altar were laden with branches of holly and ivy and pine. Braziers had been lit, taking the chill from the air, throwing out a cosy glow.

Ellie and Amy, dressed in their new finery, stood at the door. The sergeant, looking smart and neat in what Ellie guessed was a new coat, had gone to inform Daniel and the vicar of their arrival. Ellie, suddenly nervous, clutched Amy's hand. Was she doing the right thing? She had only known Daniel a matter of days, after all.

She loved him. But she had loved once before...and had been badly mistaken. She had never felt for Hart half the feelings she had for Daniel. Did that mean she had made the right choice this time...or double the mistake? She shivered, feeling suddenly cold. Amy's little hand was warm in hers. A tiny white fur muff dangled from her daughter's wrist. A gift from Daniel...

"Are you ready, love?" The deep voice came from her right. Ellie jumped. Daniel was standing there, with a look in his eyes that drove all the last-minute jitters from her mind.

"Oh, yes. I'm ready," she said, and with a full heart laid her hand on his arm.

"Then lead the way, Sergeant and Amy."

Gravely the sergeant offered his arm to the small girl. Like a little princess, Amy walked solemnly beside him down the aisle. As they reached the altar, Amy's attention was distracted. "Look, Mama, the vicar has a dolls' house, too," she whispered.

Ellie followed her daughter's gesture and her hand tightened on Daniel's arm. To the right of the aisle at the front of the church sat a Christmas diorama on a small wooden table. A stable, thatched with straw, was surrounded by carved wooden sheep and cows and a donkey. Over the building a painted wooden star gleamed. Inside the stable stood a woman in a blue painted robe, a woman with a serene expression and kind eyes. Beside her stood a tall dark-haired man smiling down at a child not his own, with love in his eyes and his heart.

Like the man at Ellie's side.

Amy stared at the diorama in fascination. She was too small to remember it from the previous Christmas. "The vicar's dolls' house has a family, too—a mama and a papa and a baby, just like us, only I'm not a baby anymore."

Ellie glanced up at the tall man by her side, looking at Amy as if he'd just received the most wonderful of gifts. She said huskily, "That's right, darling. It's a very special family. That's Mary and that's Joseph and that's little Baby Jesus."

"It's lovely." Amy was entranced.

Daniel's arm tightened around Ellie and he drew her forward as the vicar began.

"Dearly beloved…"

* * *

Daniel and Ellie returned to the cottage alone, their foot-steps crunching on the cold ground, anticipation their only companion. Daniel lit a fire downstairs, then went upstairs to light another one in the bedroom, while Ellie laid out some supper. They ate almost in silence, eating slowly, barely touching the wine and the game pie that Daniel had brought.

He laid down his knife and fork and said with a wry smile, "I can't think of a word to say or take in a mouthful of food, love, for wanting you. Shall we go upstairs?"

Tremulously she nodded.

They walked up the stairs with arms wrapped tight around each other. Ellie recalled that first frightful battle to get him up the stairs, his dogged courage as he took each step, and felt a fresh surge of love. How far they had come in such a short time...

When they reached the bedroom, she hesitated, suddenly realising she should have gone up ahead of him and changed into her nightgown. She glanced at the curtains across the sleeping alcove and wondered if she should go behind them to change. It would be a little awkward. There was not much room.

She glanced up at Daniel and the questions in her mind dissipated like smoke as his mouth came down over hers in a tender kiss. She leaned into him, returning the kiss with all her heart. Her hands curled into his hair, loving the feel of hard bone beneath crisp short waves. She could feel the place where he had been injured, where she had cut his hair away.

Daniel felt her trembling against him. He wanted her so much, wanted to dive on to the bed with her and make her his in one bold passionate glorious movement. She was his! His beloved. The woman of his heart. Ellie. Pressing small moist kisses over his face. So soft, so warm, so giv-ing. He felt proud, primitive, possessive.

But she was trembling. And it was not simply desire.

He recalled her shock when he'd touched her intimately, all those mornings ago, her surprise and bemusement at the pleasure his hands had given her. He deepened the kiss, feeling a jolt like lightning surge through him at her enthusiastic, yet endearingly inexpert return of his caresses. She was a married woman, a mother, and a widow, his little Ellie, but of the pleasures between a man and woman she seemed almost as ignorant as any new bride.

Daniel reined in his desires and set himself to introduce his love to the joys between a man and woman. He rained her soft, smooth skin with kisses, running his hands over her, soothing her anxieties wordlessly, caressing her, warming, knowing her.

The cream of the silk gown looked heavy and lifeless against the vibrant delicacy of Ellie's skin. He unbuttoned the gown, pearl button by pearl button, revealing more and more of her soft, silken skin. He slipped the gown off her shoulders and she flushed shyly under his gaze, all the way down to her pink-tipped breasts. It was the most beautiful flush he had ever seen. He bent to kiss her and when his mouth closed over one nipple she arched against him, crying out with a small muffled groan and clasping his head to her breast.

He glanced up at her and his body pounded with heat and need as he saw her head flung back, her eyes blind with passion. Mastering his own needs, he moved his attention to her other breast, and was rewarded by a long shuddery moan.

Daniel slowly divested her of her clothing, piece by piece, for once not feeling impatient with the quantity and complexity of the underclothes women wore, because as he slid each garment over her skin, she blushed most deliciously and shuddered sensually under the warmth of his hands as they pushed the soft cotton slowly over her skin.

He hazily made a note to get her silk underclothes. A few minutes later he changed his mind. It would be better if she wore no underclothes at all...

Finally she was naked, soft and peachy in the flames of the fire he had built. Blushing, she glanced at the bedclothes and then back at him and he realised she would want to cover herself while he disrobed. She was shy and modest, his little Ellie.

She surprised him. "My turn, I think." Eager hands made short work of his neckcloth and shirt buttons. She hesitated when it came to the fastenings of his breeches, then reached for him. He gritted his teeth, fighting for control as she fumbled with the buttons, frowning with concentration, her hands brushing against his arousal, her breasts swaying softly.

She unfastened the breeches and slowly pushed them down his legs. And stared. It was almost as if she had never seen a naked man before, the way she stared, enthralled. And then she reached out and touched him and he could hold back no longer. He tumbled her back on the bed, and, with none of the finesse he prided himself on, entered her in one long powerful thrust. She was hot and moist and ready for him and she arched against him, her body pulling him in, closing in, welcoming him...and as his body claimed her, totally out of his control, she stiffened, her eyes suddenly wide with shock.

"Daniel," she panted. "What is happen—?" She arched all around him and her body began to shudder uncontrollably.

"Let yourself go, love. I am here," he gritted out, himself on the brink of climax.

"Oh, Daniel, Daniel. I love you!" And she shattered around him, sending him over the edge of bliss into oblivion...

He had never known it could be like that. Daniel gazed at his beautiful, rumpled sleeping new bride with bemused wonder. He had thought he would be the one to initiate Ellie into a new world of lovemaking between a man and woman. But if he had shown her a new world, she had shown him one too, a world he'd never even dreamed existed. The world of making love with the woman you adored. Physical pleasures, he'd realised, were shallow ephemeral moments, compared with how it had been with Ellie. The moment when she'd come to climax—her first ever...

Would he, could he, ever forget that look in her eyes as she gazed into his, shouting that she loved him...as she shattered with pleasure, sending him into oblivion with her?

It was like looking at a painting all your life and not knowing there was a living breathing whole new dimension waiting on the other side of the canvas. Like eating all your life and not knowing there was such a thing as salt...

No, there were no poetical images to describe making love with Ellie. All Daniel knew was that he wanted to live to a very ripe old age so he could love her every day of his life.

He leaned down and began to wake her with his mouth, smiling as she squirmed with sleepy pleasure, reaching for him even before she was awake...

At mid-morning, a coach arrived to take them to Rothbury. It bore a crest on the side panel. Ellie glanced at Daniel in surprise. It seemed rather a grand coach for a farmer.

He grinned at her. "It belongs to the Dowager Viscountess, Lady Rothbury, my love. When I told her I was bringing a bride to Rothbury, she insisted I use her carriage."

"She must be a very kind-hearted lady."

"You might say that," agreed Daniel wryly. "I put it down to a managing disposition, myself. The woman has made my life a misery since she lost her husband and her eldest son."

"Oh, the poor lady. She must be lonely, Daniel."

He nodded. "Yes, she has not enough to do. However, she is expecting her first grandchild any day now and I am hopeful that the child will keep her out of my hair in future." He picked up a bundle of Ellie's possessions and winked. "At any rate, having no conveyance of my own as yet, I wasn't about to look her gift-carriage in the mouth."

"I should think not." Ellie frowned thoughtfully as she hurried to collect her things. It was clear that Daniel was a little irritated by his employer's managing ways. She hoped she could smooth the way between them.

Because of their imminent eviction, Ellie was already packed. She left her chickens for Ned to take, as Daniel said he already had plenty. There was nothing else. In a few minutes, their meagre possessions were placed in the boot of the coach and they'd picked up Amy and the sergeant and were heading north.

The trip to Rothbury was long, but not tedious. They passed the time with songs and games for Amy's entertainment. And with small secret glances and touches, which recalled in Ellie the magic and the splendour of her wedding night and morning and raised in her body the shivery, delightful expectation of nights and mornings yet to come.

Ellie thought of how she had told Daniel weeks before that they had already "made love," without having joined, flesh with flesh. She remembered the look on his face as she'd said it, a little quizzical, a little knowing...indulgent.

How naïve she'd been. She hadn't understood that the

act of making love with Daniel would bring another dimension to that love, a deep, powerful intimacy that was not merely physical…though it was intensely physical. She would never forget that first, almost terrifying intimacy, the intensity as she'd exploded into helpless, splintering waves of pleasure under his eyes.

She'd assumed that because the physical act had been unimportant in her marriage to Hart, it would be the same with Daniel. She'd believed it was, by its nature, crude, furtive and only necessary for the procreation of an heir. Because that's how Hart had seen it.

But nothing was the same with Daniel. With Daniel it was…a joyous celebration. A glorious, elemental claiming, in which they united in a way that she had never imagined. It was not a mere fleshly joining—it was…everything. Body, mind, soul. She shivered with remembrance. And pleasure. With Daniel it had been an act of reverence as well as earthy delight. They had made love so many times and the echo of it was with her still. It was as if in one night their bodies had become forever joined, with invisible, unbreakable threads.

The coach swayed along. Awareness shimmered between them, recalling moments of shattering delight. She did not simply love Daniel, she was part of him. And he of her.

With tender eyes she watched him, playing a children's clapping game with Amy, pretending bearish clumsiness with his big, calloused hands. She felt a ripple, deep within her body, as she watched. There was nothing clumsy about those big, beautiful hands. They had taught her body how to sing; it was singing still, within her, deep and silent.

He had transformed her in the night, murmuring endearments, caressing her in places never before caressed, creating sensations she'd never known…nor even imagined. It was as if he knew her body better than she did herself.

Ellie caught his eye, and saw the lurking wolf-smile in it. His gaze sharpened, as if he knew what she'd been thinking, and she felt herself blush as his look turned suddenly intense and hungry. He wanted her. In the course of a single night he'd loved every part of her with hands and mouth and eyes, bringing her alive as she'd never known was possible. And she'd gloried in it so that the wonder still spilled from her...

She couldn't wait for the night to come. Last night she had been the novice, reduced to a blissful jelly by his loving attentions, but it hadn't escaped her that he seemed to enjoy being touched the same way she did. Tonight it would be her turn to explore him. She felt herself smile, a small, secret triumphant feminine smile, and then she caught his eye again, and blushed scarlet as if he'd read her mind.

Passion. She'd never understood it before. An incendiary mix of primitive power...and sublime pleasure. Explosive. Ready to reignite at a look, a touch, a thought...

Though it was only afternoon, dark was falling by the time they turned in at two large stone gateposts, topped by lions. They received their first sight of Rothbury House a few moments later.

It was ablaze with light. The house was huge with dozens of windows. In every window there were candles burning. As they drew closer, Ellie could see they were red candles. Christmas candles.

"Remember how you told me about your wishing candle?" Daniel addressed Amy. "Those are wishing candles for us, to bring us all home safe and sound."

Amy's eyes shone. Ellie lifted his hand and held it against her cheek. It wasn't true—it was probably a tradition of the Big House, but it was a lovely thought, to make a little girl feel welcomed. Daniel put his arm around Ellie and smiled.

The coach pulled up at a flight of steps. "The front door?" whispered Ellie, surprised.

Daniel shrugged. "I'm under orders to present you to the Dowager without delay. She prides herself on knowing everyone on the estate. And it is her carriage, don't forget."

"Oh, dear!" Ellie nervously ran a hand over her hair and tried to smooth her travel-crushed clothing. She hoped the Dowager would not be too demanding an employer.

In the magnificent hallway, an elegant lady awaited them. Silver-haired, she was the epitome of elegance, dressed in the first stare of fashion in a black gown, a black shawl in Norwich silk dangling negligently from her elbows.

"Ellie, I'd like you to meet the Dowager Viscountess, Lady Rothbury," said Daniel.

Ellie curtsied to her new employer.

"Mother, this is my wife, Elinor, the new Viscountess of Rothbury."

Ellie, still curtsying, nearly fell over. Daniel bent down and helped her up.

"But I thought I was to be the new housekeeper!" gasped Ellie. "You mean, you're, you're—"

He bowed. "Viscount Rothbury, at your service, my dear." His blue, blue eyes twinkled wickedly as he kissed her hand in a way that made Ellie blush.

"My son is tiresomely reticent about some things," the lady said sympathetically. "He told *me* he was bringing home a cottage wench, but you are as beautiful and elegant as any of the suitable young ladies I have been flinging so uselessly at his head this age."

"Much more beautiful," growled Daniel's deep voice

and he grinned down at Ellie, who looked flustered and adoring at the same time.

The Dowager Viscountess gave a small, satisfied nod. She moved forward and drew Ellie into a warm, scented embrace. "Welcome to the family, my dear girl. I think you will do very nicely indeed for my scapegrace son."

"The scapegrace son agrees with you, Mother."

Lady Rothbury's eyes dropped to where Amy was loitering in the shadows of her mother's skirts, a little overwhelmed by everything that had happened. "And who have we here?" she said softly. "Can this be my beautiful new granddaughter? My son promised me I would love her instantly."

Ellie's chest was suddenly tight. Such welcome as this she had never dared to dream of. Her daughter would be loved in this house.

Amy examined the older lady with wide, candid eyes. "Are you really Mr. Bruin's mama?"

"Mr. Bruin? Is that what you call my son? Yes, I am his mama. May I ask why you call him Mr. Bruin?"

"That's 'cause he looked just like a bear when he came to me and Mama. He was all prickly."

Lady Rothbury laughed. "A most perspicacious young lady. A prickly bear is exactly how I would describe my son at times." She smiled down at Amy.

Amy looked thoughtful. "I haven't got a grandmother," the little girl said shyly.

The Dowager Viscountess held out her hand and said softly, "You have one now." Amy glanced at her mother for permission, then, beaming, took the older lady's hand.

Lady Rothbury smiled at Ellie through tear-blurred eyes. "Thank you, my dear. You have made my son and me happier than I would have believed possible."

Ellie couldn't say a word. She was blinking away her own tears.

"Now," continued the older lady, "I have something for my beautiful new granddaughter—a welcome home present which I hope she will enjoy. It isn't new, I'm afraid—it was mine when I was a little girl. I kept it for my daughters, but I was never blessed with any, so it has remained untouched in the attic these many years. When Daniel told me about his Ellie and her Amy, I had it brought down and cleaned up and I must say, it looks almost as good as it did when I was a child."

Ellie looked quizzically at Daniel. He shrugged and murmured, "No idea."

"Come along, Amy." The little girl's hand held fast in hers, Lady Rothbury swept down the hall.

Grinning, Daniel called, "She's a princess, Mother. You have to call her Princess Amy."

His mother turned, regally. "Of course she's a princess. She's my granddaughter."

"Come on, I want to see, too," said Ellie. But his arm restrained her.

"In a moment, love. You don't mind if I call you love, now, do you?"

Ellie shook her head, barely able to talk for the happiness that swelled within her.

"Before we see what my mother has up her sleeve for Princess Amy, you have your first duty as Lady Rothbury to perform."

"Oh, yes, of course," said Ellie, suddenly apprehensive. "What must I do?"

He tugged her half a dozen steps to the left and then stopped. And waited.

"What is it?"

His eyes drifted upwards. Her gaze followed. A branch twisted with mistletoe.

"Ohh," whispered Ellie. "A kissing bough. That duty I can see is going to be very arduous. I might need help."

And, standing on tiptoe, she reached up and pulled his mouth down to hers.

After a moment, they separated reluctantly. "You have a choice, my love—we go into the drawing room, or straight up to the bedroom."

Breathlessly, Ellie straightened her gown. "I think it had better be the drawing room. And then..." she looked at his mouth and pressed a quick, hungry kiss on it "...the bedroom."

Arms around each other they strolled towards the drawing room, pausing every few paces for a kiss. At the threshold they stopped. Lady Rothbury sat on a small footstool beside a low table. Amy stood beside her, her little face a study. Ellie gasped.

Amy turned. Her eyes were shimmering with wonder. "Look, Mama," she whispered. "Have you ever, ever, *ever,* seen such a beautiful dolls' house?"

Ellie speechless, shook her head, smiling as the tears spilled down her cheeks.

"Look, Mr. Bruin."

"You can call me Papa, if you like, Princess." Daniel turned Ellie in his arms and began to dry her tears. "I thought you told me you weren't a watering pot," he grumbled softly, making her laugh, even as she wept.

"Can I, Mama? Can I call Mr. Bruin Papa?"

"Yes, darling. Of course you can. He is your papa now."

"Good," said the little girl in satisfaction. "I told you that my Christmas wishing candle was special, Mama. It did bring Papa to us."

"Yes darling, it did."

"Look, everyone," said Lady Rothbury suddenly. "It's snowing."

Outside the long windows, across the bright, dancing flames of the red Christmas candles, it began to snow, softly, gently, blanketing the world with white, making everything clean and new and fresh again.

And so it was Christmas Eve. Filled with peace, love, and the promise of joy to come.

* * * * *

COMING NEXT MONTH FROM

HARLEQUIN
HISTORICALS®

- **BOUNTY HUNTER'S BRIDE**
  by **Carol Finch,** author of CALL OF THE WHITE WOLF
  In order to gain control over her life, a daring debutante leaves her
  fiancé at the altar and, instead, enters a marriage of convenience
  with a bounty hunter bent on vengeance! But when she does the
  unthinkable and falls in love with her husband, will pride prevent
  her from changing a temporary bargain into a permanent union?

  HH #635 ISBN# 29235-X $5.25 U.S./$6.25 CAN.

- **BADLANDS HEART**
  by **Ruth Langan,** final book in the *Badlands* series
  Kitty Conover knows a thing or two about breaking mustangs,
  but she doesn't know the first thing about love...until Bo Chandler
  comes to town. When another man claims Bo's identity, what will
  Kitty believe—the hard evidence or her heart?

  HH #636 ISBN# 29236-8 $5.25 U.S./$6.25 CAN.

- **NORWYCK'S LADY**
  by **Margo Maguire,** second in the *Widower* series
  After an embittered lord rescues a young noblewoman from
  a shipwreck, he discovers that she's lost her memory. While
  nursing the mysterious beauty back to health, he searches for her
  identity and soon discovers that she's the daughter of his most
  hated enemy....

  HH #637 ISBN# 29237-6 $5.25 U.S./$6.25 CAN.

- **LORD SEBASTIAN'S WIFE**
  by **Katy Cooper,** author of PRINCE OF HEARTS
  A world-weary nobleman is on the verge of matrimony when the
  past comes back to haunt him. A reckless pledge made years ago will
  now bind him to a desirable, but deceptive woman!

  HH #638 ISBN# 29238-4 $5.25 U.S./$6.25 CAN.

KEEP AN EYE OUT FOR ALL FOUR
OF THESE TERRIFIC NEW TITLES

HHIBC631

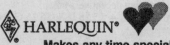